WHEN EYES DON'T LIE

AILEEN & CALLAN MURDER MYSTERIES
BOOK TWO

SHANA FROST

Copyright © 2021 by Shanaya Wagh

All rights reserved. No part of this publication may be reproduced, distributed, or transmitted in any form or by any means, including photocopying, recording, or other electronic or mechanical methods, without the prior written permission of the author, except in the case of brief quotations embodied in critical reviews and certain other non-commercial uses permitted by copyright law. For permission requests, write to author@shanafrost.com

This is a work of fiction. Similarities to real people, places, or events are entirely coincidental.

Website: https://shanafrost.com

WHEN LIES DON'T LIE

First Edition.

Paperback ISBN: 978-93-5473-757-2

Large Print ISBN: 978-93-5659-764-8

Written By: Shanaya Wagh as Shana Frost

Copyedited by Charlotte Kane

Image on the cover by Tim Hill, Arek Socha and Pixabay

Print Cover designed by Germancreative

BOOKS BY THE AUTHOR

You can find an entire (latest) catalogue on the website: Shanafrost.com/books
Here's what you can read next…

Aileen and Callan Murder Mysteries
When Murder Comes Home
When Eyes Don't Lie
When Birds Fall Silent
When Red Mist Rises
When Old Fires Ignite
When Distilled From Rage

Banerjee and Muller Mystery Series
Smokes of Death Beer

To my teachers.

Without words, I would have no story to share.

SCOTTISH GLOSSARY

Aff yer heid- Off her head
Banlaoch- Female Warrior
Bairn- Child/Toddler
Bampot- Crazy
Boaby- Bobby
Boke- Vomit
Boggin- Filthy/Disgusting
Feartie- Coward
Eejit- Idiot
Nyaff Rockets- Irritating Idiot

This book is written in English (UK)

PROLOGUE

The angry sky spoke of violent storms and worrying nights. Night had descended with an inky darkness—a bit too early for summer—thanks to the overcast sky.

She approached the windows in her kitchen and peered out.

What was that?

Something flashed out in the dark. The beam flickered, a beckoning light in the dense blackness of the night. It sparkled and remained bright.

Who was out there? Was someone stranded in this treacherous weather? In Loch Fuar, no one was foolish enough to tread the rocky Highlands this late in the evening. Perhaps she could bring the lost people to safety.

Tugging on her jacket, Aileen wrenched open the door, preparing herself.

A breeze as freezing as the Antarctic blew into the inn laced with the metallic mucky earth.

Oh Lord, was a person out there in this harsh weather? Like a good Samaritan, she called out. 'Anyone there?'

The only answer was the gushing wind with thick droplets of rain.

Aileen licked her dry lips. Perhaps she should just stay indoors, after all, it was warm and dry in here. The moonless night cried like a wolf, causing goosebumps to rise over her skin.

Placing a foot back indoors, Aileen desperately tried shutting the door when she heard herself. Was she *afraid* to step out?

No. No, she wasn't.

Carefully locking the door behind her, Aileen braved the weather, calling out again.

This time, the response was pelting raindrops that crashed over her in a flurry, their wet earthy taste leaving her mouth bitter.

She muttered a curse and shuffled backwards when the light in the distance stopped, flickered, and stilled.

Was someone playing games? Trying to scare her? Or were they young lads, out on a night like this undoubtedly not in their senses?

What day was it? It didn't take her mind long to answer: Saturday.

Saturday night and young lads not in their senses, those two were strongly correlated.

This time she huffed, anger quickly replacing fear. As a young adult, Aileen never had the urge to spend her time "socialising." She'd rather be with her books: fiction, non-fiction, or old ledgers.

That's the reason you're all alone with less than adequate social skills.

Dismissing the usual back and forth between her inner critique and her head, she trudged towards the light.

She *was* confident, Aileen reassured herself.

Thank goodness for the plastic torch clutched tightly in her grasp. She'd learnt this important lesson since coming down to Loch Fuar: nights were dark with no streetlights. Using the torch on your phone meant the phone could die.

Thus, a physical torch it was.

The downpour miffed Aileen, knowing what a mess her boots would be, but she slogged on. After a while of questioning if she was being a fool, Aileen surveyed the treacherous landscape in this blasphemous weather. At least she wasn't tipsy like the lads in the distance undeniably were. And she was well-equipped too. There seemed to be no ditches that could hurt her… Severely, anyway.

Aileen hunched, drawing her jacket tighter around herself to retain what little warmth she had. Her jeans were completely soaked!

After dragging her feet through the dirt for a while, Aileen lost track of time. She tried her best to walk faster, but the damp earth and exertion made her footsteps sloppy, especially when the wind joined in with the vicious dance of the rain.

What kept her pushing forward was the light. It had flickered again. She was irrefutably curious.

Aileen desperately tried not to swallow the rainwater that assaulted her mouth. The taste reminding her of iron, bitter and metallic. Her only reprieve was the light, which blazed brighter as she approached it.

After a while, Aileen cleared the bushes—or what she thought were bushes—pushing past them only to emerge on a landing of sorts.

An unnatural guttural cry from above made Aileen's knees go weak and her heart raced.

Golly!

She clasped her wet wrinkled fingers together, as if in prayer. Squinting, Aileen flicked the dripping moisture from her tired eyes. Right in front of her was a small cottage!

That's where the light was coming from!

She let out a soft chuckle. Aileen had never noticed this cottage before. And judging by the crack in its roof, the place seemed neglected. It was a surprise it had any electricity at all. Surely it housed stranded people. The cottage could crumble at any moment on a good day. It certainly couldn't withstand this storm.

With best wishes in her heart, Aileen walked up to the door and called out. But her voice was lost to the otherworldly calls which assaulted her ears.

Aileen frowned at the slightly ajar door.

Who'd leave the door hanging open in this blasted weather? Perhaps it wouldn't close…

She let it go; she was overthinking. As usual. Using all the breath in her lungs she called out again, Aileen's fear was long forgotten, hoping to help someone. Despite her shouts, she was met with silence.

Once again Aileen wiped the rainwater from her eyes. Her hands had gone pale and shivered. She licked her lips. What if this was some elaborate scheme to harm her?

This is Loch Fuar, Aileen! Adventurous, Courageous!

With one hand on the slippery torch, Aileen steeled herself. A moment later, she pulled the rough wooden door open. 'Hell-'

Her words died in her mouth and what came out was a terrifying scream. Her pruney hands shook, and legs trembled. Her throat burned with bile and she couldn't breathe.

Right in the centre of the room, just above where a wooden beam ran across the ceiling, a rope dangled.

And on that rope hung a ghost. White limbs attached to a blonde head tumbled over onto a shoulder, clad in a dirty milky dress.

Lightning struck, illuminating the dangling body.

A freezing breeze tickled Aileen's clenched fists

and played with the murky hem of the corpse's dress.

The swaying feet were almost blue...

Aileen's shaky hands pressed the soft fabric of her coat that kept her warm... Alive. A repulsive, rancid reek tugged at her gut.

Dead. The dangling woman was surely dead.

CHAPTER ONE

Detective Inspector Callan Cameron stood in front of the coffee machine at the police station, debating whether he should finish his shift with a black coffee. This case of that missing woman had been mind-sucking.

Why were the damned police from the next town so keen on finding her? She'd disappeared, but there was no ransom note, nor any clue except for surveillance footage showing the woman driving into Loch Fuar using a rental car.

That led him to question: who'd inform the police she was missing?

When his phone buzzed, Callan's gaze flickered over to it. Now what? Had Douglas's doaty cat played mischief again? Mischief it was not, Callan deduced. Rather, it was the overwhelmed voice of the neat and tidy Ms Aileen Mackinnon.

Cottage, she muttered. *Dead woman.*

Based on what he knew of the landscape—owing to his morning run—Callan had chanced upon a sorely dilapidated structure on Dachaigh's property. The rundown thing was in such a poor state that it hadn't been used for the past six decades.

Callan could've enjoyed the thrill of the drive through the rocky terrain and the unyielding rain if it hadn't been for the tremor in Aileen's voice. Instead, he frowned, a checklist running through his mind.

He first had to make sure Aileen was fine and not under any threat. And he needed to know what she was doing out there in this vengeful weather.

That woman was a wee bit *aff her heid.*

The light in the cottage shone as Callan's rugged car bumped along the rough road. He clasped his calloused hands over the sandy surface of the steering wheel.

The screech of his tyres could be heard over the beat of the rain. Shielding himself against the downpour, Callan jumped out of his vehicle and sloshed his way over to the dilapidated cottage.

Just outside the door, he made out a huddled figure with drenched hair and shivering shoulders. He caught Aileen's arms and pulled her from her fetal position. She winced as she moved but didn't say a word.

Was she shuddering from the cold or from the sight she'd seen inside?

Her soft coat shielded her against the rain, but her lips had turned a sickening shade of blue. Bet she couldn't feel a thing through the numbness in her body. Despite the mucky weather, Aileen's perfume reminded Callan of summer and melons.

He was standing *too* close.

Callan led Aileen to his car. The last thing he needed was for her to faint. Aileen's usually flushed cheeks appeared peaky, and her wet brown hair was black. Her pearly skin shone like a ghost against his car's headlights.

That she hadn't taken shelter inside, despite the weather, meant something terrible awaited him… Or she was concerned about contaminating the crime scene.

Callan held her trembling body close to his, offering his warmth. Those brown irises showed some signs of shock.

He pushed her into the worn leather seat of his heated car. 'Stay.'

With that, Callan marched towards the cottage again, this time for the apparent dead woman inside.

Callan, now geared up to assess the scene, scrutinised the cadaver.

A single sigh was all he allowed himself. This had to be Marley Watson, the former innkeeper at

Dachaigh. The same woman he'd spent the entire day searching for.

Now, with her feet bare to the icy wind, her almost creamy ankle-length dress flapped in the wind. Its hem was muddied and the woman who wore it was a ghost. Her skin was whitish blue. After all, she was no longer breathing.

What had saved some horror for Aileen was the dead woman's head, which had rolled onto her shoulders, hiding the face behind a curtain of long blonde hair still fluttering in the wind that gushed around the tiny cottage.

Her dress wasn't damp. Meaning she had either died a while ago and the wind had dried her, or she'd snuck in here before the storm.

Callan analysed the rest of the tiny cottage with his keen eye that left nothing unnoticed. There wasn't anything of significance, apart from the one lamp that illuminated the room. Its illuminance was bright enough to draw attention from afar.

So someone could find her.

The rest of the wooden interiors had heaps of scrap, some cut wires, broken alcohol bottles, and he scrunched up his nose. *That's boggin.* Death fused with acidic dried urine.

This cottage must have played host to some minced bampots. If he swept this place, Callan was sure he'd find emptied alcohol bottles along with an illegal powder or two.

Tilting his neck, he stared at the slumped chair beside the body.

A potential suicide? Could it be?

Another car's honk shattered through the drenched landscape, interrupting his thoughts. It must be the detective from Loch Heaven, their neighbouring town. He got here quick.

DI Declan Walsh strode in, hunched in his patent trench coat and hat.

'Is that the innkeeper?'

Callan cocked his head. '*Former* innkeeper.' And wasn't he grateful for that?

He didn't continue to scrutinise *that* wayward thought.

Callan had already decided: this was *his* case. The Loch Heaven police could definitely assist, but Callan had no interest in partnering with them on this. He was better off alone... *But Aileen had been a good partner*. Callan pinched himself.

While others described her as shy, she'd only subjected Callan to her feisty side. He pursed his lips to hold in the small smile. He loved bickering with that woman... Callan clenched his hands.

He best give DI Walsh some private time with the body. This ramshackle cottage was so small, the two burly officers barely had space to stand, let alone objectively study the scene.

Leaving Walsh alone, he approached the shivering woman waiting in his car.

Aileen, lips pinched, slouched over the heated

air vents. Her eyes were dreamy as she stared listlessly.

On Callan's rap at the window, she almost flew out of her seat, hands pressed over her chest. At least they'd been partly restored to a more human-like colour.

Callan wanted to draw those small hands into his larger ones and warm them up, warm her up.

Shut up!

Aileen painted a scowl on her face and rolled down the window. *Ah, here goes the feisty bomb.* 'Can't you be gentle?'

'It was only a knock.' Callan smirked, knowing it would irk Aileen. Anything to get some colour back into her face and a twinkle in her eyes.

'What do you want?' She snapped, although a little feebly.

Callan had found great joy in annoying the heck out of Aileen from the first time they'd met. Since that fateful encounter, she'd always had her hackles up around him. He found it rather endearing.

And now it worked, getting that flush into her cheeks again. 'Why did ye think taking a nightly walk would be a great idea in this fantastic weather?'

Tufts of white smoke wafted out of her mouth as she huffed like a child throwing a tantrum. 'I was trying to help! I saw the light, came down here.' Her voice was barely a whisper.

'It's quite a distance.' Callan squinted at his

watch. 'About fifteen minutes from the inn, considering the uneven land.'

Aileen explained her theory that it had to be young lads messing about. 'I just wanted to caution them. It's not the best place or weather to be... Not in your senses.'

And if the killer had been around? Callan let that thought go. It was not something he wanted to be thinking about. He glanced over his shoulder at the cottage. He'd pulled the splintered, creaky door shut behind him. But the scene was hard to forget. Suicide, this didn't seem like.

The lonely Scottish wilderness was a rather unusual place to kill oneself. But he narrowed his eyes. Best not to draw conclusions yet.

The medic team came, drenching the dark landscape in dancing red, white, and blue lights. Their shrill sirens joined the raging weather.

Aileen's unblinking gaze followed him as he spoke with the detective from Loch Heaven.

Callan sauntered over and sat beside her in the car, thawing his sniffing nose and rubbing his hands together. It was about to be a long night.

Aileen shivered, clearly uncomfortable in her damp clothes.

'I'll drive ye back. Do ye need me to call anyone? Isla?'

She shook her head. 'I've seen death before.' Was she convincing herself or him?

The death she had come across had been in the

bright morning light. 'Ye didn't discover those bodies alone.' Callan pointed out.

The car bumped down the Highland roads, its headlights barely a match for the heavy darkness.

Revenge, that's what nature was after. As if in a desperate attempt to seek vengeance against the atrocities inflicted by humankind, thunder struck, rain pelted with rage, and the wind spared not even the verdant trees.

Under the hateful dark clouds, the former gleeful highland landscape in the North-Western region of Scotland stretched around a lonesome century-old stone inn.

The white stone bricks and pastel blue window frames could remind a passerby of better, drier times. A warm glow from within the house reminded one of home. And Dachaigh was home to Ms Aileen Mackinnon.

Callan helped Aileen inside the inn, his hands placed onto the back of her damp coat. He didn't know what to say. Emotions had never been his forte. Especially around Aileen.

Based on her slouched figure, the innkeeper was ready to bawl her eyes out. That calm demeanour he had come across vanished, replaced by a vulnerable woman.

She ferociously bit into her tender lips. 'Who... Who was she?'

'I don't officially know.' Callan replied softly.

Watery brown orbs met his. 'Unofficially?'

Callan sighed. 'Marley Watson.'

Aileen gasped and gaped at him. 'The former *innkeeper*?'

Without permission, his hand landed on her shoulder and squeezed gently.

Aileen faced him, her bottom lip quivering. Instead of giving in to the tears fast pooling in her eyes, she nodded. 'Thank you for getting there so quickly.'

Clearing his throat, Callan tugged at his coat. 'It's my job.'

The back of his neck prickled. It *was* his job to protect people. He had sworn by it. But with Aileen? It was different.

He better get out of here before he made an utter fool of himself.

Briskly, he bid farewell.

What had he been thinking, touching her? Eejit!

CALLAN RETURNED TO THE POLICE STATION, A little weary of his behaviour with Aileen. Why had he reacted to Aileen's vulnerability in such a manner?

Bah! He wasn't the sort who thought about emotions. He'd prefer not to have any.

Shaking himself out of his vicious thoughts, he stalked over to the coffee machine. Guess he would be working overtime today.

The door to the office swung open to reveal the hunched figure of DI Walsh. It was funny how this man dressed: a trench coat and a hat that covered most of his dark cocoa skin. A clichéd detective.

Callan pointed at the mug. 'Coffee?'

Walsh shook his head and sighed. 'I hoped we'd find her alive.'

Callan took a long sip and leant his hip on the desk. 'What do ye think?'

His fellow officer shrugged. 'It's got to be a suicide. Perhaps she was running away from her life.'

This was not a suicide, of that he was certain. Callan stared out into the damp night questions running through his mind. Where were the woman's shoes? But he didn't want to cloud his colleague's thought process. He'd get there, eventually.

Callan finished his dark brew, enjoying its bitterness, and stalked towards his office.

Walsh followed behind. 'I need to call my superior.'

'I'd like to work on this case.' Callan told him.

Walsh's gaze was wary as he walked out, busy dialling.

Callan had encountered Walsh's superior officer once. The man had sat behind his desk and sent the other detectives scurrying, making him coffee and getting him his lunch. The man's job had been so sloppy that the perpetrator had almost got away.

Callan pulled out his whiteboard. It was time to start his murder board.

Marley Watson, he scrawled in his less than legible hand. Why had she run away? Had she run away? Why to Loch Fuar?

Callan scratched his chin. So many questions he couldn't answer *yet*.

He had to consider the possibility of suicide. In that case, where was the suicide note? He scribbled that question down.

Footsteps strode towards his office. Callan tilted his head to face the door, waiting for DI Declan Walsh to enter.

The man's face was emotionless. 'I'm sorry, but my superior officer thinks we should head this investigation since Ms Watson was a resident of Loch Heaven.'

Callan's jaw hardened. They couldn't leave out of solving this case! It was his. 'She was found dead in Loch Fuar.'

Gingerly, Walsh nodded. 'Someone reported her to missing in Loch Heaven, Detective. And we want to get to the bottom of this.'

Callan took a breath to calm his boiling blood. 'Detective Walsh-'

The infernal ringing of the phone cut Callan short. He stared at the handset. 'Shit!' Callan picked up the receiver.

'Callan.' It was Rory Macdonald, Callan's superior officer.

He bobbed his head, even though his boss couldn't see him. Callan's voice was clipped as he spoke, 'Rory.' Luckily Rory valued formality as an errant pupil his teacher.

When usually his boss would crack a joke, he sighed. 'I got a call from the Loch Heaven police.' He began.

Callan shut his eyes, frustration like salt on an open wound. This was going to be a long call, and Callan knew he couldn't refuse his boss.

PRECISELY FIFTEEN MINUTES LATER, CALLAN'S HEAD throbbed. Rory in his own way had asked Callan to hand this case over. They hadn't the resources or the expertise Loch Heaven had. Callan had bristled at the last excuse.

But Rory was merely repeating what he and his colleague at Loch Heaven had discussed. His boss thought their town was still recovering from the murders that had shaken it a month or so ago and handing this case over was a good idea.

Damn it! Callan wanted to solve this case. And he knew he'd do a better job than any other detective.

Not wanting to be disrespectful, Callan rubbed his forehead and conceded. Walsh nodded and left him alone in that all too quiet office in the Town of Saints.

But, Callan mused, he'd promised no one he wouldn't work this case alone, out of office hours.

He'd bring Marley Watson the justice she deserved because she'd died here, all alone. And even a rookie could figure out it wasn't a suicide.

No, as a detective, it was his duty to get to the bottom of this. It was his oath and he better live up to it, office politics be damned.

Callan set to work, meticulously pinning up pictures and jotting down notes on his murder board. He was good at this, solving a murder. How an addict craved a hit of caffeine; he craved a good crime he could solve. He would not give up until he investigated this and figured out the answer.

Aileen could've been a corpse. She hadn't slept a wink. Why had last night's scene affected her this much?

As she had told Callan, her eyes were no stranger to a dead body, even a brutally murdered one.

But this one, this one, had been like a ghost. She'd been so lonely, swinging in the blowing wind, stuck in a crumbling structure surrounded by inky darkness and the solitary Highlands.

Aileen rubbed warm palms over her spiky arms, hugging herself tightly. It felt like unfinished business.

Brewing herself a coffee, she sat by the kitchen counter, lost in thought. Just then, the back door flew open. A flustered, yet energetic, middle-aged woman with green eyes and wild hair gushed in like the wind.

'Oh, it's a storm out there! I was worried you'd face issues…' She broke off.

'Isla!' Aileen remarked. 'It's pouring out, what are you doing here?'

'Oh, oh.' She jogged around the counter and pulled Aileen in a hug. 'I heard you saw the body. Are you okay?'

Aileen patted Isla's back. ''Twas unexpected, to say the least. And it made me wonder who Marley really was. She seemed rude and disinterested when I first got here. So I fired her. But I didn't know her at all.'

Isla swatted a hand in the air. 'She worked at Dachaigh for about two months, from when Siobhan had to leave, and you came along. And I don't have to tell you, she made a mess. And despite being here for those two months, she never once showed her face in town. Andrew would cycle down to Dachaigh and deliver the bread.'

'Why did you stop delivering bread?' Aileen took a sip of her tepid coffee.

Bobbing her head, Isla said, 'Andrew told me she was being rude. She refused to pay full price and shouted awful words at that poor boy.'

Yes, the dead Marley had been a nasty woman indeed.

Aileen sighed, and a small smile broke on her

face. She'd needed her best friend and here Isla was. She confessed. 'It was a bad day, yesterday. The police are investigating the murder. Everything will be alright.'

Isla walked towards the refrigerator and pulled out a tub of ice cream. Shaking it, she said, 'Coffee won't help. This, my dearie, is the best medicine.' Two spoons in hand, Isla sank into the chair beside Aileen. 'Don't remind me about yesterday.' She muttered.

Aileen's eyebrows scrunched up in a frown. 'Why?'

A loud silence followed. When Isla didn't speak but continued to stare at the ice cream tub, Aileen twiddled her spoon, waiting.

'Daniel and I fought.' Isla's green eyes were watery pools.

Aileen laid a hand over hers. 'Oh, Isla!'

She didn't have to nudge her much, Isla picked up from there. 'He's a man! So typical! He told me I'm eating too much candy. He thinks I'm putting on weight and... He said I've been stress eating.'

Isla stuffed a big scoop of ice cream in her mouth and swirled it around before continuing. 'Me, stress eating? I'm never stressed! Besides, who is he calling me fat?' Isla sniffed, raising her chin in mock defiance.

Aileen tried to think about Daniel, the handyman who'd helped her restore the dilapidated inn she'd walked in on a few months before.

He was a delightful, polite man who made decent conversation. He would never badmouth his wife. They had genuine affection for the other and if Daniel thought his wife was stress eating, then she was.

'Did he comment upon your physique?' Aileen ventured.

Isla shook her head. 'But he told me I'm eating too much sweet stuff. What am I supposed to do? An evil eye is the worst thing to happen.'

'Eye? What's wrong with your eyes?'

Isla glanced heavenward. 'Not my eyes! A lady came into the shop yesterday. She wanted shortbread. I said I have a pack of ten, but she wanted twenty. I asked her to wait because I had to bake them. We ran out as we always do. And I want to increase capacity, but there's never enough time or space!

'But that lady made me feel all shivery. She got angry. Muttered something under her breath, but it sounded like a curse. And then she looked at me, like, like I was a rat and she was the cat. No, no, that's not right…' Isla shuddered. 'She gave me the evil eye. Oh, Aileen, it was a sign indicating something terrible! Oh, oh… Her eyes: one was blue and the other, a sinister bright green!'

Aileen blinked. Was Isla right? Did the evil eye indicate murder?

Of course not! She was being silly, overreacting. But something continued to nag.

Marley Watson.

Aileen had turned her out just months before, hadn't she? Without a thought to whether the woman had somewhere to go. Had Marley lost her life just because Aileen wanted to keep the inn pristine?

What if Marley hadn't been able to pay a debt and had killed herself because of that? Or was she living on the streets because she had nowhere to go?

When Aileen didn't speak for a while, Isla squeezed Aileen's shoulder. 'Oh, Aileen! Don't worry. I didn't mean to spook you. I assumed you don't believe in the supernatural. And they say if you focus on someone else's troubles, you forget your own.'

Aileen shrugged. 'It's not that.'

'Tell me, what's wrong?'

Aileen took a shaky breath. 'It's just, these murders. I mean... Seeing her shook me, I guess. It didn't when I saw the other body, you know, at Dachaigh back in May. But yesterday, it was so unexpected, so eerie.'

Isla reached for Aileen's hand and squeezed tenderly.

Gazing at her kind green eyes, Aileen let the last bit flow. 'I can't help but feel she died because of me. I fired her, without a single thought about her safety.'

Isla watched the rain patter against the windowsill. When it had been storming the previous evening, it was just grey and damp today. Facing Aileen again, Isla said, 'Oh, Aileen! You think too much, dearie. Work is work, and we all know what a terrible job Marley had done with the inn. You couldn't let her stay on and destroy Siobhan's hard work.'

But Aileen's conscience didn't agree with Isla. She had played a hand in the death of a person. Another wrong decision. When would she learn to think?

'What should I do?' She groaned.

Isla sat up, energetically clicking her fingers. 'I know! You should solve this case with Callan.'

Aileen snorted. The last thing the broody detective wanted was to join forces with her. He had made it crystal clear what he thought about partners.

But Isla had got it into her head that Aileen and Callan were a perfect match. She began, a fiend for gossip. 'It would be perfect, Aileen! You need to solve this case. For some people, it helps to bury what they've witnessed, but for you? The only way you can put this demon to rest is by actively fighting it.'

Aileen shut her eyes. 'I wouldn't know what to do.'

Pursing her lips, Isla said, 'Siobhan always follows her heart. It was something she taught me when I came here from Stirling, lost and in search of a new life. She was the one who encouraged me to follow my heart's desire. Your heart will lead you north. Listen to it and follow it. Nothing wrong will come from it.'

Narrowing her eyes at Isla, Aileen tried to figure out what her friend meant. It was not entirely to do with the case that much was clear.

But what Isla said made sense. The only way Aileen could find any closure was if she knew why Marley had died this way. Perhaps it would give Marley some conclusion in death. If it did nothing, at least it would correct Aileen's colossal mistake in some measure.

A bigger smile burst across Isla's face. 'Can I help?'

Aileen grinned back, her resolve made. 'Isla, no one can bring me juice on Marley Watson like you.'

Isla's nod was so rigorous, Aileen thought her head would fall off. 'Don't you worry. I don't have just my ears to the ground, I have a set of binoculars and high-tech gossip wizards at my beck and call.'

As one, both women cracked up. For another person, that statement would have been an exaggeration but with Isla's connections, her gossipmonger ways, and her strong nose for scandal, it was no anomaly she had the resources.

And with Isla's help, Aileen would find Marley's killer, whatever the stakes may be. Even if that meant browbeating Detective Callan Cameron for information.

SHANA FROST

CHAPTER TWO

That afternoon, armed with a box full of lemon tarts and other pastries from Isla's Bakery, Aileen made her way to the nursing home. Marley had been the former innkeeper at Dachaigh, so her gran would have some intel on that woman.

Siobhan was in her nineties but as strong as any twenty-year-old. Her cerulean eyes twinkled with mirth as they always did. 'I'm so proud of ye!'

'Thank you, Gran!' Aileen narrowed her eyes. 'What are you up to?'

'Up to? Why, I've always appreciated my bonnie grandwean. Ye never told me ye were that good at self-defence! I heard ye kicked really hard at that murdering bastard! Bet he still must bawl his eyes out in prison!' Siobhan cracked up, chuckling so loud it had to be unhealthy.

'Gran!' Aileen admonished. 'I didn't mean to hurt him! He was trying to-'

Siobhan raised a hand and stopped Aileen's excuse. 'Didn't it feel great!?'

Her gran was a weird one. She was short but possessed immense strength: both physically and emotionally. Besides, in her prime, Siobhan had not been one to sit around and obey rules. Neither did she follow any norms her doctors and nurses demanded she follow today.

And she was a staunch gossipmonger as any, even giving Isla a run for her money. 'Heard ye found another body.'

Aileen bit her lips. 'I wanted to know something about that.'

'Marley Watson. Wasn't that her name?'

It was best not to ask who'd given her that information. Callan's boss, Rory Macdonald, was tight friends with her gran.

Aileen pulled at her ears, her thoughts churning. 'She worked at the inn before me. Why did you hire her?'

Siobhan steepled her fingers and scrutinised Aileen. 'Rude as any brat, wasn't she? I had no choice with just a couple of days to decide. She was willing to start right away. Said she needed the work and the money. I needed her. Not the best choice.'

'Who worked at the inn before her?'

'Oh, it was Nurse Nancy's niece, Daisy McHugh. That's Mrs McHugh's daughter. But she got married right about that time and moved to the east coast, somewhere near Aberdeen.'

Aileen reached into her satchel and pulled out her yellow notepad. 'And what did you know about Marley?'

Siobhan tsked. 'Not much. Did you ask the detective what Marley was doing on the inn's property?'

Aileen handed over the box of pastries she'd brought along. Siobhan's eyes twinkled as she grabbed the box and pulled out a lemon tart.

Watching Siobhan devour the sweet goods that her doctor had told her not to eat, Aileen shook her head. 'She didn't die on the property, but at a small cottage a few minutes away. Well, it took me fifteen minutes to get there in the dark.'

Licking her lips, Siobhan swallowed. 'I know which one ye mean. That cottage lies on the inn's estate. I've never used it. That area doesn't have great access from the highway and is a little farther away from the inn. Besides, the cottage was about to fall off when I purchased the place. Funny it's still standing.'

Siobhan handed her a smaller strawberry tart. Aileen bit into its crispy crust, licking the flakes on her lips. 'Do you have any records on Marley as well as on the property?'

Her gran tapped her sharp but wrinkly chin, 'I have some records on Marley. I think Daisy collected them. Papers on the property? I lost them all one time the inn was flooded. Your pa left the bloody door open in a storm!'

Her gran couldn't be of any more help. But she'd had some headway with the visit and got a visit with her dear gran.

Siobhan had been happy with her tart and scones. She'd told Aileen she'd share it with the others. Aileen had her doubts with the way her gran's eyes sparkled as she peered inside the box.

The woman was incorrigible. Everyone knew she snuck in whisky, watched television too late into the night, and harassed her nurse into letting her eat chocolates. The best bit: Everyone loved Siobhan for her childlike ways.

In a much better mood than when she'd left, the first thing Aileen did after getting back at Dachaigh was to scour the Control Room, now secure behind a lock. If they had any data on Marley, it had to be there.

Files on files littered the desk. Bookkeeping records from decades ago sat next to old tattered check-in registers. Aileen's hands were soon coated with a fine layer of dust.

After an hour of fruitless search, she found a call directory. On the front page, Siobhan had carefully penned down a number in a clear, legible hand. Below it was the name, 'Daisy McHugh.'

It was time Aileen called her.

She clenched the phone with sweaty palms.

Would Daisy get annoyed? Would she slam the phone down?

Aileen jolted herself out of her doubts before she'd change her mind. She quickly dialled the number.

'Hello?' Came a sweet questioning voice.

Aileen swallowed. 'Um, hi. This is Aileen Mackinnon.'

The voice gushed. 'Oh, ye're Siobhan's granddaughter! I heard ye'd taken over the inn. How I miss that place!'

Aileen's heart was still hammering. 'Yes, I work here now. Is this Ms McHugh?'

Daisy McHugh hummed and then chirped excitedly. 'My friends call me Day. How's Siobhan? Tell her I said hi! I'll be down there to meet her soon.'

Aileen hummed a "yes."

There was an awkward silence on the call.

Aileen cleared her throat. 'I wanted to know about when you left. You hired another innkeeper, yes?'

'Och aye, what's her name…?' There was a pause, and then. 'Marley Watson!'

'Yes, um, could you please tell me where you kept her background data?'

Daisy thought for a moment. 'Of course! I stored it on a hard-drive.'

After a brief explanation of where it was, Aileen clicked off the phone. This was simpler than she'd thought. Humming a tune, she headed over to retrieve the drive.

But an hour later, she wasn't singing. Heck no, she was frowning.

After that call with Daisy, she scoured the entire Control Room with its old files and records. When she came up empty-handed, Aileen wanted to punch the wall.

And then, like some sick joke, she found it. The hard-drive was so tiny, dumped in the darkest part of the lowest drawer, that she'd almost missed it. She scrutinised the drive with a scowl on her face.

Aileen plugged in that tiny drive she'd found neglected in that drawer. Her slick computer was fast, but that drive? It was fickle, to say the least.

After too many attempts than she could count, Aileen could finally access the data.

When she found only one folder and one page of information on Marley Watson, Aileen pulled at her hair. It further annoyed her that the data wasn't much, in fact, most of it was useless and perhaps fake. She'd spent more time digging up the information than she did perusing it.

She needed something trustworthy, something concrete. Marley's data couldn't be cross-checked. It was what she had told Daisy when looking for a job. Thus, it wasn't trustworthy.

Where could she find clues, perhaps even evidence? Thinking to herself, Aileen walked towards the kitchen. When her gaze flickered towards the window, Aileen paused.

Should she go to the cottage again? Did she dare do that?

Maybe Isla would like to accompany her. Aileen picked up her phone, but then remembered. Isla was entertaining her in-laws this evening. Aileen was essentially alone.

Bummer! She needed to go to the cottage. If she waited too long, she might miss an important clue!

This time, armed with a larger torch, rainwear, and a small knife she'd purchased after being accosted, Aileen pulled open the door only to hear the howl of a beast.

The sky had darkened. Grey clouds hung low, but it hadn't rained yet. The forceful wind made the tall trees sway.

Her legs halted, her mouth dry. It wasn't fruitful if she went out there this evening, was it? She wasn't *scared*, but it'd be easily visible and clearer to assess the scene under the bright morning light.

The wind cried out again; Aileen squared her shoulders. No, this wasn't the old Aileen who never took risks and gave up holiday time to complete her boss's work and never asked for any recognition. This was the new Aileen. She replayed her mantra: *Adventurous, Courageous.*

Firming her resolve, she stepped out and challenged the wind: 'You can't make noises like the bogeyman. I'm not scared of you!'

She trudged towards the cottage, her mouth bitter from yesterday's memories. The fact it was still twilight helped.

Clearing away the thick foliage, Aileen came upon the dilapidated cottage. She hadn't been able to study it last night except when she'd neared, and the brown wood had lit up under blazing lightning.

Now, under the twilight, she could observe it. The wooden walls had holes in them and some roof tiles had crashed to the ground. Thick plastic sheets covered the fissures in the roof and walls.

Who'd done that? Perhaps a local, Aileen shrugged. It didn't matter; it was surely not Marley Watson who'd done that.

Marley Watson, according to Daisy's meagre notes, had come to the inn in a van. She'd needed a job immediately with just five pounds in her pocket. The van was close to dying out, and it had been her home for the past few months. She needed a job that could provide a roof over her head.

Taking pity on her and owing to the time constraints, Daisy—with Siobhan's permission, of course—had given Marley the job.

There was no permanent address on record, nor was there any mention of any family members.

Aileen had browsed the web. Being glued to a screen, that's all that Marley had done the one evening they'd spent holed up at the inn.

A *thwack* brought Aileen back to the present, eyes flittering around the serene Highlands.

First, she wanted to assess the cottage without a dangling corpse or freaky storm to hamper her senses.

Steeling herself in retrospect, Aileen pushed open the sandy wooden door.

The lamp stood where it had been last night but was now switched off. Everything was as it was, except for the body or the noose it hung from... Thankfully.

Aileen's tensed shoulders relaxed. It was dusk. The waning sunshine was enough to bolster her courage. *At least it wasn't pitch dark...*

She stepped in, studying the wooden beam where Marley had been dangling dead.

Her pale feet would've been so cold, swaying in the breeze blowing through the open window.

Aileen bit her lips, scrutinising the fragmented window. Its old mucky glass had splintered. The remaining brutal edges were as dingy and dirty as-

'Snooping around?'

Aileen jumped high, shrieking as she faced the voice.

Her heart hammered, and she stared into the electric blue eyes of DI Callan Cameron. Callan wore his patent all-black outfit and a smirk. The thin cotton of his shirt stretched across his chest, highlighting his firm muscles.

Clearing her throat, Aileen scowled. 'Why can't you be gentle?'

Callan held up his hands. 'It was only a question. Ye were the one who got spooked.'

Aileen held her chin high. 'I wasn't scared!'

He raised his eyebrows, calling out her bluff.

Aileen huffed. 'What're you doing here?'

'I had something I needed to recheck. What are you doing?'

Aileen shrugged carelessly. 'It's a part of the inn's property. And there's no police tape on the door.'

Callan grimaced. 'I noticed. Stupid Loch Heaven police want to rule it a suicide.'

Suicide? And apparently, Callan didn't agree with them. 'Why do you think this isn't one?'

Staring outside the splintered window, Callan gritted his teeth. 'Marley couldn't have killed herself. It makes no sense!'

'So what are you going to do about it?' Aileen questioned.

Taking a deep breath, Callan's determined gaze met hers. 'Solve it in my own time, of course.'

This was an excellent opportunity to team up with him. Excitement bubbling inside her, Aileen wrenched open her mouth. But Callan cut her off. 'No, I don't need help.'

'Come on, Callan. We were great last time. I won't step on your toes!' She spoke hurriedly, lest he walk out on her.

Instead, he walked up to her until she had to throw her head back to even look him in the eye. Damn, the man was tall. Or she was too short.

'It's dangerous, Aileen.'

Aileen narrowed her eyes. 'I can take care of myself. I-'

'No. And that's my ultimate answer.' His voice was hard.

Aileen felt her blood boil. Why was the man so stubborn! She was no child who needed babysitting. And she wasn't stupid to go asking for trouble. 'I never asked you to join me in the first place.'

Ignoring him, Aileen turned around and dragged a stray chair over to where the noose had hung from the wooden beam last night.

Rolling his eyes, Callan knelt to examine a spot on the floor.

Whatever he'd come here to check on, he wasn't scrutinising. This pretence was to get her off his scent.

She was not one to back down. She'd do her own thing.

Aileen climbed up to analyse the wooden beam. Had Marley been tall enough to reach it and tie the rope herself?

Studying the beam, a glint caught her eye. She gasped.

Still kneeling on the floor, Callan groaned in frustration.

Bingo, Aileen flashed a smile. She was onto

something. She dragged the chair over to where the beam joined the roof and studied it.

'Oh yes!' A cry slipped past her puckered lips. In this entire dilapidated structure with a sagging roof, the wooden beam was newly fixed. The nails used to secure it in place were shining. And she hadn't mended this place up. She hadn't even known it existed.

Someone had taken the pains to fix this older wooden beam. The nails were gleaming with not a speck of dust.

Callan sighed as he stood back up. He massaged his right knee and sneaked a look at her.

Did his leg hurt? He was an amputee, a fact he'd kept secret from everyone until she'd seen it *that* night.

That is a mystery for another day…

Right now, she had this one to solve.

The chair creaked as Aileen leapt down onto the stony floor. Her boots snapped as she landed, but she paid them no heed. Instead, her gaze fixated on Callan's.

Callan's dark gaze bore into hers like he was searching for something. 'Please stay away from this. Marley wasn't an ordinary person, she had ties in all the wrong places.'

Aileen crossed her arms. 'I won't get in trouble. I only want to find answers.'

'I'll find them for you. Please, just…'

She stalked towards him. 'I'm looking into it whether you like it or not!'

Darkness descended, casting long shadows into the cottage. A chilly breeze blew in, in anticipation of more rain.

Now Callan hissed. 'Maybe I should break a rule and gag ye, woman! Don't ye-' Whatever Callan was about to say dissolved in a *whump* as all breath left his body.

Aileen had tackled him to the floor. She ignored his cursing as he desperately tried prying her off him.

'All I'm trying to do-' She punched a fist into his chest. 'Is help you.'

Another punch.

Callan flipped them over and clasped her wrists tightly.

'First off.' He grunted, almost losing his hold on Aileen as she wriggled underneath him. 'Ye haven't a clue how to punch. All ye'll end up doing is hurting yerself.'

Instead of second-guessing herself, using all her force, she kicked Callan in the side.

He grunted and let out a string of expletives. 'Aileen!'

She snapped out of it, her eyes wide. 'I...' Aileen huffed, pushing a stray strand behind her ear. A warm blush crept up her neck.

Callan panted, watching her squirm, but didn't say a word.

'I'm so sorry.' Aileen muttered. What had she done? Frustration and guilt boiled in her gut. It was as if a dam had broken. A string of words spilt out. 'I killed her! Don't you see? I did this! I fired Marley without a thought. Cast her out without notice or thought to where she might go. I. Killed. Her.' She choked with unshed tears.

Callan watched her in horror. There was no other way to put it. It only made her more embarrassed. What was wrong with her?

Taking him unawares, she pushed past. Scrambling to her feet, Aileen ran out of the cottage, the tattered remnants of her esteem in tow.

What an idiot!

Back in his office, Callan dusted off the remnants of dirt on his trousers before plopping on his chair.

Last night's scene had really hit Aileen hard. He rubbed a hand over his eyes. It was an eerie one, but the eejits working in Walsh's team didn't think a person like Marley Watson was worthy of investigation.

The phone rang. Callan reached for it but cursed seeing who it was. What did Walsh want?

'Aye?' He asked.

Walsh's response came at once. What was he doing in the office this late? 'Detective. I was with my superior officer and, um, our Medical Examiner found a note on Marley's body. We've identified it as a suicide note.'

Callan clenched his hands into fists.

This couldn't be.

'And where did ye find this note?'

The Loch Heaven Detective didn't respond for a while, and when he did, he fumbled with his words. 'You know, in her pocket.'

'She was wearing a frock, Walsh.' At least he thought it was a frock, or was it a dress? Bah! Why couldn't women wear simple garments?

Walsh answered slowly. 'Her, uh, dress had a pocket. And we found the note there.'

But Callan was having none of this. He wasn't even sure Marley's ghostly dress had a pocket. And if there was a note, he wanted to see it. 'I'd like to read this note.' He told Walsh.

His colleague cleared his throat. 'Yes, sure! But I called to inform you, er, we don't believe there's any foul play involved. We are ruling it as a suicide.' Walsh muttered the last part.

Callan's blood boiled, a red haze settling over his body. He clenched his jaw tight, hoping to counter-argue, even ready to argue with Walsh's feartie "Superior Officer" but Walsh, the damned bampot, had already slammed the phone down.

Feartie hog!

Callan's phone beeped with an oncoming message from Walsh.

He frowned at the infernal thing. He hated technology and wanted to throw his phone at the wall more times than not. No wonder its screen had cracked. Struggling, he pulled up the image Walsh had sent. It was the image of Marley's alleged suicide note.

"As a consequence of the poor state of affairs I find myself in, I've chosen the black veil of death over the hardships I've faced for these last couple of years. For I know misfortune will never leave my side."

Callan bristled. There was no way Marley could write that well. From the rumours he'd heard about the former innkeeper, she wasn't well-educated and chose slang over Shakespeare.

Besides, why had she chosen to take her life in a ramshackle cottage?

They hadn't found the car she'd rented, nor the shoes she'd worn. Where were both these items? She wouldn't have got here without either of them.

He stood up and listed these questions on his murder board. At this moment, he had almost no information about who Marley was. He'd done a cursory search in the police department's catalogue. And rightly so, the police had arrested Marley for plenty of minor crimes.

But the real dirt? He needed to dig it up. Where did she come from? What was her business in Loch Fuar? And why were the Loch Heaven police on her trail?

And there was only one way to find answers to those questions.

Callan sent off an email to Rory. If he wasn't allowed to solve Marley's case officially, he would take time off to solve it.

The murder board faced him. Scraps of paper always littered his office. A monkey could've danced the night away.

Callan scrubbed a hand over his prickly beard. He needed to eat, take a nap and shave.

His knee protested as it always did after long hours.

This case couldn't progress much without an autopsy or toxicology report. Hopefully, Rory could get his hands on those.

Callan stood ready to call it a day when his boss tapped on his office door. 'Five years working with me and ye never took a day off. I could give ye six months off, but I ken ye aren't going on holiday. Is Aileen helping ye with this case?'

Callan clenched his teeth. 'What's this got to do with Aileen?'

Leaning against the door frame, Rory asked. 'Hasn't Siobhan asked ye to date her? Ye're well suited. And she's got a sharp head on her shoulders.'

Rory paused at Callan's exasperated groan. 'Don't meddle. She isn't solving this case with me.'

Holding out his hands in mock surrender, Rory said, 'I'm only suggesting what's best for ye. And ye two did a great job with the previous case.'

Callan pushed his hands into his pockets. 'Can I take Monday to Thursday off this week?'

Rory sighed. 'Sure. Just be careful. Roland doesn't like officers who don't follow his commands to the T.' The white-haired grandfatherly police officer stood up. 'I'll talk to them. See if I can wield out the autopsy reports as well as the toxicology report.'

Callan swallowed the residual taste of the coffee. His stomach growled. 'Thank ye.'

His boss swatted a hand. 'Oh, Callan, dinnae mention it, I ken ye. Justice and yer duty mean more to ye than simply flaunting that badge. It's officers like ye that make me hold my head high when I name my profession. Ye wouldn't be ye if ye dinnae double down on this case and find the *real* killer.'

Callan ran a hand over his face. Rory felt that way about him?

'Any help needed, ye can always ask,' Rory said.

Callan bobbed his head.

'And ye can ask Aileen for help. Ye two make for brilliant partners. Two peas in a pod.' With a wave, Rory left.

The slight ache in Callan's head intensified. He

didn't need to know how great they were together. Their evening's wrestling match was deeply etched into his memory.

It was time he got cracking. Callan rubbed at his forehead.

Eat, sleep and a shave was the next order of business. And then solving needless murder.

AILEEN HADN'T A CLUE WHAT HAD CRAWLED UP HER skin. She'd wrestled with a detective, for God's sake!

She rubbed her heated cheeks with her hands.

It was mortifying.

She sought solace in the lemongrass freshener she'd sprayed that morning.

Best to file this incident as another one of her "death scene side effects."

At the knock on the door, Aileen's palms turned clammy. Who could it be this late in the evening? Was it Callan? She hoped not.

She pulled open the door, and her taut shoulders loosened. It was just Isla. And her friend was her usual bubbly self. She waltzed in, grinning. 'Your recipe floored the in-laws! But more specifically, I got news. And I had to drive down here to give it to you!'

'News?' Aileen leant in.

'Aye! I found Marley's flat!'

'Marley's flat?' That was unexpected. Aileen

had been prepared for simple gossip, not official details.

Isla nodded enthusiastically. 'I didn't find out about her social habits, except she was a recluse. But I guess her flat's address might help.'

This was incredible. Aileen was in awe of her friend. Marley had lied through her teeth when she'd told Daisy her address. 'How did you-?'

Isla held up her hands. 'Don't ask. Sometimes you have to slide up to the right people, even if you detest them.' Like a diva, she flipped her red hair over her shoulder.

Aileen snorted at her friend. She was something else.

Isla held out a piece of paper. On it was Marley's address. 'She lived in Loch Heaven.'

Aileen read the piece of paper. 'Guess I'm heading to Loch Heaven then.'

'That's a good idea. When will you leave?' Isla asked.

'First thing tomorrow? I have got nothing else to do.'

Isla's face fell. 'Daniel's 'bout to head over to get the work started. That means I'm on child duty. Besides, Carly and I decided girl time would do us good.'

Aileen had no clue how someone spent girl time with a toddler. But Isla worked hard, so she deserved some free time with her bairn.

'You can do this, Aileen. I know you can. And

I'm always just a phone call away.' Isla hugged her close.

Aileen waved off her friend.

Shutting the door, Aileen squared her shoulders. Yes, she could do this.

It was time to dig into Marley Watson's life.

Her phone pinged. Pulling up the email, Aileen grunted. It was surely spam! She was ready to ignore it when the sender caught her eye. It was a strange name: *ilovemurder*.

A chill ran through her as an image loaded. It was an eye. A single eye, bright green and alarmingly wicked. What struck her as more terrifying was its realistically maddening gleam.

Aileen's throat went dry.

The email had no words, but just a subject line that read: "a gift for you."

This was definitely a hoax. Adventurous Aileen didn't believe in superstitions. She sucked in her bottom lip.

No, no, she was a woman on a mission and she had better get on with it.

CHAPTER THREE

Aileen trusted Daniel McIntyre. She gave him and his men a free rein over her inn.

Getting out of their hair meant Aileen got time to drive down to Loch Heaven.

She had packed a couple of days' worth of clothes.

Tall mountains ran past, a fortress glimmered under the bright sun. Apparently, the storm had passed, and summer was back.

Shades of green were smattered with white sheep lazing around. Bales of hay were rolled up on farmlands. And the highway that ran between the fields had little traffic.

Summer meant fun holidays, ice cream and outdoor games.

Aileen inhaled a lungful of refreshing air.

Her childhood summers had entailed a trip to

Dachaigh. And now Dachaigh was her home. How wonderful was that?

Aileen drove to where the GPS informed her was the closest parking lot to Marley Watson's flat.

The town of Loch Heaven was a little larger than Loch Fuar. What that meant was the city centre had a dozen more people than Loch Fuar. Loch Fuar considered two a crowd.

Trees danced as the gentle breeze toyed with Aileen's dark brown locks. It was a pleasant day.

But the content smile disappeared as she hiked up the road to where Marley had been staying. Here, the houses were two storeys tall but showed their age. It was the neglected part of town, where no one bothered to clean the litter or empty the community bins.

Aileen grimaced at the sourness of rotting garbage.

A few leftover cans from last night's forays scattered the building. Sinister syringes peeked out from a heap of crusty cardboard takeout boxes with stale pizza half-chewed by fat mice.

It didn't take a genius to know this neighbourhood was not the safest.

The afternoon sun shone its harsh light on the grey walls, highlighting the peeling paint. Aileen almost winced at the brutally splintered window at what had to be Marley's flat.

Gnawing on her lips, she stood there staring.

Now the question was: how could she get in?

Throwing caution to the wind, Aileen entered the small two-storey structure. The musky smell was overpowering, as well as the scuttles of mice in the dark.

There was no light, apart from the meagre natural light that shone on the staircase. It highlighted the termite-eaten wooden stairs. Some stairs even sported holes.

Was Marley in such dire need for money that this was all she could afford?

Inhaling a sharp breath, Aileen gingerly took a step. The stair creaked. Cautiously, she tried the next.

It took her a while to reach the first storey. It didn't matter, as long as she didn't break her neck tumbling down these stairs!

Her boots clomped over the stone tiles when she reached the landing. A steady beam of light cut through the dimness, illuminating the dancing dust particles.

Then she heard a soft feminine whisper. Aileen jolted. Who was it?

A gruff voice spoke. 'Please. Gimme a day!'

Silence.

Holding her breath, Aileen could hear her heart pounding in her chest. There was no turning back now.

She tiptoed up the last flight of treacherous stairs, careful not to make any noise.

WHEN EYES DON'T LIE

Hiding behind the broken balustrade, Aileen peered through its gap onto the last floor.

Two doors stood next to each other, sporting gashes that spoke of years of wear.

The door to the left was wide open, and in the doorway, on his knees, sat a man with a shaggy beard. His soot-black hair was dry and frizzy. Aileen could barely see his beady eyes, before another pair of legs obstructed her view.

She squinted to make out the silhouette of a broad man looming over the one on the floor. The broad man whispered something into the other's ear that had him whimpering. 'Please... Please. I dinnae ken. I'll keep an eye oot. I'll... Gimme a day.'

Just then a willow slim figure took a step into the scene. She tsked. 'A day.' Her voice was sultry, very soft and feminine. But then it grew cold. 'Or this winter you might not be so warm. Don't leave your future *hanging by a noose.*' She chuckled, her laughter like a shard of ice.

A chill ran down Aileen's arm. *Hanging by a noose?* What was she talking about?

But the lady wasn't done. Abruptly she turned. 'Didn't your mum teach you it's rude to eavesdrop?'

Eyes wide, Aileen gasped. The woman, her face hidden in the dark, laughed. 'Do you have the guts to stand before me?'

Trembling, Aileen lifted her gaze to where the

woman's face might be. Just then she moved, her eyes illuminated by a stray beam.

Aileen's breath caught, and her body jerked.

A sinister set of eyes glared back, an unnatural green and blue.

Heart palpitating, Aileen hightailed out of there. She took two stairs at a time, praying she didn't break her crown like Jill.

Her footsteps thundered in the empty stairwell as evil laughter followed.

Aileen tripped when she burst out into the late morning sun. Her heart hammered, and she panted as if she'd run a marathon.

Aileen jolted when a snicker reached her ears from across the street. She pivoted to face a group of gangly men leaning against a car, flaky with brown rust. They sneered when one murmured to the others, hooded eyes trailing her. Red-hot fear blubbered inside her.

What had she got herself into?

One man hooted, another whistled, and the third commented on her... Derrière.

The city had had dark places, but the anti-risk Aileen had never ventured in there.

Heck, she didn't know the "D" of self-defence. Would her brief online classes help if these gangly men attacked her? Or worse, the woman upstairs...

Aileen clasped her icy hands. What had she been thinking strolling into this place alone?

When one man stood up to cross the road, Aileen's limbs grew heavy.

He glanced to his right as a car hobbled past.

Taking that as a sign, Aileen clamped the mushrooming anxiety and strode back towards the centre of town.

One step in front of the other. Steady steps…

But that demand was quickly forgotten as the cat-calls grew louder, nearer.

Using all her self-restraint from sprinting out of there, Aileen kept reminding herself: *Adventurous, Courageous.*

After a moment, the dingy streets pattered with busy footfall, leaving the litter behind. Aileen puckered at the sight of an old lady trudging a heavy bag up the street.

She quickly jogged over. 'Here, let me help you.'

'Ah thanks, dearie.' She reminded Aileen of the rosy powder her Gran used.

Only then did her palpitating heart settle.

Maybe this wasn't a good idea. Callan had warned her it would be dangerous. Aileen shook herself. No, she'd find a way. Adventurous and Courageous…

The old lady lived a five-minute walk away, thanking her profusely for the help. All Aileen did was smile as politely as she could. The old woman had protected her, not the other way around.

Aileen rounded the corner hastily and kept walking.

Striding down another block, Aileen found a small cafe bursting with youngsters and the aroma of freshly baked bread, in the better part of town.

She sighed and plopped down in a corner booth.

Taking deep breaths to calm herself, she booted her laptop.

Marley Watson… Her fingers clattered over the keyboard. Who was this woman? If the address Isla had found was the correct one, Marley had barely been able to keep a roof over her head. And judging by the neighbour and that woman, Marley had surrounded herself with dangerous people.

Did one of them murder her?

Aileen shivered just thinking about *those* eyes.

Sipping her coffee, she searched for data on "Marley Watson."

In careful print, she penned down the notes on her yellow notepad. The fear dwindled, almost dissolving in the routine task of reading and taking down notes.

After an hour or so, Aileen blinked her droopy eyes and squinted at what she'd got down so far.

Marley Watson had been in her late thirties with a previous marriage that ended a couple of years ago. The husband was in prison, charged with accessory to murder.

Could the husband have got out? Killed his former wife? Marley had—as she'd told Daisy—no family or friends to reach out to.

Aileen pursed her lips. If she wanted to hack into files to know more about Marley's life, she needed a better place. A quieter one, and somewhere private since she'd be delving into sensitive files. This cafe was a little *too* public.

At the edge of her hearing, a group laughed. Someone ordered a mug of hot cocoa. Aileen's full stomach rumbled as the aroma of molten chocolate filled her nostrils.

Focus!

She continued perusing her notes. From what Aileen had gathered, Marley Watson was the sort of person who hid behind animated posts on social media.

She'd posted memes, commented on politics, and had some contrary views on society that the Victorians would've been proud of.

She was a strange woman indeed, Aileen thought as she peered at the screen. She hadn't posted a single selfie, and she hadn't bothered to make any of her accounts private either. There were a couple of offhanded comments and responses to some posts with narcissistic tones.

Perhaps Aileen could try hacking into her accounts and then into her emails-

'Told ye to keep out of trouble.'

Aileen held onto the table when her chair almost toppled over. Her wide eyes locked with Callan's blue ones.

She gaped, cheeks heating under his gaze. They could be on fire for all she cared.

What was he doing here? He was here to solve the case, of course! Would he bring up her late-night assault? Did she have to apologise for accosting him? That only made her blush harder.

CALLAN WATCHED AILEEN SQUIRMING IN HER SEAT like a child caught stealing candy.

The little eejit!

He took the liberty of sitting opposite her. 'What part of "this is dangerous, stay away," don't ye understand?'

Callan thanked the server who placed a steaming cup of bitter coffee in front of him.

Aileen raised her chin in defiance. 'Who says I was here to snoop around?'

Callan stubbed a finger on her yellow notepad.

Perched at the cafe's tall chairs, he'd been observing her for a good fifteen minutes. She'd been too engrossed fishing dirt on Marley Watson. She was Icarus, too close to the blazing sun. And she wouldn't know when she'd been burned.

Aileen smirked. 'The curious part of my brain is hungry.'

Callan leant ahead. 'Feed it somewhere else. This is dangerous.'

Something akin to fear flashed in Aileen's eyes,

but it disappeared just as quickly. He didn't for a minute believe she was scared of his warnings. What was she hiding?

Aileen laid her palms flat on the coarse table, leaning in. 'You as well as I know Marley was murdered. All I want is to find some answers.'

She wasn't letting this go. From what he knew of Mackinnon women, they were a stubborn lot. She wasn't likely to sit back just because he asked her to.

If you can't fight them, join them, or rather join resources with them.

Callan sipped his coffee. 'Aye, it wasn't suicide. But Walsh says he found a suicide note on her person. But I doubt it's legitimate. For all I ken, it's planted evidence.'

Aileen frowned. 'How can you say that?'

He handed her his phone. 'Read the image Walsh sent.'

Aileen squinted at the letter Walsh had sent. It wasn't very clear, considering Callan's phone screen was cracked, but it showed the important bits clearly.

Being the observant sort, Aileen found the anomaly. 'Is that monogrammed paper?'

Grunting, Callan savoured another sip. 'Aye. Expensive paper for a woman who died in a dingy cottage. And judging by her unemployment record, I doubt she could afford it.'

She read the letter again, her lips mouthing the

words. Finally, she looked up at him. 'We know little about Marley to know her habits. It says here she was tired of life. For all we know, she could've been.'

Callan sighed. 'We can find out everything there is to ken. Marley wasn't a person who lived on the correct side of the law. But tired of life? I doubt that's true. As ye've noted, her husband is in prison for accessory to murder. And she too has a long sheet of her own, from shoplifting to vandalism. Even a small one on physical abuse, but the charges were dropped. And she was heading to Loch Fuar. Our little town is a bit too far away to travel to, to commit suicide.'

Aileen rubbed her forehead. 'I need to know what she was doing at my cottage, Callan. And why someone killed her.'

This was it. He licked his lips as if testing the words. 'Working together as a team is twice the might. We'll get there quicker. Besides, I have the resources and ye have the money brains. We won't step on each other's toes. Would ye... Would ye like to join me?'

Aileen blinked, caught unawares. Her eyes twinkled as she asked, 'Work with you as a partner?'

He studied her eyes for a while. 'Something like that but, ye don't cross me or go hunting on yer own.'

'Touché. Everything we do, we do together.' Aileen tsked when Callan tried to argue. 'It's only fair.' He shrugged, holding out his hand. She placed her smaller, soft ones in his.

The deal was struck.

Aileen sat back and eyed the table. 'On that note, there's something I need to tell you. I went to Marley's flat…'

She told him all that had transpired that morning. Callan listened carefully, taking down notes in his notepad. When she told him about the woman she'd encountered, his jaw clenched tight. 'Ye say Isla saw a similar person at Loch Fuar?'

Aileen nodded. 'Although I think I was projecting what Isla said. It was very dingy in there, not enough light to clearly see any of them. And clearly seeing someone's eyes? I think my brain was playing tricks on me.'

Despite that, Callan wrote it all down and listened to Aileen finish her recollection of events. No wonder she was scared. He would've been too if he wasn't carrying a gun and had no training. 'We'll ask around for this woman. I don't like coincidences, brain games or not.'

When they were done, Aileen let Callan read through her extensive notes. Aileen was really good at the tech things as well as the financials. And in the short while she'd sat here with nothing but a browser, she'd uncovered a lot about Marley as a person.

But this was the front Marley put forth to the outer world. But what was she up to in private? The only place to know about her personal matters was the rat hole she called home.

They had to head back to Marley's flat.

That same afternoon—dressed inconspicuously in dark hues—they both headed to Marley Watson's flat. Their attire didn't make much of a difference to Callan who was always clad in Satan's clothes i.e. all black.

'How are we going to get in?' Aileen questioned.

Callan hissed against the drizzle. Where had the sunshine disappeared to? 'We'll see when we get there.'

'You're not much of a planner, are you? Just as you didn't think of booking a hotel room in advance.'

Callan didn't respond until they reached the crossroads: one leading onto the bustling station and the other to the fringes of the underworld where even now, in the waning sunlight, drugs were traded as if flowers between lovers. 'Nothing ever goes to plan anyway. Why waste the time?'

Aileen shrugged. 'That's one way to think of it.'

He cast a sidelong glimpse at Aileen. She straightened when his heavy hand landed on her stiff shoulders. But she didn't jolt. Yet when something rattled in the dark edges of the street, Aileen would falter, eyes flittering around them.

As they ventured deeper into the dingy streets, Callan adjusted the hand he'd carelessly thrown over Aileen's shoulder and pulled her closer. He didn't want her scared. It was best not to draw undue attention by parading down the street like predators. This way they'd be two people taking a stroll in the sultry evening air.

The street became dirtier with each house. A strong pungent smell emanated from the drains. The fairly painted blocks tumbled into red brick structures with peeling paint and then ultimately, boasted broken window panels. In the heart of this derelict state, Callan led Aileen to Marley Watson's doorstep.

A quick side glance across the road confirmed his suspicion: they were being watched by junkies. Callan shifted as Aileen stiffened next to him.

She better stay calm…

He didn't miss a beat. He led them towards the shabby house as if he lived there, trudging up the rickety stairs with Aileen still tucked beside him, her summery perfume a respite from the acrid garbage that littered the streets. The staircase was as black as the Earl of Hell's Waistcoat, thanks to the overcast sky outside. The scuttle of scampering feet belonged to mice that raced in the darkness.

Their footsteps echoed as they hiked up from the first landing to the next. Finally, they were at the last flight of stairs leading up to the second floor that had been Marley's flat.

Aileen threw her head back as if thanking the heavens for saving her neck from the utter disaster that the stairs were. Her shoulders had bunched up to her ears. So stressed was she, that she clearly missed the obvious. Callan's hand firmly squeezed Aileen's shoulder, and he pulled her against him.

Focusing, he pointed at the door ahead of them.

The overpowering muskiness in the air was more overwhelming here. Someone had forgotten to sweep this place, making it bitterly grimy.

Funny, DI Declan Walsh hadn't bothered to visit Marley Watson's flat. But someone apparently had.

The derelict wooden door stood at a slight angle to the actual doorframe. In fact, the hinges holding the door to the frame had rotten away at the top, teetering it diagonally. Long, careless gashes scratched across the door.

But the fact that it was ajar made Callan's eyes snap alert. And the shuffling noises from within the flat meant the intruder must still be inside.

He placed a finger over his lips, signalling Aileen. Drawing his gun from the holster, he stealthily climbed the stairs.

Aileen followed behind. Damn, that woman never listened. Perhaps she couldn't stand there alone amidst scuttling mice.

Carefully, with his gun still aimed, Callan gently pushed the door open with his foot. It creaked but swung open at an odd angle.

'Police! Freeze! Hands where I can see them.'

The short man inside the room yelped. He dropped to the floor like a chicken for slaughter. Hands flung to his sides. 'Don't! Stop, please don't, don't.'

Callan stalked over to him and patted the man's sides. He wore baggy shorts and had a mop of ginger hair that had never seen a comb. His dirty face was currently pressed against the floor, muffled sounds scattering the dust where his mouth had to be.

The man was so plainly thin that Callan pulled him up with just one hand.

He wiggled, eyes squeezed as if waiting for the blow.

With amusement, Callan noted his frayed "Winnie the Pooh" shirt. It had a hole or two, but apart from that, it entirely suited the short, frail man who was no more than thirty.

'Stop this and stand, man!'

He immediately stood like the Queen's guards. 'Don't shoot.'

Callan cocked his head. 'Have I?'

Aileen stepped up beside Callan. Pity for the man shone on her face. The lad moistened his cracked lips.

'What's your name?'

'TJ.'

Callan took a threatening step. 'What's yer business here?'

TJ tried wriggling from his grasp. He was almost hysterical. 'Don't kill me! I was just trying to check if Marley left some cash behind for me.'

'Why would she?' When the lad merely stared between them, Callan shouted. 'Explain!'

TJ writhed, gaping like a fish before finally answering. 'Um, I-I work-ed for her.'

Callan snapped. 'What did ye do?'

'She wasn't good with tech stuff. You know, asking the right people the right questions on the dark web. Hacking into people's computers and stealing passwords or bypassing locks... I could help you! Please don't shoot-'

Flashing his teeth, Callan said, 'Ye just confessed a handful of crimes to the police.'

The scaredy-cat was on the verge of tears.

If Callan with his badge scared him this much, would he kill an actual person?

The lad quaked in his boots and was most likely scared of his own footsteps. But appearances could be deceptive.

Aileen was the voice of patience. 'What did you search for Ms Watson?'

'She wanted intel on a few people. I work at Vicky's; the bloke owns some computers and we do our work from up there.' He hesitated. 'She met me there once, asked if I'd find intel on a few people for a fee.'

Callan cocked an eyebrow. 'And ye said yes? That's stalking.'

The lad shrugged. 'I'd do that for money.'

'Empty yer pockets.' Callan demanded of him.

'No!'

Before Callan could get a better grip on the lad, he made a beeline between Aileen and Callan towards the door. Faster than the mice lurking in the shadows, he flew down the stairs and was out before either of them could run after him.

'That sod!' Callan huffed.

Aileen drummed fingers on her thighs, thinking.

What intel could he have found for Marley? She wasn't employed, was she? And where would she find the money to give TJ?

'Whatever he searched for her, we'll find it here.'

Callan was right. They found a lot. More than either of them could have hoped.

Marley's flat was smaller than the matchboxes in London. It had one bathroom, an alcove that doubled as a bedroom, and another nook that was the kitchen. Callan desperately tried not to gag over the fungus covered takeout boxes. The singular room was otherwise littered with newspapers, books, and soiled clothes. Apparently, the woman had lived the life of a hermit.

In one corner, behind a stack of old newspapers, was a box fixed to the floor. The handle on its metallic door and the inconspicuous keyhole on its other side told Callan it was a safe. And it was firmly locked.

He hunched over it, using his tools to unlock it.

It only took him a couple of minutes before the *click* signalled it was opened. But its contents made Callan's eyes bulge.

'Bloody hell!' He cursed.

Inside, there were two heaps of cash tied together by a rubber band. Apart from cash, there was a pocket-size diary. He pulled it out and snapped the safe closed. Funny, he scratched his chin. A broke, unemployed woman had a safe, not just a safe, but one stacked with notes. The real kind too, Callan had checked.

CHAPTER FOUR

Aileen carried out her own investigation at the other end of the room.

Using a tissue from the pack she carried in her satchel, Aileen moved a few cardboard boxes and newspapers away. She swore she saw a centipede or two crawling on them. A fungus laden bread followed another reeking take-away box before Aileen found four notebooks.

Curious, she picked them up and placed them on the rickety sofa.

She dug around some more, but when her stomach roiled from the stench, she quickly abandoned her search and sat down on the sofa. Taking a small sip of water from the bottle she carried, Aileen set to work.

She leafed through the notebooks. Unlike her,

Marley had a poor hand. It was crooked and almost illegible. Her "ts" could've been "es."

The quality of the paper was the cheapest one could find. The ink almost seeped through the page. Marley had pasted pictures too, but they weren't newspaper clippings. In fact, they were surveillance images of a woman.

Aileen frowned. Marley had two books documenting this woman's whereabouts in detail. In those books, Marley had listed down the woman's trips to the grocery store, her height, weight, preferences and schedule. How creepy!

Had Marley been a consummate stalker?

That was highly plausible, as Aileen picked up another notebook. This one was about a man. He was the owner of the pub, Sláinte. Aileen had passed it today when they'd hiked up the road. Was Marley spying on her neighbours?

Callan plopped on the sofa beside Aileen. Puffs of dust rose in the air making him sneeze.

'She wasn't a clean freak.' He commented, wiping his hands.

'That's obvious, considering the state I found Dachaigh in.' Aileen shut her eyes for a moment. 'Callan, she was a stalker.'

Callan leafed through the pages of the notebook. He scratched his chin. 'Let's go to Sláinte.'

'What?!' Aileen's eyes rounded. She knew a place like that would only be the playground of the men who'd followed her that morning.

Callan raised an eyebrow, smirking. 'Scared?'

Aileen cleared her throat. She wouldn't show weakness. She inhaled, *adventurous* and exhaled, *courageous*. 'Of course not. Just thought your presence would make their loyal customers run away.'

'Probably might, but I want to speak to this man, Charlie, in his own element. Although first I have a little detour for us.' Callan sneered. 'I want to meet someone special.'

Confused, Aileen asked, 'Who?'

Callan's gaze darkened when it met hers. 'Marley's next-door neighbour. I heard he had a visitor today.'

Callan shut Marley's door as best as he could. It grated against the tiled floor like an old machine.

Biting her lip, Aileen studied the door next to Marley's. Just like the door to Marley's flat, this one had long careless gashes on it made by a sharp knife. But unlike the flat they'd just been in, this one was locked tight.

Aileen rapped her knuckles against the wooden door. Her two sharp knocks echoed in the dark stairwell.

But no one answered.

She pursed her lips. 'Guess no one's home.'

Standing so close that their arms brushed, Callan snorted. 'He hasn't left. Hold on.'

Shuffling ahead, Callan's broad shoulders blocked Aileen's view.

Contrary to her polite knock, Callan banged on

the door with his fists. 'I ken ye are in there. Open up!' He called out.

Still no answer. Somewhere on the other side of the corridor, a rat scuttled, its nails scratching against the wooden stairs.

Aileen shuddered and jolted with Callan pounded on the door again. 'I ain't going anywhere till ye open up!'

After a long minute, the light sound of bolts snapping open drifted from within the flat.

Just as slowly, the door swung open. It was the same man Aileen had seen that morning with the shaggy hair. Hair covered his entire face except for the nose and his two eyes. His potbelly protruded from a broad frame and the clothes he wore stank. 'What?' He sneered to show nicotine-stained teeth.

Callan towered over him. He stabbed a thumb towards the other flat. 'Marley Watson.'

An alarmed pair of eyes watched them. Quickly, the man stepped back and tried to slam the door in their faces.

Callan was faster. Using his arms, he kept the door open.

Marley's neighbour hissed. 'Ye can't force yer way in, ye can't.'

Callan flashed his pearly whites. 'Then how about ye answer my simple questions? We'll be out of yer hair in a couple of minutes.'

An alerted gaze flittered between them. 'Dinnae ken.'

Aileen stepped in. 'What don't you know? Surely you've seen Marley before. She lived right next door.'

The man must have moved his jaw because his thick beard rustled. 'Dead, she was.'

Callan raised an eyebrow. 'Dead?'

Fidgeting with the doorknob, he said, 'Dead. What are ye to her, eh?'

Callan grinned. 'Marley's an old pal.'

A nasal laugh emulated from between the thick beard. 'Dinnae ken Marley had friends, did I? What ye do?'

Callan flicked a hand. 'None of yer business. Tell me, who's been visiting Marley Watson this last week?'

'Dinnae see, did I?'

'Aye, ye did. Speak!'

He shook two stubby fingers. 'Uh nh. Dinnae see.'

Grumbling, Callan snapped a pound on his proffered hand. 'Who visited yer neighbour?'

'Two men, did I see. A short, timid one and the other a tall one.'

Callan crossed his arms. 'When?'

Seeing an opportunity, the man showed Callan his palm again. 'Dinnae ken.'

Callan gritted his teeth. 'Come on!'

'Uh uh.' He grunted.

This time Callan dropped fifty pence.

Marley's neighbour hissed. 'Miserly bastard.'

Callan hissed back. 'Answer me!'

'Marley left Tuesday and dinnae come back.' His gaze flittered to her flat's door. 'I dinna remember when the other two men came, did I. But she wasnae home both those times, was she.'

Aileen cleared her throat and stepped into the conversation. 'Were they together, these two men?'

The neighbour responded after a long pause. 'Nay. Now get out, I've got things to-'

But Aileen wasn't done. 'Who was that lady visiting you this morning?'

He grew agitated and pushed on the door. 'None of yer business, is it? Get lost!'

Callan leaned forward, looming over the man. 'Answer the lady.'

But he shook his head. 'I dinnae ken, do I. I won't tell. Get outta my house.'

This time Callan let him slam the door shut. The wood rattled but stayed on its hinges.

Pushing his hands in his pockets, Callan said, 'Guess he's a hermit. Doesn't ken much.'

Aileen hummed. 'Guess so. But he said two men came to Marley's flat after she'd left. Who could they be?'

Callan tipped his head to the side. 'One according to the description could be that rat, TJ. But the second one? We'll have to figure out who that was.'

Together they listened to the scuttling. Aileen shuddered. 'I think we should get out of here first.'

'Good idea. Let's go get a drink.'

Sláinte was, as Aileen had predicted, a playground for all things illegal. Even as a civilian with an untrained eye, she caught two people exchanging a tiny packet under one rickety table.

A few heads turned, a couple of them showing corroded yellow teeth.

Aileen smothered the urge to bolt out of this vinegary dump. It took all her might not to squirm.

With sure steps, Callan approached a table at the other end and sat, gesturing for Aileen to take a seat.

So much for keeping her clothes clean.

As discreetly as she could, Aileen placed a hand over her nose, trying to smell the minty breath mint she'd used before this fateful hike.

The table was as slimy as the floor, glistening with all sorts of fluids. It wasn't a surprise that this place resembled a pigsty, was it? Aileen desperately tried not to gag as the stench overwhelmed her senses.

She placed her palms on her lap, breathing in through her mouth.

Hope I don't boke!

Callan didn't reciprocate any of her sentiments. He sat as if he frequented such establishments. Before entering, he had hidden his gun and badge under his black coat.

The only reason he stood apart from his fellow

customers would be his clothes, which could've been the high fashion in the current scenario.

Aileen didn't want to fit in. She was severely out of place. If she could, she would have run miles from here, but if this helped them solve the case, she'd do it.

A lady sauntered up to them, wearing heels that were too high and a wig that hid the wrinkles on her cheeks. She flashed a dizzying smile at Callan.

Callan propped up two fingers. 'Two ales.'

'Coming right up!' She hollered before sauntering away.

'I'm not-' Aileen's protest abruptly cut off when a man slid into the third chair.

Despite the dark interiors, Aileen recognised him. He was the man from Marley's book!

The pub owner - Charlie...

'You aren't from 'ereabouts. I smell boaby from a mile away.'

Callan responded. 'Detective.'

The pub owner sat up. Despite Charlie's bulging muscles, Callan stood taller.

'I've got ma licenses to trade. I ain't do any wrong.'

'Licenses to trade, eh? Even that?' Callan raised an eyebrow towards a table where a small pouch was being passed around.

'I don't see no nothing.' Charlie protested.

Callan dismissed the comment. 'I'm not interested in that. Tell me about Marley Watson.'

Charlie sat back, flashing a metallic tooth. 'Don't ken the twat.'

'Respect, man!' Callan commanded.

The pub-owner shook his head. 'Ken nothing'

Callan leant in and sneered. 'It'll take ten minutes for me to call my friend. Invite him here for a blether with his police pals.'

Charlie considered for a moment. His gaze flittered between the table behind them and Callan. Tugging at his dirty tank top, he whispered on a sour breath of alcohol. 'Killed herself she did. An oddball, chav!'

Aileen spoke for the first time. 'Oddball?'

The man fixed her with his beady stare. 'Aye. Never left that bin she called home. My boy now, he works for Johnny delivering pizza, he goes to her flat every day.'

'Your son doesn't work here?' Aileen questioned.

Charlie grunted. 'Just a fifteen-year-old, cannae work here.'

'And now he's sensitive to the law.' Aileen muttered to herself.

Callan shuffled his feet, leaning back before piercing Charlie with a glare. 'Why do ye think she killed herself?'

The bulky man visibly drooped his thick shoulders. 'Freddie, now that's her neighbour, said how she left in a hurry four days ago or so. That lass wasn't the polite sort. Freddie likes to help himself to the cash she leaves around in her bin. Her door was bah! A tin foil easily peeled off.'

Ah, so that man with the pot-belly and shaggy hair was Freddie. And apparently, he knew how to break into Marley's house.

Did he have a motive to kill her? Aileen asked. 'Did she get into fights with Freddie over the money?'

Shaking a hand, Charlie said, 'Nah! What's she to know how much's missing from that dump of hers? Besides, she's loaded.'

Callan raised an eyebrow. 'Where did she get the cash from?'

Charlie's voice rose as he got more indignant. ''Ell I ken! I'd do it, too, shut this place down. Put my feet up and forget about these scoundrels.'

Aileen pulled out one of Marley's notebook they'd stuffed in her bag. 'Can you tell me who this is?'

She skimmed to the page she wanted and held it up to show a clear picture of the woman Marley had been stalking. Large sunglasses hid the woman's face.

'Huh.' The man's gaze flitted around, suddenly conscious of his actions. Horror shone in his eyes. 'You best keep out 'er way.'

That was strange. Aileen gazed at the heavily tattooed man. 'Why's that?'

Charlie could barely be heard. 'That's the Houndress.'

She held the chuckle. 'Houndress?'

'Shush!' Charlie waved and lowered his head. 'Ain't no one mess with 'er. Bad news, she is. She asks you give, no questions. She owns most places 'round 'ere.'

'You mean she was Marley Watson's landlady?' Aileen clarified.

'Aye. And you stay away from her if you want your head intact!' Charlie whisper-yelled.

But Callan pushed. 'What's her actual name?'

The man bent closer till his chin almost brushed the table and whispered, his sour breath tickling Aileen's nostrils. 'Morticia Luna.'

Everything was grey and damp when they stepped out of Sláinte.

'Ah, fresh air!' Aileen inhaled large gulps of oxygen.

Callan snorted. 'It's hardly fresh. I can smell all kinds of things here.'

He put his arms around Aileen's shoulders and pulled her close. The citrus perfume she wore was a respite.

Aileen swivelled to head back to the centre of town when her steps faltered, and she gasped.

Callan eyed her panicked stare and asked. 'What's wrong?'

'The… That man.' She stammered.

His eyes sharp, Callan scanned their surroundings. There were a few figures huddled in blankets on the edge of the street. A couple of eyes trailed them through splintered windows on the dark flats above.

Someone walked on the other footpath, minding their own business. The alley between the two pavements was damp from rainwater or sewage, Callan couldn't be sure.

But it wasn't any of those things that had Aileen panicked. It was the inconspicuous man, leaning against Sláinte's wall.

Aileen spoke through clenched teeth. 'That's the man I told you about. The one outside Marley's building who followed me.'

Finding Aileen's gaze, the sod grinned. He had one missing tooth and sported a bruised lip. The full-sleeved shirt he wore was rumpled, and his muddy blond hair hadn't seen a comb in days.

Pushing against the wall, he sauntered up to them. 'Hello, beautiful.'

Aileen turned her head the other way. 'I've got no business with you. Leave.'

He tutted. 'Come on, love. Ye ken we met a while ago. Did ye forget?'

Callan's skin crawled at the jeer in his voice. He held Aileen's stiff body closer still. 'Piss off!'

Now the smirk along with those slit-like thin eyes latched onto his. 'I ain't talking to ye.'

'Talk to her, ye go through me.'

'Her daddy, are ye?' He ran a hand through his hair. 'What's yer business with her?'

Now his blood boiled. Callan swallowed a growl and spoke with barely restrained fury. 'She is with me, ye sod!'

Wagging a dirty finger, he tutted again. 'Not 'er. The woman who lives up there. What's yer connection?'

Was he asking about Marley Watson? Callan placed a hand on his hip, ready to snap out his gun from the holster. 'What's Marley to ye?'

Tilting his head, the man's gaze met Aileen's and then latched back onto Callan's. 'Ye tell me first. Yer girl pal came dun 'ere first, and then ye. What's yer business with Marley?'

Callan's hand gripped the butt of his gun. Did this man know Marley was dead, or didn't he? He spoke of her like she was alive. It could be a lie. News travelled fast in these circles. And if it had reached Sláinte, all its patrons would know. Including this man who knew Marley and where she lived.

Turning to move Aileen behind him, Callan hissed. 'Were ye keeping a watch on Marley's flat?'

Crossing his hands, the man narrowed his eyes. He stood a little shorter than Callan, and an angry red gash peeked through his sleeve. 'My neighbourhood, I do what I want. Don't nose about where ye doesnae belong.'

A trembling hand grasped Callan's arm. It was

Aileen. 'Let's get out of here.' She whispered to him.

But Callan wasn't about to stand back. 'Threatening me, are ye?'

'Warning. Ye havenae seen ma threats.' He growled. Stabbing a finger in Callan's direction, he spoke, 'Come back here, it won't end up well for ye.' Turning on his heels, the man strode away.

Aileen tugged at Callan's arm. 'Come on. Please.'

Squeezing Aileen's clammy palm, Callan guided her out of the dirty streets and into safer, crowded areas.

What in the world had Marley Watson got herself into?

AFTER A LONG CLEANSING BATH, THEY RETURNED TO the cafe where Callan had first accosted Aileen.

Callan grumbled when he plopped into the chair. 'I'm starving.'

Aileen smiled at him. 'You are always hungry.'

Flashing his teeth, Callan pointed at his arms. 'I burn up calories quicker.'

'I didn't know you were that kind of person.' Aileen propped her satchel on the empty seat.

A server placed menus on the table and poured steaming coffee in two white mugs.

Rubbing his hands together, Callan took a sip. 'What kind of person is that?'

Aileen flicked a hand, picking up the colourful menu card. 'The fitness enthusiast who calculates every calorie.'

Perusing the menu, Callan chuckled. 'If I'd had a sedentary job with sane hours, and could cook, perhaps I would be more health-conscious. Since I keep ungodly hours and can only manage burnt toast, beggars can't be choosers.'

They placed their orders and turned back to business. 'I think we should make sense of this situation.' Aileen began.

Callan lifted an eyebrow. 'Isn't that what we've been doing?'

Aileen stuck her hand in her bag, ruffling for something. Callan rolled his eyes. Women and their bags.

She slapped her yellow notepad on the table. Her eyes twinkled when she said, 'Let's make notes.'

Callan smirked. 'Ye are such a nerd.'

'So what?' She challenged.

He had expected her to deny the fact. 'It suits ye.'

She looked at him oddly but went back to her notes, scribbling something down.

Aileen's handwriting was as neat as she was. That made it easy for Callan to read it upside down. 'What are ye doing?'

She'd written a handful of names: The landlady,

aka Morticia Luna, the pub owner Charlie, the former husband, TJ, Marley's neighbour Freddie, the man with muddy blond hair, "The Bicolour eyed Woman" and Walsh. The last one made his eyebrows rise.

'What's wrong with Walsh?'

'You said the police could be clueless or hiding something.' She explained. 'They can be clueless as per your description, but Walsh? He came down to Loch Fuar in search of her. If they were sloppy at their jobs, why take the trouble to come down to Loch Fuar to search? And then just declare her murder a suicide.'

Callan's stomach grumbled at the mouth-watering aroma of potato chips floating through the room. The server placed a large plate of juicy well-stuffed sandwich and chips in front on him and a generous serving of coleslaw. Callan had to smack his lips.

Ah, food at last! Licking his lips in anticipation, he turned his attention to Aileen's list momentarily. 'I hardly spent a day with that man. From what I gathered, he's a hardworking sort. But his boss?' Callan grimaced.

Aileen bit into her own sandwich, enjoying small bites. 'That bad, huh?'

Callan nodded. 'Worked with him once. He's real sloppy but does he do it purposefully? Dinnae ken.'

Unlike Aileen, he inhaled his sandwich.

A server refilled his coffee.

Gulping down the last morsel, Callan wiped his hands. 'I think instead of a suspect list, these are our "persons of interest." For example, this man we just met, why was he so interested in Marley? What's his connection to her? Let's find that out first.'

Aileen swallowed her sandwich down with some coffee. 'When do we dig into those notebooks? They might hold some answers.'

Callan nodded. 'In a minute. What about this former husband?'

Aileen told him what she knew. She had done thorough research on him. Callan scribbled down the data on his own notepad. He lifted a finger. 'Where did ye find all this information?'

Aileen pursed her lips. 'I read all the news articles and bulletins which reported on the murder Marley's husband was accused in.'

'Let me get Rory or Robert to send us a file on him. But to be honest, if he is in prison, it's unlikely Marley went to visit him. They probably haven't spoken to each other since they filed for divorce.' Callan reasoned.

Aileen tapped her pen on the notepad. 'There's no harm in trying, is there?'

No, there wasn't any harm. So Callan asked Aileen, who was much better at using his phone than he was, to type a message to Rory. 'We need records on,' he read through Aileen's list. 'Charlie, Morticia Luna, Freddie and TJ.'

Her fingers flew over the screen. She looked up and smiled. 'Done.'

It was late in the night, and Callan didn't expect a response, but his phone vibrated, signalling a message.

Aileen read it. 'He'll email them as soon as he can.'

Great, they'd made some headway. Callan glanced at his watch. 'I think we should head back. Hopefully, Rory sends those records soon.'

The air was heavy and warm, thanks to the brief shower that afternoon. Whiffs of smoke wafted through the air. Loch Fuar had a much cleaner air than Loch Heaven but then again, this was a bigger town.

Callan tsked glancing over his shoulder.

'What is it?' Aileen asked.

'Someone's set a tail on us.'

Aileen's eyes rounded. 'What! Why?'

'Guess we'll find out.'

Callan led Aileen up the street. They were essentially walking blind. Neither she nor he had a clue which roads led where. They had no other option but to stride down one lane into the other until they found somewhere to hide and startle their tail.

Aileen had to jog beside Callan, her shorter steps unable to match his long strides. But they couldn't afford to slow down.

She pointed at a sign at the corner of the road. 'Come on, down this lane.'

Callan hesitated, but Aileen caught his forearm and yanked him down the darker alley.

The tall establishments that stood on either side of the road were quiet. In contrast to their previous foray into dingy dark streets, this one was clean. No one loitered about needlessly, and not a single rat scuttled.

In fact, white flowers loomed above them, hung from tall trees. Street lamps cast a golden glow as twilight painted the sky a mesmerising shade of purple. This street could be a perfect vista for a romantic couple to stroll arm in arm. To Callan's eye, it gave them an excellent escape route from the person behind.

They were entirely lucky when a group of youngsters strolled into their lane. The group chortled guffawing, frantically gesturing to each other about some movie they'd just watched.

Aileen whispered to Callan, 'Apparently the cinema theatre—so the board announced—is just around the corner. The cinema draws a crowd. It'll be easy to shrug off our tail.'

He had to hand it to her. It was a smart move.

Callan picked up his pace, eager to dash into the group. He caught Aileen's arm firmly in his and timed it well.

They ploughed into the group, Aileen muttering her "excuse-mes" while Callan refused to let her arm go. The group parted, still chuckling as they pushed past. Callan tugged harshly at Aileen's arm and rounded the corner into a back lane.

She toppled over but found her footing. The lane was a little noisy with the hum of the air conditioners, but thankfully it didn't reek of unwanted fluids. They might be behind the cinema hall.

Callan immediately tip-toed over to the edge of the lane and squinted behind them at the street they'd just left.

Immediately, he braced himself, gesturing to Aileen, ready to accost their shadow.

Waiting for the right moment, Callan observed the hunched figure of a man in a dark t-shirt and jeans surveying the surrounding scene. The man had been following them, maintaining a safe distance since they'd left the cafe.

The group disappeared into another alley, still ignorant of what was happening.

Callan made out the dark silhouette. The figure came to a halt, still analysing the street scene. Patiently, he waited for the shadow to move.

Only when it made its way towards the end of the street, did he brace himself. It was now or never.

As the man jogged past their hiding place, Callan reached out. Wrestling with the burly man, he shoved him face-first into the cinema's wall. An overpowering stench of nicotine hit Callan's nostrils.

'Who sent ye?' Callan ignored Aileen's gasp in the background, holding on firmly to their tail.

Judging by the man's bulging muscles, he was strong. He stood a little taller than Callan was—over six feet.

In this back alley, no one would come to rescue them if things went south. They didn't even know this area. Callan only hoped Aileen ran for help instead of fainting or shrieking as some women did… In the movies.

'Who sent ye?' He repeated.

To make his point, Callan pressed the man into the wall harder, clasping his struggling wrists behind his back. He wasn't sure how long he'd be able to hold him down. Hopefully, he'd get some answers first.

The man kept wriggling, struggling to get free, and ignoring the question.

Callan awkwardly faced Aileen, trying to keep control over their captive. He wanted to search the man's pockets but needed someone's assistance. 'Could-'

What he was about to say got lost as Aileen's eyes rounded into saucers. She reached for him, shouting. 'Call-'

Too late. Callan just made out the glint of a knife before the man escaped his grasp.

Their captive lunged for Callan.

His training kicked in, in the nick of time. He deflected the blow. The knife skidded further into the alley, but not before slicing into Callan's right bicep.

'Hell!' He cursed as that huge mass of muscle threw a punch at him, blood stained his coat sleeve. Callan reached for his gun, but the man kicked it out of his hand. It landed on the ground, out of reach. Callan revved up for the fist fight, despite the zinging pain.

Punch after punch he fought, but the cut on his arm only hampered him. The pain became too unbearable.

Damn it!

CHAPTER FIVE

Dread wrapped its claws around her throat. As if on cue, her brain chanted: *Adventurous, Courageous.*

When adrenaline flooded her veins, Aileen leapt, desperate to help Callan. But she made no progress when an iron hand clasped her arm. Someone shoved her against the opposite wall. Her teeth clattered at the impact with which her head hit the brick wall. A huge rough hand closed around her throat.

She fumbled, gasping for oxygen. Why did they always go for her throat? A dark shadow blocked her view.

Callan was losing, blood oozing out of the gash on his arm. Her heart thudded, worried for his safety. She needed to save him.

What had her online lessons taught her to do? She couldn't remember a thing!

Aileen tried to kick but found herself trapped. The more she tugged, the more her throat closed up.

Stupid, idiotic know-it-all! Why had she led Callan here to their end in a quiet street?

She kicked out but to no avail.

Her mind was dizzy, almost woozy. Her limbs ached, tiredness crept into her.

Should she just let go? Guess she should. She was so tired.

Aileen slipped into the tempting mist of darkness. How wonderful it was to let go-

The tight grip on her throat loosened. She gasped as abundant gulps of fresh air entered her lungs. Crumbling to the floor, she placed a hand over her aching throat.

Hands gripped her shoulders, jerking her up. She tumbled into a warm chest.

The alley was flooded with gloom, the strange hum of machines reminding her of hospitals. Was she dying?

The firm hands on her shoulders shook her like a rag doll. Why couldn't they let her sleep?

Someone called. 'Aileen!'

Coughing, she blinked and winced meekly. 'My back.'

It was pitch black and the familiar fumes of

blood were thick in the inky air. Could they be her own?

'God damn it, Aileen.' That voice, she knew that voice. She lifted her chin.

'Aileen!' She gazed into the electric blue eyes of Callan Cameron.

Suddenly, she stood, realising she'd fallen into his arms. 'You-you're okay?'

The beautiful twilight shade of the sky had given way to a moonless night. No stars hung in the sky, but the warm glow of a street lamp cast shadows into the alley.

Aileen heard Callan curse. She took his right arm in both her hands, assessing it. The sight of it made her snap out of her dizziness. She gawked at him. 'You need a doctor-'

'Ms Mackinnon?' Came a third voice.

Callan, still holding onto her, moved them out of the dark alley and into the well-lit street.

Aileen eyed the trench coat clad figure. 'DI Walsh.'

The detective scrutinised the two of them, searching for answers.

Aileen wiped the sweat on her upper lip. Beside her, Callan winced, surely in pain.

That knife had been sharp.

'Could you tell me why you had two men tailing you?' Walsh enquired.

When he got no answer, he merely dropped his shoulders. 'Cameron, you need to get that hand bandaged. I've called for dispatch. They'll drop you off at your hotel. Get cleaned up. I'll be waiting in the lobby. We'll talk once you're done.'

Callan tilted his chin in acknowledgement, muttering curses.

Aileen held his better arm, throwing him a glare that ordered, "Behave."

'Detective.' She addressed Walsh. 'I can't thank you enough for saving our lives.'

Walsh waved his hands. 'All I want in exchange are some answers. You've surely ticked these people off.'

The police car took them to their hotel after making sure Callan's arm was no longer bleeding. The ride back was silent except for the cackle of the police radio.

Once inside the safety of their hotel, Callan spoke. 'It had to be Morticia Luna, the Houndress.'

'What?' Aileen's voice was raspy.

'That man, men.' Callan amended. 'They had a tattoo on their torso. I saw it when he threw a punch. It was of a hound. The man who tried to choke you had one too.'

Aileen had had no opportunity to know that. She'd almost lost consciousness.

They stepped inside the lift, each lost in their thoughts.

She cursed as the door to their floor opened. 'We should've asked for a first aid kit for you.'

Callan huffed. 'My arm's not bleeding anymore. Besides, it's not a deep cut.'

'You have to get it cleaned!' Aileen protested a little too loudly.

Ultimately, they ended up at Callan's place. Aileen grimaced at the mess he'd made in his room. At least he had a First Aid kit.

Sticking her tongue out in concentration, she bandaged him up. Even if it was temporary, it had to do.

'How much do we share with Walsh?' She asked

Callan breathed through his teeth, clenching and unclenching his jaw. Aileen wasn't a consummate wound dresser. Her clumsy movements had to hurt, but he didn't complain. She felt a little guilty but if he didn't want to go to the hospital, this was all they could do.

He addressed her question. 'It's a little tricky, this situation. We don't ken whether Walsh is in on this. First, let's understand his involvement.'

Aileen only grunted, she was rather focused on his arm, muttering to herself as she tied up the wound without causing him too much discomfort.

It took them half an hour to meet DI Declan Walsh in their hotel lobby.

The man eyed them, noticing Callan's badly wrapped wound. 'You'll need to get a shot for that.'

Callan shrugged. 'What were ye doing following us, Walsh?'

The detective tucked his hands into his coat

pockets. His dark skin glimmered under the warm lights in the hotel lobby.

Dressed in his beige trench, his head hidden under a hat, hands in his pockets, Walsh would be the typical detective. All he needed was a pipe.

Aileen got their attention. 'Shall we, gentlemen? Let's make our way to the police station?'

Walsh scrutinised her. 'There's a tea shop just there, why don't we go there first?' He suggested.

Tea shop it was, but Aileen sniffed at the lingering fragrance of coffee.

The place had a pleasant ambience with picture windows showing off a serene summer vista. There weren't many people on the street considering it was late in the night.

Walsh had briefly smiled, introducing the woman behind the counter. 'That's my wife.'

Apparently, they shut shop early, but being his spouse, she'd kept the doors open for them.

Declan Walsh sat in one of the chairs and gestured at the two seats in front of him.

Aileen loved the rustic wooden decor of the place. Mrs Walsh welcomed them with a beaming smile. After taking their order, she'd hurried back to fix their beverages.

Empty cookie jars sat behind the counter. It was a place Aileen would love to hang out in with a good book. Or a place she could visit with Isla.

A warm fuzziness burbled in her heart. Aileen had a friend now, to hang out in places like these.

She'd usually only frequented such establishments to enjoy a nice tea with biscuits and hide behind a book envying people who were busy chatting and chuckling with their friends.

But now, well, she had to discuss the wrongdoings of murder and *whydunits* before thinking about hanging out with Isla here.

Mrs Walsh placed their drinks. Aileen's order of mint tea steamed, wafting delicious minty aromas around her, a welcome respite from the cold breeze outside.

'Why are you here?' Walsh asked

Callan retorted. 'Why were ye tailing us?'

The man sighed, eyeing his steaming mug. 'You weren't happy I ruled Marley Watson's death a suicide. So you've come here. I wanted to know why you were so interested in her.'

That response caught Aileen's attention, as irritation and anger bubbled. 'Interested! Detective, she was murdered. You have to find out why!'

'We have no evidence to prove she was killed. And we found a note, didn't we?'

Aileen snapped. 'A note? Was that even real?'

The man stared outside. When he remained silent, Callan tried his turn. 'Why did ye come to Loch Fuar to search for her if she didn't matter?'

Declan Walsh remained silent, thinking into his dark brew. He took a sip and thought some more. Then he said, 'We got a missing person's report on Thursday, the same week we found Marley Watson.

I went through it. It had come from her flat. The person on the phone—it was a male voice—told us she was to meet him the day before but hadn't shown up for their rendezvous.'

Aileen leant forward with elbows on the table. 'This report. Who filed it?'

Walsh shuffled in his seat. 'He introduced himself as her brother, someone called TJ.'

Aileen and Callan shared a knowing look.

Callan asked. 'Did he say anything else?'

Walsh shook his head. 'Just that he was her brother. He told us she'd left her flat two days ago. We asked him if he knew of any person she'd want to run away with or anyone who could harm her. The boy didn't respond. Instead, he hung up. We assumed it was a prank call. Let it slide.'

Callan prompted, 'There's more to it.'

'Aye, there is.' The detective slid forward. 'We got another call. This time an older voice. He told us Marley Watson was missing. But,' the detective hunched forward further, 'according to him, Marley had never returned from her trip to Loch Fuar as she was supposed to two days ago. And this call came on Saturday morning, the day she died.'

Walsh adjusted his hat. 'This older man gave me the wrong vibes. I asked my partner to go check Marley Watson's flat. Her neighbour says she'd left a few days ago. A Tuesday most likely. It jibes with the brother's phone call.'

'And as for the second one, Marley died that Saturday and thus, never returned.' Aileen finished.

Walsh nodded. 'Thus, the only explanation is Marley Watson killed herself in your cottage.'

Aileen saw red. How can he be a detective and still not see the evident clues? Passionately, she spoke. 'But the beam! It was newly fixed.'

DI Declan Walsh squinted at her. 'What beam?'

'Exactly!' To punctuate her meaning, she slapped her hands on the table. Aileen leant over. 'Did you find her phone? If you'd searched, you'd have noticed that woman was never without it.'

Walsh scowled at Aileen. 'We found it! It was outside the cottage-'

'Why would such a woman throw her phone outside the cottage? For you, she was another suicide statistic and too lowly to cast a second glance at!'

'Hey!' Walsh's chair screeched as he stood. A muscle in his jaw twitched. 'You have no right throwing accusations at a police detective. Cameron! You better hold your dog on a leash.'

Aileen slammed her fists on the table, ignoring the zinging pain that shot up her arm. She spat at him. 'Dog! How dare you-?'

Callan pulled her down, desperately trying to stifle his sneer. 'I'm sorry, Walsh. She's a wee touchy. The murder has been a bit too much for her.'

The detective sat back. 'At the end of someone's life, why'd they take their phone with them?'

Aileen was not finished. She tried to struggle free from Callan's grip from around her shoulders. 'Did you see any electronics at her place?'

'No.' Walsh said flatly.

Aileen was a little too loud, but she didn't hold back. 'Then we've got to find them! She'd need a laptop to do research and read emails. If not her, then TJ uses gadgets. He's a hacker. We need to know what he's been researching. That's what got Marley Watson killed.'

'How do you know this TJ? We don't know where he works.' Walsh growled. He obviously didn't appreciate being told what to do.

Callan ran a hand through his hair, ready to leave before Walsh lost it and pressed charges on them. But Aileen rummaged in her satchel and produced her yellow notepad.

'Vicky's.' She told the men. 'TJ works at Vicky's. Do you know where that is?'

'Perhaps.' Walsh settled. 'But this case is closed. At least that's what my boss says.'

It was late in the night when Aileen and Callan left the cafe. The cool air smelt of sweet summer flowers.

Before they strode back to the hotel, they made sure no one was following them.

'He seems to be a decent man, Walsh.'

Callan pursed his lips. 'Let's not jump to conclusions but he was helpful.'

A tremor ran through Aileen when they walked into the warmth of their hotel lobby. Being threatened, followed, and almost choked to death didn't help her fleeting confidence.

She stifled a yawn. Beside her, Callan chuckled. ''Twas a long eventful day.'

Unable to hold it, the yawn finally slipped. 'Sorry, it's just that I woke up very early.'

They stepped out of the lift. Callan halted by his room door. 'The adrenaline's wearing off. Get in a good night's sleep. You'll need it.'

'Good night.' She bid Callan and opened the door to slip inside her room.

His face was furrowed, a little worn. He winced every time he moved his injured arm. Yet he refused to get his arm checked.

'Aileen.' She came to a stop when Callan whispered her name.

Glancing at him from over her shoulder, she arched an eyebrow.

'Good job holding up today... Partner.' Callan dipped his chin and stepped in before she could string two words together.

Aileen gaped. Had he just "semi-complimented" her? Had Callan just called her a *partner*?

The soothing scent of tea tree tickled her nose as a thought wafted into her mind: Callan thought she'd done a good job today when all she'd done was flail her arms as if she were a damsel in distress.

A "good job"? Aileen bit her lips. Was he finally warming up to her? Or had his remark been to keep her from going completely insane?

Aileen grasped the handle of her room door and pulled it open.

She thudded against the door when it clicked in place. This was the first time Callan had ever complimented her. And that thought struck her, made her heart doozy, and her lips turned upwards between flushed red cheeks.

Whichever reason he'd said that for, it was a step. A step, Aileen didn't mind. A step that had plastered a smile on her face for the rest of the night.

THE NEXT MORNING DAWNED AS DREARY AS A DAY could be. Dark clouds gathered in the sky, threatening inevitable rain.

Callan's mood was no different. His arm hadn't allowed him peaceful sleep. But a message awaited him in the morning.

He met Aileen for breakfast.

Luckily, she didn't comment on his parting words to her last night. Thank god, because he hadn't a clue where those words had slipped from. Instead, Aileen suggested they go to the hospital.

'No. We've got work to do.' His tone brokered no argument.

Callan held out his phone. 'Walsh says they've caught a man named Martin Luther Hussey who Marley was involved with, professionally and romantically.'

Aileen raised an eyebrow. 'I never caught a whiff of any boyfriend.'

Setting his phone aside, Callan dug into his bacon and eggs. 'Do you remember the physical abuse charge on Marley's records? I told ye about it yesterday.'

Chewing, Aileen bobbed her chin. 'I remember. You said the charges were dropped.'

'Aye, they were, but there was someone else with her that day, a man. His name's Martin Luther Hussey. Fancy name, if ye ask me, but he's always skirting the law.'

Aileen cocked an eyebrow. 'And Marley was associated with him, are you sure?'

Callan shrugged. 'Apparently.'

WALSH WAS WAITING FOR THEM WHEN THEY arrived. 'We caught that idiot yesterday in a drug's bust. Sorry, the boss is out for the day or he would have greeted you.'

Callan stuffed his hands in his pockets, not before wincing.

'You look like hell.' Walsh observed. 'Officer Crawford could help you out-'

'No. I'm fine, thank you.'

But Walsh continued. 'Officer Eleanor Crawford is our mother hen. She's bandaged her share of officers in our station. Better than any nurse.'

'N-'

'He'll love for her to check it out. Thank you.' Aileen piped in, ignoring Callan's scathing glare. If he was going to act like a child, she would treat him like one.

Walsh studied Aileen and pursed his lips. 'Perhaps after the interview?'

Fifteen minutes later, Aileen found herself in the Observation Room, peering through that weird reflecting glass facing the Interrogation Room.

When they led Martin Luther Hussey inside, Aileen gasped. Beside her, Callan stilled. 'Bastard!'

Her throat dry, Aileen rasped. 'That's... That's the same man we met yesterday outside Sláinte!'

Callan gritted his teeth. 'That sod. No wonder he was loitering outside Marley's house.'

Under the bright lights of the Interrogation Room, his features were more prominent. His forearms were bare too.

Martin Luther Hussey had tattoos all over his arms, along with some angry gashes. The man could've been in his forties, with poorly cut muddy blond hair. He by the looks of it worked out and lived a rough life.

His bruised lip was still a little swollen, and he smirked. 'Hi, Ellie.' He said to Officer Eleanor Crawford.

Officer Crawford had neatly pinned salt and pepper hair, giving her a motherly feature, but looks could be deceptive. She wore her uniform as sharp as any new officer. Aileen respected all women in uniform. They brought a softer touch and sharp brains to a profession that historically had been dominated by the other gender.

'There are times I think you want to be here.' She reprimanded the man.

Hussey jeered. 'I get to see yer beautiful wrinkly face.'

Pulling a chair back, she sat as Walsh entered. 'If you'd learnt manners, you wouldn't be here.'

Walsh plopped on to the other plastic chair. 'Hello, Hussey.'

All he got in response was a snort.

Officer Crawford observed the man keenly. 'Marley Watson.' She folded her hands. 'You know that name.'

'What about that blood-sucking bitch? Havenae seen her in months.' Walsh dismissed with a wave.

Crawford flashed a pretty smile. 'What did I say about those manners? Now, don't lie. Didn't you murder Marley at Loch Fuar last week?'

In the Observation Room, Callan snorted. 'She's good.'

Yes, she was. That salt and pepper hair wasn't for nothing.

Hussey jerked up, hissing expletives at Crawford. She didn't even blink.

Agitated, Hussey yelled. 'I did no such thing! She, that wench, blackmailed a lot of wrong people. They'd have finally done her in.'

'Did she blackmail you?' Walsh asked.

Sitting back, Hussey snorted. 'Lived with me, she did. Needed a man to take care of her. The agreement was she'd share twenty percent of blackmail money with me.'

Crawford chuckled and made a flippant comment. 'Only twenty? You must be slipping.'

Angry, Hussey lunged at her but was refrained by his handcuffs. 'Hey, ye pansy! I-'

'Why'd you leave her then?' Walsh cut Hussey off.

He settled back and huffed. 'Got bored of her yak-yak. Clingy she was, always asking where I went and why I dinnae come home that night. She ain't my mum.'

'So ye killed her.' Crawford persisted.

'Hey, ye eejit!' Hussey jumped again, almost rattling the desk pinned to the bland floor. His voice reverberated through the dull room. The one grilled-off window let a little sunshine in.

Walsh leant over threateningly and growled. 'If you didn't kill her, then what were ye doing at her flat?'

Hussey sat back, licking his lips. He crossed his arms over his chest and jutted a chin out at Walsh. 'I was never there.'

Walsh tilted his head. 'I've got a witness.'

But Hussey didn't relent. 'Ye got nothing on me. Ye cannae pin her death on me. Check that landlady she desperately wanted to con. Yapped to me about it.'

Crawford sat back and pressed, 'What was your business at Marley's flat?'

'Her flat? Her flat?' Hussey cackled. 'Sounds so fancy. She lived in a rat hole. And dragged me with her. I never went there again. I haven't seen her in months.'

Walsh placed his elbows on the table. 'Didn't you report her missing?'

Hussey snorted, staring at his shoes. 'Ye cannae pin her death on me. We were done a long time ago.'

Officer Eleanor Crawford interlinked her fingers and placed them on the table. 'So, you haven't seen her in months - dead or alive?'

Hussey narrowed his eyes at her but quickly dropped his gaze, muttering. 'Ask the landlady.'

Aileen and Callan met with Walsh in his cramped office. It was at least a little larger than Callan's.

Callan plopped into a chair, rubbing a hand over his arm, gritting his teeth at the pain.

Just when Aileen opened her mouth to rebuke

him for not seeking help, Officer Eleanor Crawford walked in with a First Aid kit.

'Now let's have a look.' She barely gave Callan a chance to protest when she poked his bandaged arm.

He hissed. 'Ow!'

Crawford beamed and got to work. The astringent smell of antiseptic swirling through the room.

Callan swallowed the pain. 'Ye did great today, with Hussey.'

She smiled sweetly. 'Thank you. He's a nasty man. It's wasted potential.'

Walsh assessed the group. 'But I don't think he's capable of murder.'

Officer Crawford snorted. 'I won't put it past that man.'

Walsh sighed.

Pulling out a cotton swab, Officer Crawford crouched beside Callan. 'Hold still.'

Callan hissed.

Aileen cleared her throat. 'Could Hussey have attacked us yesterday?'

'Don't think so.' Walsh explained, 'Cameron punched the other guy in the face, so he'd have bruises. When I got the second man off you, I got him in the face too. And they both ran away before I could arrest them, but Hussey is a bit shorter than they were and doesn't sport a bruise apart from that lip he's been parading this week.'

'Aye.' Callan spoke through clenched teeth as

Crawford worked on his arm. 'It was dark, but the height doesn't match.'

Aileen contemplated the situation. 'Then we have someone else on our backs.'

Walsh leant in. 'Perhaps, and they are out for your blood.'

CHAPTER SIX

Callan wouldn't admit it out loud, but his arm didn't smart as often after Officer Crawford had worked on it. Her touch had been maternal, a balm in itself.

The ceasing of at least one throbbing limb made it easier to think about the case.

They returned to Aileen's room.

Callan strode over to the window. Hands crossed, he gazed outside. The sky had opened up and rain pelted, sending ice cream vendors and tourists scuttling for shelter. Only the well-prepared or brave dashed through the pitter-patter.

Behind him, Aileen shuffled through her satchel and sank into the chair by the desk.

He'd initially known Marley Watson was bad news. But he'd never imagined getting entangled in such a mess. People threatening and attacking them was indeed far too dangerous. But if he asked Aileen to return under Dachaigh's safe roof, she'd refuse.

Taking a deep breath, Callan rubbed his eyes. He desperately needed food and sleep. But the case called to him. The sooner they could solve this, the quicker he could get Aileen back to safety.

His phone chimed. Pulling up the email, Callan grunted. 'It's Rory. He's sent all the records we'd asked for.'

Aileen perked up. She pulled out her fancy laptop and tapped a few keys. 'Login here. Let's see who our "persons of interest" are.'

Callan typed in his password, which luckily he could remember. 'There.'

Aileen took over, her fingers flying. Quickly she pulled up the records. There were five of them belonging to Charlie, Freddie, Morticia Luna, Marley's former husband and TJ.

Leaning over Aileen's shoulder, he scanned each of them.

She looked up at him. 'Did you ask for Martin Luther Hussey's record?'

'Damn it! I forgot. Ye type.' Callan handed Aileen the phone. She sent off the message with a swoosh.

They turned their attention back to the records. She accessed the former husband's record first.

There wasn't much of significance there. They had caught him almost red-handed. Marley had divorced him soon after, and they hadn't seen hide nor hair of each other since.

Moving on, Aileen pulled up data on the pub Sláinte's owner: Charlie.

Callan dragged a chair over and sat, knees brushing Aileen's. She scrolled through his data. 'He's been active.'

Rightly so, Charlie had a long sheet. His offences ranged from drunk and disorderly to vandalism and threats. But never murder. There were several parking tickets he hadn't bothered to pay and one arrest, on record, for possession.

'Bet he meets a handful of interesting people in that pub of his. Must have made several friends that way.' Callan pointed out, jotting down notes.

Aileen highlighted some facts and clicked some more keys. 'Do you think one of his friends put him up to it?'

Callan scribbled some more before shaking his head. 'First, let's go through all this data and then brainstorm. Plus, there are those notebooks ye found at Marley's. Didn't ye say there was one on Charlie as well?'

Leaning forward, Aileen pulled open the next file. This one was Marley's neighbour.

Frederick "Freddie" Breck was a very unusual person. He too sported a long sheet. It included several breaking and entering charges. He also had forgery added to the mix. But, Callan mused, he had broken into laboratories and university libraries.

'What in the world?' Aileen too noticed and kept scrolling. 'He's stolen test tubes and microscopes, even fuse boards and switches. Look, they've found some chemicals he's stolen from the labs too.'

Callan laughed. 'It takes all kinds, eh? Looks like he's a science geek. See there's a history here.'

Aileen gawked. 'Geez, he's got a PhD too.'

'I wonder what happened that he lives in that rat hole.' Callan scribbled more notes. 'I think we should go to meet with him.'

Next up, Aileen pulled up Morticia Luna's record. She scrolled, then looked over her shoulder. 'She's relatively clean.'

Rightly so, there were no major offences recorded on Morticia Luna's list. She had a couple of speeding and parking tickets, but nothing else. Not even a drunk and disorderly.

Too squeaky clean. It reeked of forgery. 'Something's wrong with it. If Charlie was that scared of her and Marley was spying on her, she can't be a Jane Doe.'

Aileen frowned. 'Something to dig into then?'

Callan nodded and watched as Aileen opened up the last person on their list. 'TJ.'

'Wow!' Aileen pointed at the screen. 'He has

been to prison for holding sensitive files for ransom. He's hacked into a bank's database and stolen their customer's data. There's another credit card fraud charge. Good lord, it's a never-ending list!'

As she scrolled, Callan found more offences, but they were all committed using technology. 'Guess he isn't just some tech guv. He's more like a master.'

Aileen hummed her agreement as she highlighted another set of information. 'But he could be a hit for hire. Look, there is one charge here for possession of drugs. He might even commit these frauds in exchange for some, you know.'

That could be true, since TJ didn't seem to have loads of cash with him unless he was a closet millionaire. Marley was a hoarder too and look where she lived.

Reaching the end of the file, Aileen sat back. 'Should I get Marley's notebooks out?'

At his nod, Aileen reached into her leather satchel and pulled out four notebooks.

Two of them were pocket size and the other two full-scape sheets. All of them were bound in sandy card paper.

Marley had used the smaller notebooks to maintain a log of sorts, and the other longer books had data on Marley's unsuspecting targets.

Callan picked up one pocket-size book and inspected it. 'She didn't spend a lot on these.'

He went through a log detailing Charlie's

whereabouts and the various times Marley had visited the pub. Marley went as far as to document who sat where along with a brief sketch of the pub's layout.

The other book on Charlie had some irrelevant details about him. The man apparently was fond of ice cream soda and spent his Thursday evenings watching reality TV with his wife.

How had Marley found out such personal details? It was as if she'd had her eyes and ears inside Charlie's house.

Suddenly, Callan froze. 'Aileen?' He called out slowly.

Blinking out of her haze, she asked. 'What's wrong?'

'Marley. What did Charlie say about pizza?'

Thoroughly confused, Aileen scrunched up her nose. 'Pizza? Hold on, his son works at a pizza place. Johnny's was it?'

He swivelled the book to show her the information Marley had gathered. 'She ate pizza every day from Johnny's. And it was Charlie's son who'd deliver it. Bet she used it as an excuse to ask him questions about his father. Where else would she find such personal details about Charlie?'

'What was she up to? I mean, was she blackmailing him as Hussey said?'

Callan chewed that thought for a while. 'Maybe he was a potential victim? Perhaps she was trying to find some juice on him. She could squeeze him dry then.'

Aileen tilted her head. 'She's also got extensive data on Morticia Luna, including her ledgers. It must be TJ's doing, to find these ledgers, although someone's cooked the books.'

'Cooked books?' Callan asked.

'Misstated records, creative accounting especially to embezzle cash or evade tax in this case, I reckon.' Aileen explained.

Callan smirked, excited. 'So her record isn't as clean as it shows in her official data?'

Aileen shrugged. 'Seems to be the case. Although this is what Marley has. There's no proof this is concrete or that these are Morticia Luna's books of accounts. We need the actual books with the complete data.'

She leant in, pointing to a few numbers. 'For example, these expenditures are inconsistent with the-'

Callan waved his hands to stop Aileen. 'Don't waste yer breath. I won't understand a thing. What I know is that we need to look into Morticia Luna. And let's visit Charlie to get a feel. What if Marley blackmailed him and he snapped, killing her?'

Aileen pursed her lips. 'That's the most likely motive. But it's hard to imagine a man who likes ice cream sodas and reality TV dates with his wife murdering a woman.'

Callan raised an eyebrow and chuckled dryly. 'Ye'll be surprised at what some people are capable of.' He tapped a finger on the desk. 'And let's add Freddie to the list, see why he's so fond of science equipment.'

The pelting rain outside had waned into a dull afternoon.

Just when he was about to close the notebook, something caught his attention. It was a picture of Morticia Luna with two hounds. The image was grainy, but next to it was a log entry.

Ah!

Considering the logistics, Callan said, 'Come on. Let's rent out some property first.' He jogged to the door and was out before Aileen could string two words.

It wasn't until he reached the lift that her lighter treads followed. Aileen panted as she came to a stop next to him.

Glaring at him, she asked. 'Where are you running off to? Want to move to Loch Heaven, do you?'

Callan smirked. 'Nope.'

WHERE WERE THEY GOING?

Callan refused to tell her.

Instead, he climbed into his well-worn car and

made an impatient gesture for her to follow. It surprised her, given that they'd made most of their investigative journey on foot.

Aileen maintained silence as Callan drove. Compared to his languid movements, he drove as if they were being chased.

She gripped onto the edge of her seat, sending a quick prayer for their safety. If she thought they were unsafe in the city, there was nothing to stop Callan when he drove away from the habited streets.

As the scenery changed Aileen could spot small cottages in Loch Heaven which soon gave way to rolling moors and farmland. The road became narrower, winding around trees and mounds. Instead of slowing down, the empty roads urged Callan to drive at a breakneck speed.

Tall mountains that stood on the edges of Loch Heaven grew larger and the forest thickened, restrained only by the tar road.

'Are you planning on murdering me and burying my corpse in the forest?' Aileen joked, her shoulders bunched, hoping they didn't crash into an oncoming vehicle.

Callan only smirked. 'Trust me.'

Trust him when he could collide with a tree and send them to an early grave? Aileen dug her nails into the seat. 'C-Could you please drive slower?'

He shrugged. 'We are in a bit of a time crunch. Don't worry.'

Aileen's heart thundered, and she faced him with wide eyes.

'Live a little.' Came the response from the police detective. When she continued to clutch the seat, Callan waved a hand. 'Why did ye leave that fancy job behind?'

What?

That was the last question Aileen had ever thought he'd ask, given the moment. She fumbled for something to say, entirely forgetting about Callan's rash driving. Carefully, she responded. 'It was an uneventful job. I had to leave it before I turned ninety and had an uneventful life behind me. There is boredom in being risk-less.'

Callan let out a deep bellied laugh, startling Aileen. What had got into him? 'Risk-less, ye?'

Utterly surprised by that response, Aileen stared at her interwoven hands on her lap. 'I was a different person back then. Hardworking, sometimes taking over my boss's work and sitting mum when I got passed over for a promotion, *seven* times in a row.'

Callan chuckled. 'No wonder ye spit fire at me every chance ye get.' He raised a calloused hand. 'All ye've done since I've known ye is invite murders, two in yer own inn plus a theft and now one on yer property.' Callan laughed again. 'Might I also add ye got yerself attacked, several times? You, Ms Aileen Mackinnon, are a magnet for trouble. I doubt there's even a bone called, how'd ye put it?

"Risk-less" in yer body. Ye are yer gran. Yer boss must have been an eejit.'

By the time Callan finished his brief speech, Aileen sat there, eyes wide, staring at him, blushing a deep shade of red right to the roots of her hair. She desperately tried stringing words together, hoping to speak anything except the squeal that threatened to spill out of her mouth.

Her gran? Callan thought she was like the strong-willed, energetic and witty Siobhan? He respected her gran, was even terrified of her.

And Aileen was that… Strong? Confident?

'Ah, here we are.' Callan grinned.

Still fumbling, Aileen looked around.

Callan drove through a street lined with a small cluster of houses. They were weekend homes, some almost as big as mansions. Judging by the few high-end cars parked in the driveways and the surrounding vista, this was a place for the elite.

He parked opposite a mansion which befitted an eighteenth-century-palace-cum-fortress. Huge barricaded gates closed off the property. Through the gaps, Aileen stared at the lush manicured green gardens. Someone took care of those plants.

And behind the gardens stood a fortress, there was no other word for it. It had watchtowers of sorts, complete with turrets. Gothic arched windows made Aileen think of Windsor Castle. Perhaps the Queen herself lived there. The cream colours of the mansion glittered under the sunlight.

Did Callan want to break in? The base of Aileen's neck tickled. There was something sinister about that place. And she wasn't sure she wanted to find out what it was.

'What?' She stuck her head out of the window, taking in the fresh air sweet with a flowery scent.

'That's Morticia Luna's place according to Marley.' Callan smirked.

Aileen gasped in surprise. Who knew there was much money in renting out property in dingy areas?

She squinted, getting a better view, blinking when a sharp gleam caught her eye. It had come from the tower.

'Are those…?' She trailed off.

Callan leant close to her to get a better view. 'Aye, armed guards.'

Aileen's breath hitched. What was Morticia Luna up to? 'So her business is more than merely renting property. It has to be. Just like we saw in Marley's notebooks with the creative accounting.'

Beside her, Callan patted Aileen's back. 'Smart, accountant.'

She swivelled to face Callan. Who was this man and what had he done with the grumpy oaf who never complimented her?

'Ah, it's time!' Callan exclaimed, hopping out the door and striding across the street.

Aileen pried her gaping mouth shut and scrambled out of the car. When was the last time she'd heard Callan talk so much?

She jogged behind him. But Callan hadn't waited for her or cast her a backward glance.

Surely Morticia Luna's guards were aware of them by now. Aileen could've been shot dead. For all she knew, there were a couple of guns trained on her at this moment.

And Callan didn't care. Which was typical of him.

She panted behind him, glaring at the black-clad figure of Callan. He'd done an excellent job throwing her off her stride. It was way easier to be angry at him, but she didn't mind this happier man either.

Raising her voice, Aileen asked, 'What if she doesn't let us inside?'

'She won't.'

'Then why are we here?'

Finally, he looked at her over his shoulder. 'Marley did a thorough job, that's why.'

Instead of knocking on those enormous gates, they rounded the house and strolled down a narrow path.

The trees intertwined to create a beautiful, peaceful avenue. Birdsong filled the air and a light breeze made the smaller shrubs rustle. Flowers bloomed, and the distinct gurgle of a fountain pattered through the trees. Soft sunlight flashed between the thick foliage onto the green grass, making the diamond-like water droplets glitter.

Behind the avenue was the marble fountain,

right in the centre of the lawn. The air smelt of fresh earth. There was no one else around, giving a certain tranquillity to the air.

Callan led her further into the park.

Aileen gasped when the closed avenue opened up to a resplendent waterbody where smaller fountains burbled. White swans swam in the loch, surveying their territory.

'It's gorgeous.'

'That's why she walks her hounds here each morning.'

'Huh?' Aileen was thoroughly confused.

Callan finally explained. 'According to Marley's log on Morticia Luna, the landlady brings her hounds here every afternoon for a walk.'

A lightbulb sparkled to life when Aileen recalled a hazy photograph of the landlady with her two hounds right here next to the loch.

She had to hand it to him, Callan had found the perfect time to interview Morticia Luna.

As if on cue, Aileen stared slack-jawed at the two beasts heading their way. Between their fiercely muscled bodies sauntered an elegant lady. What the pictures didn't show was this woman was really tall. Almost as tall as Callan, but as slender as a willow tree.

What was Callan thinking? She could let her hounds loose on them. Did they stand a chance against these fierce animals?

Taking Aileen's hand as if they were just another couple out on a morning stroll, Callan ambled forward. He smiled, speaking in a muted tone to Aileen just loud enough for a passerby to hear. 'Hounds! My grandad had one on his farm. What fine dogs!'

Callan halted in front of the lady: Morticia Luna, in the flesh.

The woman lifted her lips in a sneer before casting a loving glimpse at her two hounds. 'They are ferocious…'

Callan bent to pet them, but the dogs raised their hackles and barked at him.

'They don't take well to strangers.' Her voice was sultry, her eyes hidden behind the customary sunglasses.

'Apparently.' Callan continued to beam, not once letting go of the charade 'Say, Madam, are ye the one who runs that skincare business my girlfriend here is nuts about?'

He pulled Aileen closer.

Aileen bobbed her agreement. 'You are familiar.'

What the hell? She let her inhibitions loose. Shaking her head at Callan, she admonished. 'You aren't good at remembering faces, love. We watched this lady on TV, remember? You were on that commercial-'

Morticia Luna spluttered. 'I'm neither. I have a real estate business.'

'Ye rent out property?' Callan spoke with an enthusiasm Aileen never knew he possessed apart from when it was time to catch murderers. He was a good actor. Aileen on the other hand was ready to choke on her spit.

Without waiting for a response, Callan grinned as bright as the sun. 'Honey, weren't we just talking about renting a house?'

He said to Morticia Luna. 'We want to move in together. Exciting times. But she doesn't trust the internet. So we wanted someone real to help us find a place. And now we've met ye.'

'It's a miracle.' Aileen piped in.

They sounded sleazy.

'Aye, could ye help us?'

They'd all but accosted the Houndress. In a polished yet painfully polite manner, she tilted her chin and smiled thinly. 'Sure, just call my agent at this number.'

She handed over a card to Callan.

'Thank ye!'

Before they could so much as bid her farewell, she swished around, sauntering back the way she'd come. The wind carried her last words. 'You should study the boyfriend she spent all her time with.'

'What?' Aileen asked

Callan clicked his tongue. 'She's smart. She ken we are on her scent.'

'How?'

Callan held out the sheet of paper. On it was scrawled. "I didn't kill her."

'Haughty.' Aileen stared as Morticia Luna retreated.

She peeked up at Callan to gauge his mood, but his face had set into a stoic mask.

'Morticia Luna mightn't have killed Marley. But she could've arranged for her murder.' He muttered.

Aileen's heart thumped. Yes, she definitely could have.

BACK IN CALLAN'S CAR, HE TAPPED HIS HAND ON the steering wheel, waiting for Aileen to buckle in. As soon as the seat belt clicked in place, he took off.

'Where are we going now?'

Callan didn't respond. Instead, he thought out loud. 'How does she know about us?'

Aileen shrugged. 'News travels fast. Besides, she must have her ears to the ground.'

As the car raced through the countryside, Callan focused on the road. 'So how does Charlie ken about Marley's death?'

Aileen swallowed the panic. But her heart palpitated. She clutched the seat. 'Um, a pub's a place where gossipmongers meet, isn't it? Barbara's Tea Room for example at Loch Fuar is one such place. And Barbara hears everything.'

Callan agreed. 'That could be a reason Marley was paying such close attention to Charlie. He kens everything.'

'Why don't we go there and speak to him again? Like you suggested, get a feel?' Aileen suggested.

CHAPTER SEVEN

It was almost half-past five when they entered the main city of Loch Heaven. Needless to say, they got stuck in a minor traffic jam.

Callan cursed at the slow pace of traffic but finally, after a delay of ten minutes, turned into the parking lot of their hotel. 'Let's hike up to Sláinte. I doubt my car's safe there.' He explained.

Hopping out of the car, he stretched and gestured to Aileen. 'Let's see what sort of gossip goes around at Sláinte. Bet it won't be about how much weight Mrs McHugh gained.'

Aileen laughed. 'I didn't know you paid attention to that sort of thing.'

'I don't. Rory does.' Callan shivered, making Aileen laugh harder.

Like the previous day, he held her close when they crossed the crowded streets towards the gloomy ones. Due to a rainy afternoon, most people were huddled in the darker edges and under awnings of dilapidated buildings.

The puddles on the streets were mucky and the air heavy with moisture.

Gingerly, they stepped over the puddles and avoided the littered garbage bags. Thankfully, the clouds were parting to reveal the sun's rays.

No one loitered outside the pub. In fact, business seemed to be slow.

When Callan reached for the thick wooden door with one tiny glass window, it opened to reveal a man with muddy blond hair.

'Ye!' Martin Luther Hussey exclaimed.

'Kicked ye out of jail, did they?' Callan taunted.

'If they find nothing on ye, they can't just nail a crime on ye, ye bampot!' Hussey growled.

Callan's face was set in a scowl. 'What are ye doing here?'

The man almost lunged for Callan and got into his face. 'I told ye: My neighbourhood, ye stay away or I'll-'

The door opened wider to reveal a scowling Charlie. He slapped Hussey's back. 'I ain't having ye pick yer fights outside ma pub, ye prick! Get lost.'

Hussey snarled at Charlie. 'This eejit ain't giving ye no business. Ye better ken who to sidle up to.'

Charlie flicked Hussey's head. 'Yer thick ye are. He's a boaby, ye eejit.'

'Ah, bobby.' Hussey crossed his arms and

walked up to Callan till they were chest to chest. Flashing the missing tooth, he snapped. 'No wonder ye reek.'

Hussey was so close, Callan could smell him. Unlike the last time, the man smelt of nicotine mixed with an exotic perfume, not the cheap floral one.

Callan dipped his eyes to Hussey's neck, where a golden chain glinted under the dim light. He could also see an angry gash that was just healing.

And that day, under the harsh lights of the Interrogation Room, there had been a couple more bruises on his arms, and another cut on his jaw.

Where had the money come from? Or was it stolen?

Callan smirked, jerking his chin towards Hussey's neck. 'Nice chain.'

With a sneer, Hussey pulled it out. 'Coulda snatched it from an eejit tourist. But it's nice to go pay cash for it, almost hassle-free. And what do ye think about this watch?' Hussey held his wrist up and shook it. 'Fancy, ain't it? All purchased in cash. Got the receipt. Ye can't arrest me now, can ye, ye bastard?'

Charlie cursed and closed the pub door behind him. 'Move on, ye. I willnae have ye fighting with a boaby on ma front door.'

Hussey looked over his shoulder. 'I got no time to spend it on stinking pigs.'

With that, he sauntered off, whistling to himself.

A small crowd had gathered around, wanting to witness a fight. Sorely disappointed, they scampered off when Callan shot them a glare.

Turning to Aileen and Callan, Charlie spat. 'What do ye want?'

Callan jabbed a thumb at the pub. 'Need to speak with ye.'

'Nay! Not inside, I won't have the likes of ye hampering ma business.' He strode towards a side alley.

It was filthy to say the least, with water puddles and a garbage bin no one had bothered to empty. The outer walls of the buildings had turned black with chimney fumes and a cockroach or two hung onto exposed bricks, making Callan's skin crawl.

Beside him, Aileen's breath faltered. She was quiet as she took in the surrounding scene. As if in reassurance, she pulled the strap of her satchel closer.

Rounding over to the back, Charlie came to a halt. He leant one shoulder on the wall. Behind him were more garbage cans that had gone murky with age and were littered with dustbin bags. 'What?'

Crossing his arms, Callan stood with his legs apart. But Aileen spoke first. 'Freddie. Who is he?'

Charlie chuckled. 'What do ye want with 'im? Smart kinda stupid man. Teaches youngsters to cook and brew, if ye ken what I mean. A professor he was, but then his teaching methods didn't sit well with the stiff collars.'

Aileen linked her hands. 'So what does he do now?'

'Breaks-in, steals the odd science stuff. And spends most of his time hauled in that house. Like I told ye, Marley's his source of income along with his side business of selling illegals.' Charlie explained.

A shout rose from inside the pub, followed by a curse. Charlie ignored it.

Callan veered the conversation. 'Saturday between four and six in the evening, where were ye?'

Charlie boomed with laughter. 'Why do ye ask eejit questions?' He thumped his chest. 'I'm a pub-owner. Saturday is a busy night.'

'Answer my question.' Callan demanded.

'Just did.'

Callan tsked. 'Ye never said where ye were on last Saturday, yer "busy day"? The night Marley died.'

Standing upright, Charlie shook his head. 'Dinnae kill that chav! Ye can't say I did 'cause I dinnae.'

Narrowing his eyes, Callan spoke slowly. 'Where. Were. Ye?'

Charlie said, stabbing a finger at Callan. 'Ain't telling ye nothing without ma lawyer. I ken ma rights.'

Of course, he knew his rights, thanks to his stellar criminal record. He might even have a lawyer on payroll for all Callan knew.

Throwing one last glare at Callan and then Aileen, Charlie turned around and slipped through a back entrance inside the pub.

Shit!

Callan looked up to see the floor above the pub. 'Why's the first floor boarded up?'

Aileen sighed. 'Could be a storage unit. Boarding it up protects stock.'

When he spied a rickety ladder, Callan grunted. 'Looks like ye're right. A storage room.' Callan looked around the back alley. It had one flickering light that revealed a secluded street.

Holding out a palm to Aileen, Callan said, 'Come on, let's pay Freddie a visit and see whether anyone is lurking around Marley's flat.'

Aileen placed her softer hand in his. 'Do you think he'll even notice? He seems to live in a world of his own.'

Callan considered what she said. 'He's also the sort who might notice things. Besides, didn't ye say he asked for a day to keep his eye out, to whoever was threatening him? Something to look into.'

Holding Aileen close, Callan led them to Marley's flat. Now that the rain had dried up, more people prowled the streets. The humid day had given way to a sultry night. Callan snorted when an omnipresent stench abused his nostrils. There wasn't a single star twinkling. The sky a dark abyss threatening to swallow all of existence.

Plenty of the street lights were dead, instead used by street urchins to lean against.

Quickly, they turned into the rundown building. Better the scuttling mice than those unblinking eyes.

Pulling out his torch, Callan flashed it around. Their climb up to the second floor was uneventful, apart from the few gasps from Aileen when an insect or mice scurried by.

Like last time, Callan had to bang on the door several times before they heard a curse from inside. Something crashed and was followed by another curse.

Several seconds later, the door opened partially to reveal hair.

'Buzz off! I took nothing, just a quick errand.'

When Freddie moved to shut the door, Callan spoke. 'Just a few questions about Marley Watson.'

'Marley who?' Came the muffled question. Freddie was still hidden behind the door, with only his hair visible.

It was dark inside the flat, and all Callan could make out was the dim white light.

Callan reiterated. 'Yer neighbour, Marley Watson.'

Suddenly, Freddie opened the door. A black veil shrouded the room inside. Freddie had boarded up his windows too to create some sort of black room. In the centre illuminated by a white lamp was a desk scattered with all sorts of scientific apparatus.

Freddie waved a hand behind him. 'I'm working, I am. I ken who ye are. Ye are the police, ye are. Like I told ye, there was this eejit who thought it would be fun to smash my equipment. I had to run, get stuff that was broken, I did.'

Aileen leant around Callan to peer at the room inside. 'You stole all that?'

Pressing the backs of his hands on his hip, Freddie looked left and right. 'Nope. I put the equipment to good use, I did. Those bampots don't know how to use it well. I do, do I.'

Flummoxed, Aileen said, 'But ye might get arrested.'

'Nah! It's a small price to pay, is it? Hey, almost free,' Freddie wiggled his eyebrows. 'Now, what's this about this Marley woman?'

Callan pointed at the other door. 'Marley Watson, the woman who lived next door.'

As if shaken from his stupor, Freddie blinked. 'That's what her name was, was it? The cash machine? Oh. I hear she's dead, she is.'

What was wrong with this man? Hadn't he spoken to them about Marley last time they were here?

Ah, now he got it. *The eejit sod!*

Callan reached into his pocket and pulled out a penny.

Freddie chuckled. 'Ye started with a damn pound, ye did.'

'That was supposed to be yer entire payment. Now a penny's all ye get.'

Taking the offered coin, Freddie wagged it. 'I like ye, I do. At least ye dinnae threaten physical harm. I cannae afford more damages, can I? What do ye want to ken about Marley?'

'Has anyone been to her flat since yesterday?'

Freddie shrugged. 'The lad TJ. Wanted his share of her cash. I got a lock pick. Gave him his share and took mine, I did.'

Wow, what a lovely neighbour! Callan didn't roll his eyes, instead, he asked, 'Who was the lady who was threatening ye yesterday morning?'

At that Freddie wagged a finger at them. 'I like ye, but not enough to risk my life. I gotta get back to work, I do. If that's all.'

'Hold on.' Aileen spoke. 'Did Marley ever figure out you helped yourself to her cash?'

Freddie shrugged. 'Never came to me asking if she did. We never spoke, kept my distance, I did. And she was always cooped up, left once in a day for a couple of hours. That was my window to get in and out.'

'And can ye get us inside now?' Aileen lifted an eyebrow.

'Sure, I can.'

Five minutes later and two pennies lighter, they were inside Marley's flat. Everything was as dirty as it had been yesterday.

Callan didn't switch on the lights, lest they attract unwanted attention. Instead, using gloves and a torch, he tried to go through the litter. When his stomach protested at the sight and the smell, Callan gave up.

Gingerly seated on the sofa, Aileen used her torch to leaf through the notebooks. Callan sat beside her, careful not to upset the settling dust. She was going through Morticia Luna's log.

Aileen, frowning, turned to him. 'Didn't you find a pocket-sized diary in the safe yesterday?'

It took him a while to recollect. 'Och aye! I'd almost forgotten. It's in the evidence bag, back in my room.'

Shooting him one exasperated look, Aileen went back to the notebook on her lap.

In the dark, with nothing else to do, Callan thought back to the day they'd had. It had been as long and eventful as the previous one. From interviewing Hussey to the encounters with Morticia Luna, Charlie, Freddie and Hussey as well.

Leaning his elbows on his knees, Callan spoke aloud. 'If Marley was a cash-machine as Freddie put it, he's got no incentive to kill her. It's like slitting the goose's throat for that golden egg.'

Twirling a finger, he said, 'Then there's Charlie, who can be lying about his whereabouts. The time of death, at least to my knowledge, is between four and six. Half-past six at the maximum. I think she died before the storm which picked up at around fifteen minutes past six that evening. I remember.'

Aileen halted her perusal of the notes. 'What about the autopsy and toxicology reports?'

'Damned Loch Heaven police won't hand them over.'

'There's one address here. It says it's the Houndress's lair.' Aileen stabbed a finger on the page.

Holding out a hand for the book, Callan settled it on his lap as Aileen swivelled her torch to illuminate the page.

'I don't think so.' Callan shook his head. 'This is too dangerous to do without backup.'

Aileen pursed her lips. 'Come on!'

'What happens when a thug makes us out and brings us to Morticia Luna? It's essentially one and a half versus Morticia Luna's well-trained goons.' Callan reasoned.

'One and a *half*?' Aileen's voice was soft, a little too quiet.

Oh no. Callan realised his mistake.

Aileen punched him in the arm. It didn't hurt, but for good measure, he scrunched up his face in a pained expression. 'I-I meant…'

'I might be short but I'm not a weakling!' Aileen's outburst was loud in the silent room. Callan could swear she scared some vermin away.

She sure scared him. His eyes widened. 'I didn't mean it that way! What I wanted to say was ye aren't trained. And with just one gun between us and ye not knowing how to punch or shoot, is a bit of a one-sided match. Morticia Luna will have her lair guarded tight.'

Aileen shrugged. 'If you put it like that, then it's true. But can't we spy from a distance?'

Callan wanted to say no and mean it. But he was rather curious about Morticia Luna's lair. What sort of things could go on there?

'One hint of trouble and we are out of there and back to our hotel.'

Aileen grinned. 'You bet!'

THE STREETS WERE BUSY WITH GRIFTERS COUNTING their share, as hustlers handed out money to huddled groups of young people loitering about minding their own. A couple of squatters lounged about in the abandoned houses, their eyes trailing Aileen.

Thankfully, Marley had a map of how to get to the "lair" from her flat. That woman had been thorough. If she'd put half that energy in innkeeping, Dachaigh would have never been loss making in the first place.

Aileen sighed. To each his own. Marley liked to live precariously, and that got her killed.

They stuck to the dim light cast by the scattered streetlights, not daring to slip into the shadows. As the night waned on, the street grew darker and the shadows deeper.

Were they foolish to seek Morticia Luna on their own?

Following the map, they turned left and into a narrow alley. It was just like the one beside Sláinte that Charlie had led them through just an hour or so ago.

According to the map, they had one other turn left before they reached their destination. Slowing down, Callan spoke in her ear. 'Let's not take this turn. We should have a vantage point from this alley.'

He pointed around them. 'I don't think there are any windows looking into this street. We'll remain inconspicuous.'

Aileen gave him a thumbs-up sign and jogged over to the end of the alley.

The other street was a larger one but silent. It was awash with a golden glow thanks to one streetlight.

It seemed to be relatively clean with not a single street dweller crouched in the shadows. Why were people so afraid of Morticia Luna?

Callan's hand landed on Aileen's shoulder, and his front brushed against her back. Aileen was pressed between the wall and Callan. She shuddered to think about the grime she was brushing against. Her shirt was surely spoilt now.

Still whispering, Callan discreetly pointed at a structure where the grey concrete hadn't cracked. 'That's the cleanest and best-preserved building we've seen hereabouts. Bet that's the lair.'

Nodding her agreement, Aileen too spoke in

Callan's ear. 'Guess we'll wait and see what's happening.'

As if in response, a light shimmered in one of the rooms. There was no curtain to obstruct their view. And the darkness in the alley made it easier to see, albeit the window was high enough for them to just make out the figures.

The window filled with a broad man. They couldn't decipher his features, but he had to be burly. He stood there a while, facing the room.

With bated breath, they observed.

When he moved out of view, Aileen let out a groan.

'Shush.' Callan admonished. 'Patience.'

They both knew she didn't have much of it. Gritting her teeth, Aileen shuffled to a more comfortable position, still hidden in the shadows.

Somewhere far off, an owl hooted, and smoke puffed out of a chimney in the street they were crouched in. The fumes burned Aileen's nostrils, but she didn't complain.

She'd asked for this adventure.

Suddenly, there was a movement in the window where the man had been. This time it was a cloaked figure. It didn't move, not until it swivelled to stare right out of the window.

Gasping, both Aileen and Callan hunched lower and deeper into the dark.

From somewhere far away, they heard the

rumble of a car's engine. Goodness, had they been made out?

But Callan didn't ask her to move. He too waited silently. Aileen's heart was beating fast. She was afraid someone could hear it.

Headlights turned the corner, and an inconspicuous black car came into view. It had tinted windows and no license plate.

Was this even legal?

Callan's breath tickled Aileen's neck and she shivered.

Right in front of them, the car slowed to a crawl. But it didn't stop until it reached the entrance to the building with the cloaked figure.

The car's engine cut off, sending everything into silence.

Aileen's hands grew cold.

When the entrance door swung open, her heart almost jumped into her throat.

As if on cue, the boot of the car popped open. The driver must have done that from inside the car.

Two men walked out with large suitcases. Judging by the way they struggled to haul the luggage in, the suitcases had to be heavy.

When the two men disappeared, a giant man walked out. Rounding over to the back of the car, he inspected the luggage.

Satisfied, he shut the boot and turned, examining the street.

Aileen almost pressed her face to the wall,

trying to disappear. He clearly hadn't seen them yet. The dim glow of the streetlight caught his face. 'Oh.' The gasp slipped from Aileen's lips.

Callan clamped a hand on her mouth and lightly squeezed. But he still didn't move.

They didn't breathe for a long moment. That one moment was like a lifetime.

The giant man's gaze swept the road one last time and then he took a few steps towards the street Aileen and Callan were crouched in.

Aileen's breath faltered when the sweetness of nicotine wafted the air. The man reeked of it. He was that close.

Oh shit!

Two steps in, he halted and inspected something in the dark.

Another moment stretched on. Turning around, he shouted. 'All clear!' And went back in.

On his heels, two other figures stepped out. One was the cloaked figure and the other a gentleman dressed in business formals. They stood hidden under the porch, but the light from within highlighted their silhouettes.

Turning to each other, they spoke until the cloaked figure stretched out a pale hand. They shook hands, and the man walked towards the car and slipped inside.

The cloaked figure stood with hands linked in front until a beast of a hound slid out of the building and ambled towards the figure. A second hound followed.

When the figure patted their heads, Aileen knew. That was Morticia Luna.

Now her heart was in her throat. And her mouth was parched.

What if the hounds sniffed them out?

Aileen bit into her lips.

Barely coherent, Callan spoke. 'Get ready.'

When the car rumbled to life, he tugged at her shirt.

Limbs shaking, they retreated the way they'd come before anyone had a chance to look in the shadows. They could be sitting ducks then.

Tip-toeing out of that alley, they found their way to another street. Luckily this one was well habited, even if by pickpockets and seasoned thieves. At least they won't shoot them at sight.

Aileen panted, her hand firmly in Callan's as they retraced their footsteps to Marley's building. But a wrong turn led them askew.

After ten minutes of walking blind, Callan halted. Using his torch, he pulled out the map. 'Bloody hell.'

Leaning into his side, Aileen peered at the map. 'Where are we?'

Callan circled his figure on the map. 'Somewhere close to Sláinte. Hey, ye okay?'

Aileen stared at the ground. 'It was exhilarating

to say the least. Better than any haunted house or even those rollercoasters at amusement parks.'

Callan chuckled. 'Definitely, but for a moment there I thought we'd been made out. Why did ye gasp?'

Looking around them, Aileen leant in and whispered. 'I think I've seen that man before. The giant. But I can't remember where. These past two days have been so,' she waved her hands. 'It'll come to me.'

'Hope it does. Let's get back and, after a cleansing shower, get a good night's sleep. The bloody arm kept me up all night.' Callan said.

CALLAN NAVIGATED THROUGH THE DARK STREETS, trying to make sense of the direction they were going. The damn technology was useless with no connectivity. Aileen's phone had died a while ago, and Callan's was barely holding on.

Studying his arm, now hidden behind the black coat, Aileen asked. 'Does it still hurt?'

Callan waved a dismissive hand. 'Negligible. Nothing great, it'll heal.'

Aileen bobbed her head. 'Of course, it will, but you've got to take care of it.'

They fell into silence, their footsteps echoing.

Aileen trembled a little, but Callan had his arms

around her again. To another passerby, they were just a couple out for the night.

Considering the map, Callan figured they were a few buildings away from the pub. All he had to do was take this turn. Following the route, he led them into an adjoining alley.

It was colder here as darkness swallowed them, laced with the overpowering acridity of urine mixed with alcohol. Rats scuttled around in the edges of the blackness. A body or two hunched in those darker corners.

Was it safe to have brought Aileen here? She was a grown woman who didn't need his protection, but they were lost for all he knew. They could spend the entire night just navigating these vicious streets!

Why on earth would Marley choose to stay in this area? She had the money to move out. Enough cash that her neighbour helped himself to some of it and she apparently hadn't even noticed.

The road broadened as they inched further. One lone street lamp flickered on the opposite side and illuminated the broken neon sign that read "Sláinte."

Callan exhaled a relieved breath. They were one house down from Sláinte's backyard.

But there was something wrong. His gut jumped, alerting him. Eyes sharp, Callan looked around. It took him two seconds to spot the cause of trouble.

There was a silhouette standing on the other

side of Sláinte, leaning against a rusted railing. It was hidden in the shadows, barely lit by a faint dancing light from behind it.

Callan gauged it to be a lean man, six feet in height, give or take. The rising hair on his neck was enough to alert Callan that he watched them.

The man moved, a brief shuffle before a click brought a dancing flame to life. Just then, the man lit a snout. White smoke wafted where his face would be, adding the taste of nicotine to the thick air.

Callan tensed, his arms squeezing Aileen closer. Slight tremors coursed through her body. But her gasp suggested she hadn't made out that man on the opposite side of the road, not until he'd lit his cigarette.

Focusing back on the road, they soon reached Sláinte. A rickety ladder rested next to the backdoor and the upper floor was boarded, just as it had been. No one loitered at the back entrance when the party was out front.

Instead of halting near the pub, Callan led Aileen through the back alley. An erie silence descended onto the street, hugging them as a cloak might. Not a soul stirred in the dark.

Just as Aileen wrenched open her mouth to speak, Callan abruptly stopped and dipped his hands in the inky darkness.

His empty hand emerged holding a trembling bony lad.

'Ye again.' Callan sized up the lad he was holding, similar to a rat held by its tail.

He wriggled but quickly gave up the act. The eejit had been following them all along.

TJ fumbled with his words before he spoke coherently. 'I just-I just wanted to know if you have ma money.'

Callan rounded on him. 'Why would we have yer money?'

The lad shrugged, shuffling his shoulders. 'I did the job Marley asked. I ain't waiting around much longer. They'd get me, too. I know they would.'

Crossing his arms, Callan glared at him. 'Ye have a stellar record. How much do ye charge for bank fraud?'

TJ's eyes flittered around. 'I need the cash. Hard cash. Now. I don't do that anymore. Ain't freelancing.'

Aileen bit her lips. 'What do you do then?'

'This and that. Smaller crimes, digging for data.' TJ slipped his hands in his pockets. 'Okay fine! I might have held some data ransom, charged a hefty payment. I don't do charity. And Marley paid peanuts anyway. She can't die and leave me nothing.'

Callan tsked. 'But didn't ye help yerself to her money just yesterday?'

Caught, TJ's eyes widened. He lurched, ready to run, but Callan was quick to catch him this time. He picked the lad with one hand, as he'd done before. 'Had ye worked for Marley Watson long?'

Whimpering, TJ muttered. 'She came in, wanted a job done, I was the best at the rate she was willing to pay. I did the work, she paid me in instalments.'

Callan dropped him to the ground and got into his face. 'Why are ye planning to run away? Who do ye think is after ye?'

TJ's voice trembled, fear clouding his eyes. 'The same one who got her. Stay away from them, I tell ya. I told Marley too, but she didn't listen. Stay away.'

Aileen pressed for more information. 'How many people have you checked out for her?'

The bony man ran a tongue across his cracked lips. 'Two, just the two.'

'You sure?'

'Hmm.'

Callan bent to his height. 'Tell me names. Who did ye search for? Who is after you?'

The lad's gaze flittered around as his legs quaked. 'She wasn't in the right business, that boyfriend got her into it, he did. Tried staying away, but I gotta earn-'

Callan lifted his cheeks in a sinister grin. 'Of course ye do, to keep yer pockets full. Who. Is. After. Ye?'

The lad shook his head, kicking out again. 'Leave me alone! I need ma money and I need it, or

I cannae think right. She paid peanuts, she did. But I accepted. Marley was a miser, but her targets pay well, they do, but messing with them as she'd planned to. That's what got her killed.'

'Who are they, TJ?' Callan was losing patience.

The smell of nicotine filled the air again, but Callan ignored it as he peered at TJ.

The urchin leant in, speaking slowly in hushed tones. 'Hound-uh,' the lad choked. Blood gurgled and poured from his pale mouth.

What? Callan jumped back, pulling Aileen with him.

Aileen's scream shook tremors through Callan's body.

Horrendous red spots splattered TJ's Winnie the Pooh shirt where a large dagger had ripped it, piercing his young heart.

Trembling, TJ collapsed onto the reeking wet floor. All they could do was stare as life left his dreamy eyes.

CHAPTER EIGHT

Callan had been one moment too late, preoccupied listening to the lad, then to make out the life-ending glint of the whetted dagger.

The fragrant sharp swirls of nicotine floated through the sultry air, playing with his nostrils just as the knife had flown unbidden into the body of the bony urchin.

'Hey!' Callan shouted as he flicked his torch on, flashing it into the darkness.

There was nothing there apart from the yellow illuminated eyes of rodents. Not a man in sight.

As if he'd stick around.

'Damn it!'

He ran over, flashing his torch further into the darkness. A few figures crouched there, huddled into moth-eaten blankets.

His torch highlighted a piece of paper, weighed down by a stone. It had a message printed on it.

"You Will Be Next."

He pocketed the note, before pivoting to notice Aileen trembling, staring at the mucky street near their feet, petrified.

A heavy astringent odour of blood suspended in the sultry air. Aileen's skin glimmered, whitely pale as she stared at TJ.

The dead lad's eyes were entirely too large and lifeless.

'Callan.' She muttered through her teeth.

But Callan couldn't respond, a thick layer of sourness wrapped around his own tongue. He had to call this in. It was his duty to.

Swallowing the rising bile, Callan used the last bit of battery left.

Out of the corner of his eyes, he saw Aileen clutching her hands over her mouth, eyes wide and unblinking. He hoped now more than ever she'd keep her heid. The last thing he wanted was for her to have a meltdown in this dingier part of town.

Callan needed to secure the scene and get her away from the body. But first he trudged over to her and led her some feet away from the corpse, shoes squishing in the murky puddles the rain had left behind.

Emotions had never been this strong point. But his mouth wrenched open without permission. 'Ye okay?'

Aileen raised watery eyes to his. Her lower lip trembled. Unable to handle the pain he saw in her eyes, Callan snaked a hand around her waist and pulled her close. She sniffled against his shirt. 'So-Sorry.'

The dark alley lit up in shades of red and blue as sirens rounded the corner. A shadow or two made a run for it as a police vehicle came to an abrupt halt.

Momentarily, they were blinded by the luminance of the headlights.

Uniformed police officers strode towards them, smartly dressed in their yellow jackets.

Callan flashed his badge, eager to get Aileen back into the safety of their hotel.

'Ah, it's a mess.' One officer hung his head, shaking it.

'Aye, the man had a good aim. Poor sod got it in his heart.'

'Never saw it coming, judging from the angle.' The police officer knelt beside the lad.

Callan didn't want to wait. He urged the officers to get them back to their hotel. For them, this was just another street urchin. One of the many who were born and died on the streets.

People like Walsh's boss won't care for him. Callan's heart beat harder. He clenched his jaw. No, it was his duty, as per the oath he'd taken. He would take care of TJ now. Protect him, at least in death. Even if that's the last thing he ever did.

Aileen couldn't think straight. She was still leaning against Callan like a damsel in distress.

Eyeing the scene, she tried shoving the vomit rising in her throat. He was dead. Her breath hitched.

Noticing her gaze, Callan spun to block her view.

Breathe, she instructed herself. But one inhale and all she wanted to do was boke. Burying her nose in Callan's coat, she inhaled his woody scent.

Callan squeezed the hand he'd wrapped around her. 'They are dropping us off at the hotel. Come on.' He nudged.

She shuddered, the air suddenly growing colder than it had been a moment ago.

At Aileen's nod, Callan ushered her into the backseat of the police car and hopped in beside her. 'We've been asked to go to the station first thing in the morning.'

This was the first time Aileen had sat in a police car, let alone in the backseat of one—a criminal. She cared little about this unexpected experience. All she heard her mind assert was: "You are a criminal."

If she hadn't pressed TJ for answers, if she hadn't come here, he wouldn't be dead.

Aileen wrapped freezing hands in an awkward self-hug.

She cast a side glance at Callan. He sat, his demeanour as indifferent as it always was, invincible. A slight prickly beard marred his chiselled jaw. He was staring out of the window, warm glowing street lights highlighting his features before casting it into blackness.

Strong. That he certainly was. And Aileen needed to be strong. She needed to find who'd do this.

Perhaps Marley Watson was up to no good, perhaps TJ was nothing more than an urchin making money through stalking others for payment. But no one had the authority to take their lives.

Perhaps no one'd mourn their loss, no one to even report they'd died. But that didn't mean their killer would be let off the hook. After all, Marley Watson and TJ were young people. Death had called on them far too early.

No, she had to bring them to justice. And whoever their killer was, was getting bolder. The longer they took finding him/her out, the sooner he'd/she'd slip through their fingers.

That wouldn't do.

Aileen trembled as a shudder ran through her. Adventurous be damned, she slid her cold hands across the hard seat into Callan's warm ones.

He squeezed hers.

Together as partners, they'd do this.

AILEEN DIDN'T KNOW HOW SHE'D GOT THROUGH THE night.

She'd made a beeline for the bathroom as soon as they'd got in, emptying the noxious contents of her stomach. She purged till she was simply heaving.

It might have been sheer exhaustion, which most people experienced through drinking too much, but for Aileen, the brutality of murder had laced her eyelids with lead.

She barely made it to the bedroom where, drunkenly, she sprawled out on the itchy carpeted floor and snored the night away.

Now, late in the morning, she sat at a table in the hotel's restaurant, toying with the crusty edge of her cold toast. The black coffee she'd poured in the cup had gone tepid a while ago. Aileen's head pounded like someone was wielding a hammer against it.

Callan slid in the chair opposite hers, his face stoic and voice gruff. 'Morning.'

Aileen didn't even try to lift her chin in greeting.

They sat in silence as Callan gobbled a full English. The smell making her feel more nauseated than she already was.

Aileen stared at her plate when Callan assessed her.

'I-I'm sorry about last night.' She muttered.

Sighing, he placed the cutlery aside. 'The scene shook me as well, and I'm a homicide detective. All we can do is find who did it. The more we introspect, the lesser time we have in finding TJ and Marley's killer. And first things first. Ye need to eat. Yer brain won't work without fuel.'

Callan hadn't ever been this gentle or understanding. So stunned was she that he plated up some warm eggs and toast for her. He also refilled her cup of coffee. When she continued to stare at the table, he urged. 'Come on, partner. We are strapped for time.'

In companionable silence, they munched until Callan's phone beeped. He muttered some curses at it. 'Eejit thing. Why do I need it?'

For the first time in a long time, Aileen chuckled. She picked his phone and frowned. 'It's an email from Robert Davis.'

Callan grunted. 'What does he say?'

Aileen rolled her eyes. 'Unlock the phone, Callan.'

Finally, she pulled up the email and read it aloud. 'Dear Callan. I was scrolling through the surveillance footage recorded on the day of the murder. I saw something that might help in the case. I've attached the files. If you need help to download them, ask Aileen.' She finished. 'He's a smart one.'

Callan flicked a hand. 'He's learning to use that tongue of his. Bet Rory asked him to add that last sentence in. He's a little too excited that we are here together.'

Aileen groaned. 'That means Gran knows.'

Swallowing the last bite with coffee, Callan wiped his hands. 'Sure she does. Nothing happens in Loch Fuar without Siobhan knowing about it. Come on, it's time to meet Walsh's superior officer.' Callan made a face. 'Brace yerself.'

The police station at Loch Heaven was busier than Loch Fuar's. They had more of a police force than the three-member team back home.

Aileen trudged into the station, following Callan like a puppy as they were led into an office stacked with boxes of papers and files.

It would have usually annoyed her if she'd had to follow Callan. But today, she marked as an exception. Even though eating some breakfast made her feel better, her head still throbbed.

It made her sick that she'd have to narrate last night's events. Aileen decided to keep mum and let Callan do the talking.

An older man with a rotund belly took a seat on the high-backed chair. He barely fit. The centre part of his head was bald with a light dusting of hair marring the sides.

His beady eyes scanned Callan. 'Detective Cameron.'

Callan merely tilted his chin. 'DCI Roland.' He mumbled nonchalantly.

The beady stare moved to Aileen's face, not before landing a little lower. Aileen slanted her gaze away, uncomfortable.

'So I hear you murdered someone.' His voice was nasal.

Aileen gasped when the man sniggered at his own words.

Beside her, Callan flashed his teeth, clearly not amused. He'd told her DCI Roland had a good reputation, but Callan didn't hold him in high regard. As for Aileen, there was something about this man that just didn't sit right with her.

This was Walsh's superior officer?

The scowls between Callan and Roland were uneasy as if strong undercurrents creating a tension in the air.

TJ's unblinking eyes staring at her.

Aileen snapped herself out of it. Focus!

'So,' DCI Roland sat forward, joining his fingers in front of him. 'Tell me what you two were doing there. Getting into some bad habits while I'm not looking, Cameron?'

'We were there to check out a tip we were given.' Callan lied.

DCI Roland chuckled. 'And you killed him after you got what you wanted.'

Aileen had had enough. She hissed at the man. 'We didn't kill anyone, Mr Roland!'

The man pierced Aileen with his black eyes and waved a hand. 'Kevin, please. I never meant it that way. It was just a joke. Just trying to be nice.'

When he gazed at Aileen's chest again, he was definitely not being "nice." Aileen fisted her hands wanting to say something to wipe that jeer from his face.

Callan clenched his teeth. 'We were making our way towards Sláinte, checking a tip. When I realised we were being followed, I led Ms Mackinnon away as to not raise suspicion-' From then on, Callan went to recount the incident to the T.

He told Roland about meeting TJ and that the questions they asked him.

'The lad lurched forward when the knife got him but be didn't fall face down. Instead, he tried to right himself, however, I think his legs gave out, and he crumpled to the ground, landing on his side.' Callan finished never telling Roland about the adventure they'd had before running into TJ.

'Never thought about using your police issue, eh?' Roland taunted. Was the DCI trying to get a rise out of Callan?

Callan didn't take the bait. 'He was a short lad. I had to bend low to listen to what he was saying since he was whispering. I never saw the knife till it flashed under a flickering light. Before I could push him aside, the blade pierced his heart.'

DCI Roland lifted a lip, smirking. 'And?'

Callan muttered. 'Damn it!' He continued, frustration etched in his voice. 'TJ was dead the moment the blade entered his body. It was a good aim. In a split reaction, Ms Mackinnon tried to steady him, but I knew if his killer was still around, they could aim at us next. And if they were long gone, that would only result in Ms Mackinnon contaminating the scene. Thus, I held her back.'

'It was a dagger attack. No one carries multiple of those to kill people. Not like a Chinese movie, anyway.' DCI Roland flashed tiny yellow teeth.

Callan shrugged noncommittally. 'The killer was gone when I flashed my torch. I didn't think it was safe to leave Ms Mackinnon behind on her own.'

Roland raised an eyebrow. 'So it was safe to lead your… Girlfriend to that place.'

It wasn't exactly a question, but Callan leant forward, imitating his colleague. 'I prefer to keep my girl close. She's safer that way.'

My girl? Aileen blushed. Did he really think of her that way?

Of course not, Aileen! He's trying to keep Roland away!

DCI Roland flashed a smile at Aileen that wasn't at all genuine. 'You are a lucky woman to have such a man at your beck and call.'

Aileen didn't respond. She continued to study the prickly carpet with interest.

Roland turned to her. 'Well, can you tell us what happened?'

'That young man would never live to see his thirty-first birthday.'

After that, Aileen repeated what Callan had told the detective. She lied through her teeth about the "tip" they'd received and never mentioned their foray into Morticia Luna's lair.

Roland nodded, grinning at her when she was done. 'You've had a nasty night, eh? Is that how to take care of a civilian woman? Dragging her along to the police station as if she were your shield, Cameron!'

'Ye said ye'd-'

Roland cut Callan off. 'Don't give excuses, man!'

Beside her, Callan gritted his teeth.

But Roland wasn't done. 'Let me warn you. That area's too dangerous to take a lovely woman out for a stroll or drinks. My rat tells me stabbings in that area have increased tenfold. Besides, didn't I tell DCI Rory Macdonald that the case is closed?'

Callan gritted out. 'He has nothing to do with this. I'm on leave.'

A nasal laugh filled the room. 'Kicked you out, did he? Well officer, enjoy your time off instead of running riot in vicious areas. You are lucky it wasn't you or Ms Mackinnon here. Next time you might not be so… And if I find you lurking around places you shouldn't be…'

Callan's jaw was clenched so tight that it took him a while to respond. 'Got it.'

Roland bobbed his head, his double chin swinging as his beady eyes landed on Aileen's chest.

What a creep!

Aileen cleared her throat and tugged at Callan's sleeve.

She sighed when they were out into the fresh air and away from the police station.

Callan led them towards their hotel again, and he held her hand firmly.

They hiked back in silence before emerging in the crowded city centre.

'That scoundrel!' Callan growled suddenly.

Aileen knew who the "scoundrel" was.

She wanted to know. 'Do you think these detectives seriously investigated Marley's case and now TJ's? Roland seems to be a little…' Aileen had no clue how to describe him.

Callan clenched his jaw. 'Either they are trying to keep us out of it…' He thought for a minute. 'Or they are genuinely clueless and want to file this a suicide. It's not like anyone would take notice.'

'Is Roland always this…?'

Clenching his jaw, Callan muttered. 'They call him an ideal detective. "Ideal Detective," my arse!'

Aileen shivered. 'I hope they don't all follow his example. I wanted to scratch those beady eyes out. Bet they'd continue to look where they shouldn't.'

'He's an eejit. And I can bet my year's pay he's about to cast TJ's death as an accident. And also give some sloppy speech on how crime is rampant in those lowly areas. Those would be his words, not mine.'

Callan was on a rampage. He obviously detested the Detective Chief Inspector. Aileen could respect Callan on that one opinion of his alone.

Roland was the type of man who didn't give two hoots about people like TJ. For him, it would just be a way to garner more public attention and sympathy.

But the one thing Aileen wanted to do was wipe that damned smirk off his face.

They returned to Aileen's room, where she took her place behind the desk and Callan stared out of the window. She pulled out her laptop and booted it. 'Callan, want to check the surveillance footage Robert sent?'

The sun peeked from between the trees, making the chlorophyll in the verdant trees glimmer. There was not a hint of rain in the blue sky.

Callan pulled up a chair beside Aileen and sank into it. 'Remember what TJ said last night?'

Aileen shuddered. It was hard to forget. The scene was etched in her mind. She sipped some water. 'What about it?'

Callan caressed his chin. 'Marley was blackmailing people. TJ confirmed that last night and he was the one getting her intel on her "targets" as he called them. And there's no other way she could have so much cash. Marley had been unemployed since May.'

A little guilt tickled her heart. Aileen had fired Marley.

Shaking those thoughts from her mind, Aileen

figured out what he was trying to say. 'You think Morticia Luna and Charlie were Marley's latest "targets" and one of them snapped.'

'Could be. I mean, I won't put murder past Morticia Luna. But then again, it's jumping to conclusions. Let's just keep that bit in mind, that Morticia Luna and Charlie could've been Marley's victims.'

Aileen agreed, scribbling that bit in her yellow notepad. 'And what about the pocket-sized diary you found in the safe?'

Muttering, Callan stood. 'Hold on, let me get it.' He jogged out of Aileen's room only to return half a minute later. 'I was going to read through it last night but, well, I was exhausted.'

She didn't want to think about the previous night again. She'd rather wipe it out of her memory.

Instead, Aileen opened the book Callan had brought with him. Scanning it, Aileen nodded. 'It's a detailed account of Marley's monetary affairs.'

Callan leant on the desk. 'Do we have any names of potential "targets" or past "targets"?'

Still reading, Aileen shook her head. 'Either these are some hastily taken notes or Marley didn't know any accounting. She's merely listed the date she's received money with an initial. And in the other column, she's listed where that money was spent. There is a daily log of it. She counts the cash as per her books and the real one she's got by the end of every week.'

Elbow on the desk, Callan caressed his prickly beard. 'Ye mean to say she calculated how much she had left at the end of every week? That's a good habit, isn't it?'

Aileen agreed. 'It is. I keep thinking she'd have been a good innkeeper only if she'd channelled her energies in the right direction.'

Callan waved a hand. 'It was her choice.'

It was. Aileen let it go. Pointing at her laptop's screen, she said, 'Log in to your email. Let's see some surveillance footage.'

Five minutes later, after cussing at the fickle Wi-Fi, Aileen downloaded the surveillance footages Robert had sent.

Sides pressed together, Aileen and Callan watched. It was footage captured on Saturday morning.

Callan squinted at the screen, watching. 'Slow it down.'

They watched again with bated breath. There were several cars which entered Loch Fuar that morning. 'Damn the weekend!' Callan swore.

Aileen paused the footage. 'Hold on. Watch this car.'

She rewound the footage and they watched a car rash driving. It entered their town. Pausing the video again, Aileen zoomed in as far as she could. 'Oh gosh.'

Callan grinned. 'Guess we found the time Marley reached Loch Fuar that day.'

Yes, they had. But Aileen had seen something else too. She grinned back at him. 'That's not all. See this car. It's literally following on her heels.'

She pointed to it and rightly so, it followed Marley's rental, driving just as rashly. It was a compact vehicle with just two seats. But the driver was more cautious than Marley.

Callan scrunched his nose as if he couldn't believe his eyes. 'What in the world?'

Aileen snorted. 'It could be a joke, but you know how you hate coincidences?'

The driver of that rental car was wearing a mask. Not the sort that hid his face, but the one that looked like a hound.

Callan hummed a "yes." 'Hate coincidences. What's the license plate? I'll ask Robert to run it.'

Aileen dictated the license number, and he noted it. 'Marley's car's a rental. You might need a warrant to get information about it.'

Then Callan listed the details of Marley's rental car as well and sent them off to Robert after hurling a couple of expletives at his phone.

Aileen tapped a few keys on her laptop. 'Here's the other footage Robert sent. According to him, this car is way fancier than any he's seen.'

Rightly so, they found a top-of-the-range slick car gliding into Loch Fuar, not an hour after Marley's rental. Unfortunately, it had tinted windows and the camera couldn't capture the driver's face. But the license plate was visible.

Callan asked Robert to search the database for this car too before leaning on the desk and watching the last footage.

The footage was recorded in the evening, just before the impending storm. And rightly so, amongst the plethora of cars leaving, they found the slick vehicle that had entered Loch Fuar only that morning. It stood out from the rest of the mundane vehicles.

Aileen listed the time at which the car left. Beside her, Callan tsked. 'Fifteen minutes to six. Fits within our time frame. Commit the crime and hightail it out of there.'

But that wasn't the only car they spotted. Half an hour later, the car with the driver wearing a hound mask followed. They couldn't see the driver's face, just the license plate.

'Bloody hell!' Callan slapped a hand on the desk.

Aileen drummed her fingers on the table. 'Now what? We can't identify any individuals just that three cars entered Loch Fuar and only two left. There's no sign of this rental car Marley hired.'

Callan faced Aileen. 'So where is this car? The Loch Heaven police never found it. Heck, they never even asked around for it. Add to that, they never even found Marley's shoes. We need to find all these things to catch the killer.'

Where would they find these items? Aileen didn't know. The killer could've disposed of them for all they knew.

Just then Callan's phone signalled an incoming. Apparently, Robert was quick.

'He's sent the details of each car. The car driven by the person wearing a hound's mask belongs to a "Houndress & Co." and the other fancier one is registered to a "John Doe."'

Callan read the message and thudded a fist on the table. 'Bloody hell! John Doe? How come the authorities allow someone to register their car under that name? It's definitely a hoax.'

Aileen sat back, thinking. 'Hold on.' She tapped a few keys and loaded a directory in which they could find the name of any registered company. When she didn't find any company registered under the name "Houndress & Co Limited" Aileen tutted. 'There's no such company called "Houndress" but there is one called Morticia Luna Limited.'

She scrolled through the details. The company was a private one and had filed its accounts on time. And, Aileen grinned. 'It's registered to the same address where we saw Morticia Luna with that man yesterday, her "lair." And it says here Morticia Luna Ltd is engaged in real estate and rental property.'

Callan noted that down. 'It's got to be Morticia Luna's company then. Who is this "Houndress & Co."?'

Aileen thought for a moment. 'It could be Morticia Luna trying to register a car under an alias or an imposter who knew the police would dig into the details of the car. If you ask me, the latter's the most likely option. The person driving the car is trying too hard to hide himself or herself with that mask.'

Hissing, Callan said, 'This leads us nowhere!'

But it gave them something to dig into. Aileen shook her head. 'Look, we know that there were potentially two cars who entered and left Loch Fuar that day. One followed on Marley's heels and the other left at the time of her death. It could be a coincidence, but I think we should look into it.'

Callan pursed his lips. 'They could've gone anywhere, parked the car anywhere. Most tourists visit the loch on the weekends, and they don't take the treacherous road through town. They go to the other shore where it's easier to get to the loch.'

'We can at least give it a try, Callan.' Aileen persisted. 'How many parking lots can Loch Fuar have?'

Aye, they could give it a try.

Callan said to Aileen. 'We might have a lot of parking lots with no surveillance footage.'

Aileen's face fell.

He grinned. 'It's Loch Fuar. We've got something better than that!'

CHAPTER NINE

That same evening, Aileen and Callan set out in their respective cars for Loch Fuar. It felt good to leave this darker city behind for Loch Fuar's more close-knit community.

On the way home, Callan's phone rang. It was Aileen. 'Hey! I thought since your car is ancient and without a radio, you'd want some company.'

Callan rolled his eyes. Aileen was too impatient. 'Can we give this case a rest please, at least till we get back?'

'I just called for the company.' Came the reply. After a long pause, Aileen asked. 'You never told me why you are doing this for Marley and TJ?'

Wanting to keep those questions at bay, he cut his answer short. 'It's my duty.'

Aileen tsked. 'The truth, Callan.'

Callan didn't answer immediately. Instead, he

focused on the road. 'It's not always about being paid for the work ye do. Duty is duty, ye can't measure it in money's worth.'

'Have you always wanted to be a detective?' She asked.

Tapping a finger on the steering wheel, Callan thought about it. 'There are other ways to perform yer duty than being a detective.'

The line fell silent. Callan was sure she'd clicked off, but she spoke after a while. 'You don't speak about yourself, you know.'

'Neither do ye.' Callan retorted.

Aileen chuckled. 'I told you, I left my risk-less life behind. You might deny it, but it was very boring. Gran had a better life than I did!'

Callan allowed a small smile for the ninety-year-old. She was a fierce pain in the butt. 'I didn't always want to be a detective. But I've always wanted to give back to society.'

Aileen didn't press for more, instead, she diverted the conversation to more common, safer matters. Lord knew he wasn't ready to share anymore. Not with her, especially when his mouth lost its filter when she asked him questions. He'd told no one. And here she was, Ms Aileen Mackinnon from the city, a brilliant forensic accountant. And he hadn't thought twice before babbling about his past to her.

He sighed and watched the sun setting on the horizon. He had to investigate what was wrong with himself…

The tiny police station was quiet when Callan clicked open the door.

Officer Robert Davis sat behind the desk, his forehead resting on the wooden table. Callan rolled his eyes.

The Town of Saints…

Apparently.

Aileen pushed past him into the warmth of the station. The weather was cooler now that the sky had turned dark.

Callan walked over to the coffee machine. At its hum, Robert Davis startled awake.

'Cal-Callan…' He stuttered.

'Morning.' Callan quirked an eyebrow with a small smirk. 'Sleep well?'

Robert ran a hand through his hair and looked at Aileen sheepishly. 'Hi, Aileen.'

She waved at him. 'You did excellent work with the surveillance footage.'

The young officer gave her a shy smile and then held out a drive. 'It's all on here for the files.'

Mug in hand, Callan shot a glare at the officer. 'Didn't ye think it's customary to ask permission before ye hand over pertinent data to a civilian?'

The sod gaped at Callan, alarmed.

Aileen elbowed Callan. 'Leave him alone. Come

on, we've got work to do.' She took the drive from Robert and led the way into Callan's office.

Callan scowled at Robert before striding to his office and slammed the door closed behind him.

Aileen was already at the outdated murder board. She pointed at it when he walked in. 'We've come a long way since Sunday.'

Callan pushed his left hand in his pocket. 'Aye but not far enough to catch the killer.' Gesturing to Aileen with his mug, he said, 'Ye sure ye don't want to check Dachaigh out? We can meet in the morning.'

Aileen leant a hip on his table. 'What's the point of driving here in the dark if we aren't going to work? Besides, I can't leave you alone to slog the night away. We're partners, remember?'

It was hard to forget. A small smile played on his lips.

Callan walked over to his murder board. 'I'll get this updated. Would ye be able to trace Marley's car until then?'

'On it, sir!' Aileen mock saluted him and marched out the room.

He chuckled at her unending enthusiasm and got to work.

Drinking the dark sludge that passed as coffee, Callan meticulously transferred his notes onto the board.

❅

In the other room, Aileen sat in front of the ancient computer which had helped her crack the previous case.

The sparse closet-shaped room closed in on her, but she had no time to dwell on its tiny size. She'd best get cracking.

Using the notes she'd made in Loch Heaven, Aileen dug into the car rental companies that operated in this region of Scotland. Thanks to a tag Aileen had spotted on Marley's car, she found the company quickly. And luckily, they had twenty-four-hour customer service.

Aileen dialled their number and sat listening to it ringing.

In the minute that followed, her heart rate soared, and doubt began trickling in. What would she ask them? What if they thought she was being an idiot or worse, a prankster? She clutched the phone tighter, her palms sweaty.

'Hello, I'm Emma from Rent Your Ride. How may I be of assistance to you?' Asked a sweet voice.

'Emma! Hi. I'm Aileen Mackinnon, um, I wanted to know if you could tell me a few details about a car my friend had rented from you.' Aileen drummed her fingers on the desk as she spoke.

There was a long pause. 'I'm sorry, ma'am. I can't divulge those details to you.'

Aileen sighed and bit her lips, thinking of a way to get the information she wanted. 'Could you at least tell me where the vehicle was dropped off?'

Another pause followed before Emma replied. 'Sorry, I can't. Although we have fixed drop-off points. I can list those in your area for you if that's helpful.'

Aileen perked up. She was getting somewhere. 'What's the closest drop off point for Loch Fuar?'

'Could you hold on a moment, please?'

A few clicks drifted down the line, and Aileen drummed her fingers impatiently.

A couple of minutes later, Emma spoke. 'We have only one drop off point at the outskirts of the town at this parking lot…'

Callan was hunched over his murder board when Aileen waltzed back in.

'Ye are in high spirits.' He remarked.

'That's 'cause I am. The drop-off point for Marley's car? It's exactly at the place our "could-be killer" would've parked his/her car.'

Callan frowned. 'Ye mean it's the one near the cottage?'

Aileen nodded. 'Guess we should go there.'

Glancing at his watch, Callan hummed. 'Aye. First thing in the morning. They open at seven. I think we should call it a day. I'm back on duty tomorrow.'

Callan struggled into his coat and walked out with Aileen.

His phone pinged in his pocket but Callan ignored it. It could be an important email. But damn technology. Tomorrow was soon enough to read it.

WHEN EYES DON'T LIE

Armed with a coffee cup and sunglasses to fend off the blazing sun, Aileen watched Callan park his car in the parking lot nearest to the cottage.

She had got there five minutes earlier and sat observing the young family of four, trying to decide which hike they should take.

'Morning!' She greeted Callan.

Callan nodded. 'Good morning.'

They strode over to the tiny office at the parking lot.

It was a tourist information office and a place to pay your parking fees, all in one. Colourful pamphlets giving information about Loch Fuar and the various activities to do here sat on a revolving shelf. But most slots in the shelf were empty.

Despite it being a weekday, the parking lot was operating at full capacity.

A blond-haired man greeted Callan. 'Detective Cameron.'

Callan bobbed his head. 'Sean. Busy day, eh?'

'A sudden burst of pleasant weather brings in the hiking enthusiasts. What can I do for ye?'

Callan gestured to Aileen. 'This is Aileen Mackinnon, the innkeeper at Dachaigh.'

Aileen nodded her greeting.

Sean's eyes lit up. 'Are ye off on a hike together? There's a perfect one for couples.'

'No,' Callan's denial was quick and curt, snubbing out the light in Sean's eyes.

Did everyone in town want them to get together? Aileen kept herself from rolling her eyes.

Callan stood with his hands on his hips. 'I want to see yer log for Saturday, last week.'

Sean pursed his lips. 'Ye ken I need a warrant for that.'

'Or maybe ye could use that memory of yours that Rory's always praising. The night of the storm. Do ye remember anyone who came here from Loch Heaven?' Callan pressed.

Sean thought, staring out of the window. 'I wouldn't ken. Many cars were parked here that morning. It was a pleasant day. And we don't maintain an account of where the cars come from.'

Callan pursed his lips, thinking.

Aileen stepped up beside him. 'Perhaps you could tell us if you had any rental cars park here?'

Sean's eyes twinkled once more. 'I ken! There was a car here parked for a couple of days. We had a person from the rental agency come dun here for it. Took it away just last Monday.'

At Callan's raised eyebrows, Sean explained. 'The man came from the company. He said the lass who'd dropped off the car didn't hand it over to the official as she was supposed to. And the car was here for a while, since that storm. He took it away on Monday.'

'What did this girl look like?' Aileen placed her hands on the counter between Sean and them.

Sean tapped his chin. 'Funny ye should ask because she was weird.'

'Weird how?'

As if conspiring, Sean rested an elbow on the counter. 'For starters, she wore a white dress, just as a ghost might. And her hair was all long and loose. She came dun here to meet a man, I think. That was Saturday morning.'

Aileen tapped her fingers on the glass. 'A man?'

Sean bobbed his agreement. 'Hm, a man with red hair, lanky sort. I saw him again that evening. He drove his car that way to Loch Heaven.'

'And this weird woman?'

Pursing his lips, Sean said, 'She never came for her car.'

CALLAN FOLLOWED AILEEN'S SEDAN TO DACHAIGH and waved her off. She squinted past the bright sunlight to watch his car tumbling down the road and out of sight. It had been an adventure ever since she'd come to Loch Fuar and met him.

'Hey, Aileen!'

She turned to see the sturdy Daniel McIntyre on her roof.

Smiling, she skipped to the whitewashed stone inn with the blue framed windows. The summer flowers in the garden gave the scene a very homely feel, very Dachaigh.

'What are you doing on the roof?' She had to shout to be heard.

'Getting yer work done. How's Callan?' Daniel yelled back.

She rolled her eyes at his not-so-subtle question. 'Did Isla put you to it?'

He laughed. 'She ordered me to tell ye, that ye're summoned to the bakery the moment ye return.'

Aileen groaned. Isla was better at harrying a person into telling details than professional interrogators. She'd want to know the whole scoop. But what was there to tell? Besides, she had to go to the police station and dig dirt on their suspects.

'I'll be on my way then. Best not to keep your wife waiting.'

Isla's Bakery was buzzing. Children sat munching on chocolate cakes, and mums with strollers huddled around the tables sipping coffee and gossiping.

An average day in Loch Fuar.

'Aileen!'

Her red-headed friend rounded the corner and drew her in a bear hug smelling of baked goods.

She pulled away just as abruptly and wiggled her eyebrows. 'Well?'

'Well, what?'

Isla hopped on the balls of her feet. 'Don't be daft! How was Loch Heaven?'

Aileen scowled. 'Very dangerous if that's what you're asking.'

'Och! Dangerous, eh?' Isla wiggled her eyebrows.

Aileen narrowed her eyes at her friend. A fiend for scandal if she ever saw one. 'Yes, dangerous. The kind where you could lose your life.'

That levelled Isla's energy. 'Oh?'

Aileen nodded. 'We had quite the adventure, but it wasn't something I'd want to live through again.' She shuddered.

Isla pursed her lips and pointed at her ginger-headed nephew packing the orders. 'Andrew! Man the till.'

With that, she dragged Aileen behind the counter and into her tiny office. A small crib sat in the corner.

Aileen peered into it, smiling.

Little Carly, with her pink cheeks and pink lips, slept soundly on a soft blanket. Her tiny head showing strawberry blond hair.

Aileen cooed at the sleeping toddler. 'She's so cute.'

Isla sighed. 'Aye, when asleep. We just witnessed an ear-splitting tantrum an hour ago. Too tired, she's asleep now.'

Aileen sat in the single visitor's chair.

Isla leant against her desk. 'Tell me what happened.'

Sighing, Aileen told her all she and Callan had been through. Her friend was the perfect listener. She shuddered at the terrifying bits and paid close attention to the details. Isla never missed a thing.

'You are now reading those notebooks and files then?' She asked when Aileen was done.

Aileen nodded. 'Since the case is officially closed, we get to keep the books, I think. I shudder to think what might happen if Roland gets his hands on them.'

'What a nasty man that Roland! I'd have scoffed his ear!' Isla huffed.

Aileen laughed and pulled out one of the notebooks. 'I'm sure there'll be something in this that I've missed.'

Isla's proffered hand gestured for the book. Aileen handed it over, peeking at the sleeping Carly again.

The notebook's pages ruffled as Isla leafed through it rather quickly. She gasped. 'Oh!'

Aileen turned to see her friend. 'What... Isla, what is it? You've gone pale.'

With wide green eyes, she pointed to a page in the notebook. It was opened to the image of the Houndress with her two hounds.

Aileen sent a quizzical glimpse at her friend. 'That's Morticia Luna, I told you about her.'

'But, but that's the same Bicolour eyed Woman

I told you about! She's the one who cursed me with the evil eye!'

Callan rubbed at his eyes as he got the mounting paperwork done. Why did they need to file reports when an eighty-year-old thought she had the right to pick apples from her neighbour's garden?

What were eighty-year-olds doing climbing trees in the first place?

He sipped his third coffee of the day. And it wasn't even half-past eight!

The tell-tale footfalls of his boss's boots reverberated through Callan's office. Rory Macdonald appeared at his office door, very grandfatherly in his plaid shirt and trousers with shrewd eyes that spoke of years of experience in the police force. 'Aye, ye're having one of *those* days.'

Callan scowled at the paperwork. 'I missed filing this, apparently.'

Rory waved a hand at Callan's paper-strewn office. 'I wonder how ye missed it given that ye are so organised.'

'Haha, was Aileen whispering in yer ear?' Callan scribbled down the required information.

His boss sat on the visitor's chair, the one Aileen had cleaned yesterday for sitting. 'Nope, she didn't but she's right though. It's high time ye cleaned this place. Ye might find some vegetation under these papers.'

Callan chuckled sarcastically. 'More like vermin that breeds paper.'

Rory laughed with him. 'It's good to have ye back. How did it go?'

Hanging his head, Callan told Rory about the crazy rollercoaster that had been Loch Heaven.

'Wow!' Rory gawked. 'That's something. All I did for the past three days was to badger Roland to send those autopsy and toxicology reports. And there's still no response. Although I tapped the police grapevine.'

Callan stopped writing and gave Rory his full attention. 'And what does the grapevine say?'

'That it was all hurriedly done, the autopsy. The medical examiner found some splotches of alcohol on Marley's dress. Most likely it's champagne. And there were some bruises consistent with being choked to death. The cause of death was Hangman's fracture, but she had scrapes and bruises on her arm. Perhaps she fought her killer.'

They had known about the bruises and still ruled this a suicide? Bloody Roland! But it was the alcohol bit that confused him.

'Why would Marley consume champagne the same day she was murdered?' Callan stared back at his board. This made no sense. What was she doing at the cottage?

Rory swished a hand. 'Ye'll figure it out. Now

let me try asking Sean at the parking lot some questions. We go back a long way.'

Satisfied, Rory walked out, and his voice drifted down the hall as he greeted. 'Hey, Aileen!'

'Hi!' Aileen dashed into the room and panted. 'Ca-Callan! Isla… Morticia Luna… Bicolour eyed Woman…'

She plopped into the chair Rory had just vacated. Pulling out a bottle of water from her satchel, she unscrewed its lid and guzzled the water.

Callan watched her, amused. 'Did ye run here from Isla's Bakery?'

Aileen nodded, still panting.

'When was the last time ye even exercised?' Callan tsked. 'Isla's Bakery is not even 750 metres away from here.'

She shot him a glare. 'Don't sit on your high horse, Mr I Exercise Every Morning. Some of us have to cook breakfast for their guests.'

Callan cocked an eyebrow. 'I thought Dachaigh is closed for repairs?'

'You know what I mean!' Aileen scowled.

This woman was unique. She could argue with him till *he* was out of breath. Lord knows she had the stamina and the arguments. 'Ye said something about Isla and Morticia Luna?'

Finally calm, Aileen spoke. 'Yes! Callan, Isla says the Bicolour eyed Woman she ran into the day of the murder? Morticia Luna is the same one!'

'Bloody hell!' Callan slammed a hand on the

file. 'No wonder she always has those dark glasses on. I thought it was odd that we'd never seen her eyes. And that afternoon we met her in the park, it wasn't sunny either and she still had sunglasses on.'

'What do you think she is hiding?' Aileen asked.

Hurriedly, Callan said, 'I got an email last night. I ignored it and thought it was spam, but now that ye mentioned her eyes.'

He tapped a few keys on his old laptop. It took a while, but the image loaded. 'It was an email from an account called *ilovemurder*.'

Aileen propped a hand on his desk and peered at the screen. 'Oh Callan…'

Callan sat sipping his fourth cup, listening to Aileen tell him about a similar email she received. This was bad.

'Why didn't ye tell me sooner?' He demanded.

'I forgot!'

Slamming his palms on the desk so hard that the laptop rattled, Callan growled. 'Aileen, don't ye see? That day ye went to Marley's flat alone and met that goon along with this Bicolour eyed Woman. Ye dismissed it as a trick. But it wasn't. It was Morticia Luna! And this email could have come from her as a threat!'

Huffing, he sat back and typed off an email. 'This might be futile at this point, but I've asked a colleague in the Electronics Division to check out this email account for us.'

When Aileen sat mum, Callan dipped his chin.

'Sorry about the outburst. But it all links now. No wonder she knew who we were when we met her at the park. She'd already seen ye at Marley's flat.'

Aileen's voice was barely coherent. 'But... But that thing about hanging by a noose. What do you reckon that is?'

Caressing his smooth chin, Callan considered. 'To remind ye of that night? A warning perhaps?'

'She could have done it. That's how she'll know!'

He mulled it over. 'Charlie ken too. News travels fast and she has her goons informing her.'

Aileen pulled out her yellow notepad. 'It's time to scratch off one suspect from my list. The Bi-colour eyed Woman and Morticia Luna are the same person. How didn't we see this before?'

'Ye never saw her that afternoon, just her eyes. There was no way to be sure it was the same woman. That leads me to the question: where did Isla see Morticia Luna's photograph?'

Aileen smiled sheepishly. 'I was with Isla and she... She happened to read Marley's notebooks-'

Callan tilted his head and in a low tone said, 'Happened to read?'

Aileen dismissed it with a wave. 'I've got to get back to Dachaigh. There are some tiles and cabinets that need my attention.'

Callan frowned. 'And I've got bloody paperwork to file. Although I should be done by the afternoon.'

Aileen fixed the satchel on her shoulder. 'Lay off that coffee. See you soon.'

FOR ONCE, HE LISTENED TO AILEEN AND LAID OFF the coffee, meaning where he normally would have guzzled twelve cups he stomached six. But the deficit in caffeine meant he was desperate to do something, anything, by the afternoon. His head throbbed from all the mind-numbing paperwork and his right knee protested from all the sitting-on-his-arse.

Thus, for a break, Callan made his way to the dilapidated cottage. Maybe it could give him some clues. He hadn't been there ever since Aileen had wrestled him to the ground.

She was something else. He smiled.

The ramshackle cottage stood as it had that day, albeit the weather was better now. The bright afternoon light made it easy to study the structure. Termite-eaten wood, some rusted planks owing to all the monsoons the cottage had withstood. Someone had draped a plastic sheet over its roof.

Callan grinned. It was the perfect spot for errant youngsters and junkies. But Loch Fuar had only a handful of the latter.

He parked a couple of feet from the cottage and mused about its lonely spot.

This rugged road was secluded, skirting around

Dachaigh's estate, but it put the cottage on the outskirts of the inn's premises. This area was so far out that the road was more of a mud track, making for a bumpy ride. Definitely not safe for most cars, but his SUV could make it.

Where had Marley found such a spot? *Being the innkeeper for two months, she'd have either scoured for such a spot or stumbled upon it.*

According to the footage, all the suspicious cars which had driven to Loch Fuar that day couldn't brave this road. Using a normal city car to get here would be close to assassinating it.

Hence the parking lot.

But why did the killer murder Marley at this lonesome cottage? Why not kill her in her own flat?

Callan strode towards the cottage. Its sandy door shuddered open. Bright sunlight poured in through the splintered window, reducing the musky dampness that had been present the last time.

He stared at the enigmatic beam. Who had fixed it? And why?

And the lamp placed by the window. Did the killer want to be caught or did he or she place the lamp here thinking they were well hidden from other eyes?

He inspected the lamp again, but it gave no clues. It didn't require any electricity; it was battery operated.

The killer must have known this place had no

electricity. Or was this Marley's doing? Why would she bring a lamp along?

They had to have transported it to the cottage. Aileen hadn't seen it before, had she? No one else could have seen it. And Aileen was the observant sort.

He cast another glance around the cottage and stepped out.

Shrubs danced, and the breeze tickled his hair. He took in the refreshing summer air and cast a wary gaze at the Highland mountains and Loch Fuar, serene but frosty.

What had Marley and her killer seen?

Callan frowned at the ground. He crouched, studying the now dry mud. Closing his eyes, he pictured the day of the murder.

There had been a forecast for rain, but the day had dawned pleasant enough. Why hadn't he chosen to run through the forest trail before dawn?

The air had been light, just cool enough to sweat during an enduring run. And then he'd gone to the office to listen to Robert tell his wife they'd take their toddler to the park.

'It's a beautiful day, hun.'

Callan opened his sharp eyes.

Marley had been sipping champagne, that's the only way she could have got some on her dress. Why would she consume alcohol, a celebratory drink, inside a rundown cottage?

He narrowed his eyes.

Och aye. She hadn't been in the bloody cottage, she'd been here, out of the cottage, enjoying the Highland scenery and celebrating.

But celebrating what? What was her business at Loch Fuar?

What about her killer? He or she was either lying in wait or celebrating with her.

Still crouching, Callan stabbed a finger in the ground. 'The phone, yes! Didn't Walsh say they'd found her phone *outside* the cottage? And as Aileen said, Marley was never without her phone.'

And then there were the bruises.

The murderer had tried to kill her *here*, not inside the cottage, no. That's why Marley's phone was outside.

She hadn't thrown it there; it had fallen when the killer got to her.

It meant that whoever the killer was, they were strong enough to drag Marley inside the cottage and keep her there.

Callan smiled crookedly. It made a lot of sense now.

CHAPTER TEN

He didn't care that his shift was long over or that it was dinnertime. He shot off a quick text, after a lot of swearing, to his "partner."

When he'd received no response, he dialled her number.

To his surprise, it took her a while to answer. 'Where are ye?'

Aileen only hummed. After a while, she cleared her throat. 'Sorry, what?'

'Where ye asleep? It's hardly seven!'

'I read your message! I'll be there.' She huffed and hung up.

Despite his incredible breakthrough, it took Aileen a good half an hour to arrive. It usually took her ten. And he knew that, owing to her impatient nature.

Sinking into his visitor's chair, Aileen grumbled. 'There are entirely too many varieties of tiles and cabinets. Adding to the strange week, I'm ready to crash.'

Callan tutted. 'Not so soon. Long way to go before we sleep.'

She looked at him from under her lashes. '*Miles to go* before I sleep. If you are referring to the poem.'

Shutting off his laptop, Callan steepled his fingers. 'Ye understood what I wanted to say.'

He only received a grunt as Aileen sank against the backrest. 'What did you find?'

Callan stood, shrugging into his jacket. 'I could offer ye coffee, but ye need something stronger. Come on.'

He tugged her hand, ignoring her protests. She tumbled into him, her citrus perfume playing with his mind. He held her at arm's length and led her to his car.

'I'm not in a mood for games. Where are we going?' Aileen questioned as soon as he strapped on his seat belt.

'Ye'll see.' He smirked.

Like a petulant child, Aileen crossed her arms and stared out the window.

Ten minutes later, they pulled up in front of the only pub in town. It was packed full. People were milling about, young and old, out to enjoy the light summer air.

Someone shouted. 'Callan!' He waved at them, ignoring the scrutinising eyes, and led Aileen inside.

'Is this your idea for a date? Where the decibel level is such that we can't hear each other?'

Callan shrugged and pulled her along.

'Everyone's staring. You could've just let me go back to Dachaigh. The last thing I want is gossip. And the entire town's waiting for it-'

Callan signalled to the bartender.

Aileen continued her tirade. 'If you are that interested in dating… I gave you the option of shoving this stupid promise under the carpet and-'

He held up a tumbler of whisky. 'This.'

Lines formed on her forehead. 'I don't want a bloody drink!' She hissed.

But Callan was adamant. 'What do you see in whisky?'

Aileen crossed her arms and narrowed her eyes. 'Amber coloured liquid. What else should I see in whisky?'

Callan tutted. 'The ability to loosen tongues.'

That's when she understood. Her eyes widened, and she noticed Sean from the parking lot office sitting at the bar with his friends.

Callan's breath hitched. Perhaps it was the first time since they'd met that she'd grinned at him that way—an open smile with some pleasantness in her eye… Directed towards him.

His heart thumped. What was wrong with it? He hadn't even had a sip of whisky and his body was playing tricks with him. It had to be his heart; it wasn't functioning normal lately.

Whisky in hand, he jabbed a finger at Sean. 'Come on.'

They both slid onto the barstools next to the blond man. It took Sean's ears no time to perk up. Another fiend for gossip.

Bingo!

Aileen greeted the man. 'Hey, Sean.'

With a busted pout on his face, he smiled back. 'Hey, ye two!'

'Nice night, isn't it?'

'Och aye. What ye two doing?'

Callan drooped his shoulders.

Aileen leant over, her perfume making his heart palpitate. 'This case has got him tense. I'm just being a good friend and helping him unwind.' She winked.

Sean's eyes glinted. 'Aye? That's nice of ye…'

The older man's eyes flickered around the room. 'So, how's the investigation going?'

At Callan's wince, Aileen whispered. 'Not well. It feels like we're going in circles. Poor Marley…'

Callan dropped his chin, staring into his whisky. Aileen placed a hand on his shoulder in solidarity.

It took Sean precisely five seconds of squirming in his seat to react. He licked his lips and leant towards them. 'I'm not in the office and well, I was never here, okay?'

When Callan nodded, Sean continued. 'I

checked out the car license plates after ye left. And I asked the lad on duty that day. He's young and keeps his heid out of his arse…'

More like his nose in other's business.

'What did ye find?' Callan asked.

If it was possible, Sean leant in further, until his shoulder rubbed against Callan's. Despite the lack of respect for his private space, Callan kept mum and listened.

'Marley, that's her name? She drove in and was followed by a red-haired man.'

'Dyed red or ginger hair?' Callan tipped his head until it was an inch away from Aileen's.

Eyes wide, Sean explained. 'Red. He was medium height, so the lad told me. He can't be sure though he remembers the red hair. But-but the lad thinks the hair wasn't natural.'

In the meagre space between them, Aileen leant in too, until her hair fell on Callan's shoulders.

Citrus perfume. He clenched his jaw.

'What do you mean? Are you sure it wasn't natural?' She questioned.

Sean peered over his shoulder to make sure no one heard him. 'He couldn't tell but said the red was far too bright to be natural.'

Aileen bit her lips. 'Did this red-haired man have any moles or distinct features on his face?'

'No, at least I dinnae ken.' Sean shrugged. 'Sorry. But, aye, there was another thing. When they, this red-haired bloke and Marley, took the countryside trail, another car came into the lot. It was fancy. A man and a woman stepped out, so the lad told me. He remembered them 'cause the lady seemed funny. She had two dogs. The man took the dogs with him and followed the couple down the trail.'

'And what about the lady?' Aileen was still leaning into Callan. Her scent was too distracting from the topic at hand.

Sean sipped from his glass. 'She went into town.'

'Could you describe her, please?'

For the first time, Sean cracked a smile. His voice was barely audible over the noise of the pub. Somewhere, someone shouted "cheers" and glass pints *clanked*. Someone laughed a belly hurting laugh and someone called out to the bartender.

Callan took a sip of his malt whisky and swallowed with a grimace. 'Sean, describe this woman.'

Sean sneered. 'He's a lad, mind ye, green but a lad nonetheless. And this woman, let's just say, was a sight for sore eyes. He described her to me in great detail.'

Aileen crossed her legs and pressed into Callan's side to catch what Sean was saying.

Geez! Callan all but hissed.

Sean's eyes twinkled. 'The lad said she was tall, willow slim and um, had a beautiful physique. Long hair and an elegant build.'

'An older woman?' Aileen tapped a hand on the bar.

Sean nodded.

Rummaging in her satchel, she produced Marley's notebooks and flipped it open to a page. Showing it to Sean, she asked. 'This her?'

His grin widened. 'Aye, that could be her!'

It was a picture of Morticia Luna.

CALLAN AND AILEEN LEFT WITH HUGE GRINS.

'That's the second person to confirm Morticia Luna was here that day and parked her car at the parking lot!' Aileen exclaimed.

Ah, so the enthusiasm was back. She skipped down the road. 'I can almost feel it. We are close.'

Callan wagged a hand. 'So, I've got another puzzle for ye.'

'Puzzle?'

He told her about the details Rory had found, and what he'd deduced at the crime scene that afternoon.

'Bruises, you say?' Aileen raised a hand. 'But if she fought back, won't a DNA sample from under her nails be her killer's? Like if she scratched him/her?'

Staring at the clear sky, Callan huffed. 'Bloody Roland didn't ask for DNA samples. It was a mangled job, at least that's what the tattle says.'

They settled into his car. After a bit of jostling, Aileen clicked her seatbelt in place and faced Callan.

'Two cars followed Marley's rental. She never went to fetch her car because she was already dead. And then this red-haired fellow, he's the same man who wore the hound mask. He was extra cautious, wasn't he?'

Callan started the car and pulled onto the road. All was silent and dark, his car's headlights barely breaking through the darkness. 'Yes, too cautious like he knew something bad could happen.'

Playing with her coat pockets, Aileen said, 'Could he be Morticia Luna's goon?'

He focused on the road. 'Two people saw Morticia Luna. Remember how clean her record is? That means she has goons do the legwork for her and hides in the shadows. *She* is extra cautious too. Then what was she doing showing her face in Loch Fuar when she had plans to kill Marley?'

They turned into the street where the police station was. Aileen stared ahead. 'She wouldn't have come to Loch Fuar at all, rather sent a goon to do her bidding.'

'My thoughts exactly.'

They both hopped out of his car and ambled towards Aileen's.

Awkwardly, she tugged at the handle of her satchel. 'So um, what's the plan for tomorrow?'

'Let's go to Isla's Bakery and ask her about

Morticia Luna. She's the queen of tattle next to Siobhan. Isla would have heard something.' Callan suggested.

'She definitely would have heard about our visit to the pub together.' Aileen rolled her eyes. 'I'll have a lot of questions to answer to tomorrow.'

Callan chuckled. 'Ye can do what I do.'

Hands on her hips, she asked. 'And what is that?'

'Trade secret.' Callan mimed zipping his lips. Laughing at himself, he bid her a good night.

AILEEN SHOULDERED THE DOOR OPEN AS SHE marched into the tiny police station with two bitter coffees and scones freshly baked by Isla. She'd strutted into the bakery, purchased what she wanted and left before Isla had a chance to question her. But from the twinkle in her friend's eyes, she knew Isla had heard.

The light in Callan's office was on, the only one in the station's darkness.

Where was everyone?

She heard some cussing from Callan's office and smiled. He was alright then.

Turning into his office, she halted. "What are you doing?'

As if caught with his hands in the cookie jar,

Callan bounced up from the floor where he'd been sprawled. 'Ever heard about knocking?'

She cast a glance over his unkempt table strewn with papers and coffee cup stains.

Her nose twitched from the odour. 'It's stinking in here. When was the last time you opened the windows?'

Callan huffed. 'Good morning to ye.' He took a go-cup from the tray. Holding it up, he bobbed his thanks. 'Lord knows I need it. I can't find anything in this dump.'

'Clean it, one paper at a time.' She suggested.

Sipping his coffee, Callan walked to the murder board. 'We'll clean this mess first.'

Aileen settled in the chair and made space for the yellow notepad on the desk. 'As per what Sean said, Marley Watson parked her rental car at the parking lot. This red-haired man followed her.'

Reading the words she'd penned down, Aileen said, 'We saw this man in a compact car, wearing a Hound's mask follow Marley from Loch Heaven. And then there's this fancy car which followed again from Loch Heaven and left around the time of death. With enough time to commit the crime and leave.'

Callan picked up from there. 'But we ken that Morticia Luna along with a goon drove in that fancy car. She had her hounds with her. So, if the goon is with Morticia Luna in her car, who is this red-haired sod?'

He scrawled that question on the murder board. 'Something to look into.' Pointing to another question he'd listed, Callan read it out loud. 'What was Marley doing at Loch Fuar?'

Aileen hummed as she thought. 'Why would she fix that beam? And why would she have two people following her? Had she asked them to, or were they spying on her?'

Callan sighed. 'Let's start at Isla's Bakery.'

When Aileen groaned, he chuckled. 'Ye are going to have to face the music someday.'

In the wee hours of the morning, Aileen and Callan walked to Isla's Bakery, which was teeming with people.

Loaves of bread were flying off the shelves, and every customer left with their favourite cup of coffee.

The glint in Isla's eyes hinted at an impending interrogation. She kept glancing between her and Callan coyly. The one drawback of having a best friend.

Aileen ignored the sneaky glimpses people sent her way. Did they all know about their visit to the pub? She blushed. But it had been for purely professional purposes!

Isla yelled over the murmur of the crowd. 'I'll be right with you. Two minutes…'

It wasn't two minutes, but almost ten. Callan had a steaming mug of coffee in his hand, much to Aileen's disagreement. He drank too much of it.

Isla sat in her office chair, eyes gleaming. She steepled her fingers and wiggled her eyebrows. 'So, you two showed up at the pub last night and left together. Aileen comes here this morning and fetches breakfast for two and now here you are.' She pointed at Callan. 'Hungry again.'

When Isla smirked, Aileen snapped. 'Isla! We didn't, we... Don't hint at things that never happened.'

Blinking innocently, she countered, 'Didn't you go to the pub last night? Or grab coffee and scones this morning? And aren't you here?'

'We're here about the case.' Callan said gruffly.

Isla rolled her eyes. 'Whatever you say.'

Small town wonders and gossip. It still took Aileen by surprise. But it had helped them last night, and it might prove useful again.

Callan ventured. 'Isla, Aileen said ye told her about a lady who'd come here.'

Isla pursed her lips. 'Morticia Luna? Wasn't that what her name is?'

'Ye said she had bicolour eyes?' Callan confirmed.

Isla shivered, the gleam disappearing from her eyes. 'Sinister eyes as well.'

Aileen shuffled towards Isla's desk. 'Did you speak with her about anything, why was she here and such?'

Isla sighed. 'I've been thinking about the incident since yesterday when I saw her picture. She was a weird woman, but the elegant sort who dressed immaculately. You know, the kind a woman such as me would notice and scorn over…'

Aileen huffed. She knew all too well about how she'd envied other women for their confidence.

Isla swatted a hand. 'I didn't say much to her. Not until we had our little disagreement. But she also purchased a tart and sat outside nibbling on it for a while.'

'When did she leave?' Callan piped in.

Isla slammed her hands on her desk. 'Don't be impatient. Listen to me!'

Callan exhaled heavily and muttered. 'Women!'

'She was checking her phone. And I was angry, wasn't I? So I sat at the till scowling at her through the window display. And thought to myself. Isn't it odd how she keeps checking her watch? She wore one of those fancy watches, you know, so she wasn't checking the time. And she wasn't staring at her phone either, just checking the watch.'

'As if waiting for a signal?' Aileen supplied. 'A message?'

Isla nodded. 'And to answer your question, she left at about two that afternoon. But I saw her hurrying towards the outskirts at about five, just before it rained. Which is odd given that there's nothing there.'

Callan threw his cup into the bin. 'Nothing there for a tourist… But the parking lot leading to the cottage? That's where she was going…'

Aileen stood. 'Right at the time of the murder…'

Outside Isla's Bakery, Callan gestured for Aileen to continue down the road.

A light breeze played with her hair, messing her hairdo. For God's sakes! She spent an eternity trying to set them into place this morning!

Callan cleared this throat. 'I reckon it'll take at least twenty minutes to reach the parking lot.'

Aileen shielded her eyes from the harsh sun and scrutinised the landscape. 'It doesn't match the timing or the surveillance footage. If they left at say half-past five, it would take them approximately another half an hour till they'd show on the surveillance at the exit from the Highway into Loch Fuar.'

'Cutting it close, I think.'

Aileen halted and pointed at a break in an old wooden fence. 'What if we walked through here?'

He tsked and stuffed his hands into his pockets. 'It's called trespassing.'

'It might be the route she took. Looks like a short-cut to me. And what are the chances someone might object?'

Callan shouldered through the narrow opening. His shirt's hem caught a stray splinter.

'Damn it!'

The brief wrestling match tore a part of his shirt. He mumbled at the torn hem.

At Aileen's chuckle, Callan sent a glare her way.

She simply shrugged. 'You won't miss a black shirt, you've got a closet full of them.'

He shook his head, mortified. 'But a shirt's a shirt. God forbid I'll have to go shopping for one!'

They made it across an uneven plot of moorland. The dumpy, unkempt area made it tough to move faster but it was definitely quicker than taking the main road. The earth was damp, its fragrance engulfing them.

A man came dashing down the mound. 'Oye! What do ye think ye're duing?'

Callan pulled out his badge. 'DI Callan Cameron and this is our civilian consultant.'

'What do ye want?' The man snapped.

He was old, his day's scruff turned white. But he still sported salt and pepper hair. His teeth had seen better days and were now half corroded. 'What is it about ye youngsters, running about ma land. Nyaff rockets!'

Aileen stepped forward. 'Youngsters, Mr…?'

He didn't introduce himself but continued to bark at them. 'Aye, youngsters! Just last week that woman ran through here. Almost destroyed my grass garden.'

Aileen didn't want to know what he meant by "grass garden." But she was interested in this woman who'd trespassed his land last week.

She pulled out Marley's notebook with Morticia Luna's photograph. 'This her?'

The older man squinted. 'Aye, the same. And going the same way ye're going.'

The man didn't allow her to ask more questions. Instead, he shooed them away. 'Get off ma land now! Out, the both of ye. Police or nay I dinnae care!'

Once out of earshot and back on the tar road, Callan clenched his jaw. 'Now we ken how she made it back in time.'

'Did she know about it or get lucky?' Aileen asked.

Callan studied the fence. 'Lucky if she's never been here before. But what spooked her enough to make a run for it? Did her goon kill Marley in anger and deviate from the plan? This fence is easy enough to climb over. And she is a tall woman.'

Aileen stuffed the book back in her satchel. 'But risk getting caught?'

'Spooked, wasn't she?' Callan observed. 'Most people don't think when they're scared.'

A bird chirped, and something rustled behind the hedges. A squirrel sprinted up the tree.

Everyone seemed in a hurry lately.

'Morticia Luna spent the entire day in Loch Fuar and hurried to the lot as if she was about to miss the bus.' Callan scratched his chin. 'Why don't ye enquire after her at the village and check Barbara's Tea Shop. It's somewhere she could've spent the day without drawing attention to herself. But it seems she did a bad job of it. Everyone remembers seeing Morticia Luna.'

Aileen narrowed her eyes towards him. 'What about you? What will you be doing?'

Hands on his hips, Callan said, 'I'll check if Sean's lad is up for a chat. Make sure we got those timings right.'

CHAPTER ELEVEN

Callan took his time to get to the parking lot. He enjoyed the summer sun and took ten minutes longer than he should have.

Walking into the claustrophobic office at the parking lot, he took a double-take. Callan hadn't expected to meet the white-haired man.

'Rory.'

His boss swivelled from his position in front of the counter and grinned. 'Ah, Callan! Good to see ye. I was just telling young Josh here how he's done an exemplary job helping the police.'

Callan cocked a brow. 'Has he now?'

Josh smiled shyly as Rory praised him. 'Why he was just telling me about the evening this woman at the cottage died.'

Callan placed both elbows on the counter, essentially trapping the lad behind it. 'I want to hear all about it.'

Josh visibly swallowed. 'It was the end of my shift, but Sean was late that day. Ye ken, he had to wait till his wife got home or something. I do the extra hour to help him now and then…'

Rory thumped him on the back. 'Good lad!'

The boy blushed. 'Um, the lot was almost empty, 'cept for those three cars dun from Loch Heaven. The weather was turning, and a lot of tourists had left. I'd seen those three cars park here at the beginning of my shift. It's rare to have cars parked overnight. This lot's in the middle of nowhere, this car park is. The occasional tourist may stop to take the hikes here, but no one stays overnight. The inn, Dachaigh, have their own parking.' He pointed a thumb over his back.

Callan shuffled his feet and studied the parking lot. It was almost noon, and the lot was filled with cars. Apparently, many people wanted to enjoy the Highland sun just like yesterday.

Rory tapped on the open logbook. 'You said ye had it in here?'

Flipping open the page, Josh pointed at the check-out time. 'Now I'm not sure I can show this to ye but if it helps.' He shrugged. 'We don't have an electrical system. Our lot's empty all winter, so it's difficult to maintain the system and all. It's my job to note down the time each car leaves.'

Callan studied the entries. Rightly so the car

he'd now come to recognise as Morticia Luna's left at precisely twenty minutes past five. What was the rush?

Marley's car wasn't mentioned, but as per their surveillance footage and this log, Marley's companion's vehicle had checked out about half an hour later.

Were both those men planted there by Morticia Luna?

Stabbing a finger at Morticia Luna's car he said, 'Did ye see who got in the car?'

Josh's boyish face scrunched in thought. 'Cannae have missed it. A woman...' He gulped. Besotted he was, too green to know better. 'This woman crossed over old Harry's land and ran to the waiting car. A man was sitting in it already. The same she'd come with that morning. And he, he raced away without a second glance. Just minutes before he'd thrown cash at me for the parking fees, not even waiting for the receipt.'

Callan scrubbed his chin, a wee scruff already growing. 'Could ye describe this man?'

Josh shrugged. 'Ordinary. Two eyes, a nose and a mouth.'

Ordinary as in not good enough for her... Callan rolled his eyes. Lads...

'How tall was he?' He pried, trying to squeeze out as much information as he could from Josh.

'Tall's not the word, no. He was a giant, a misfit for the er... The elegant woman. He was thick around the middle, had a bit of a belly but bulging muscles. And yes, he reeked of cigarettes.'

Whipping out his phone, Callan pulled up a photograph. 'Is this him?' It was an image of Charlie. But Charlie, despite being tall, wasn't a giant.

'Na, that man had hair, almost a mop. Blond hair.' Josh said.

'What did his face look like then?' Callan asked.

Josh blinked twice. He blushed again. 'I didn't take a closer look. I was busy um…'

Rory bit his lip to keep a chuckle from escaping. 'Comparison is no good laddie.'

The young boy hung his head. 'But, but now that you mentioned it, he was wearing a cap. Took it off when he stepped in 'ere. And that's when I thought… How odd. He comes here with such an… An elegant lady with a black eye and a bruised jaw.'

Callan frowned. 'Black eye, eh?'

Josh nodded, Callan's grin widened into a sneer. 'Funny, 'cause I ken someone who should sport one and reeks of cigarettes.'

Stepping out from that tiny office, Callan stared at the sky and thought things through.

Rory's footsteps crunched the gravel under his feet. 'Well?'

A grin was permanently etched on his face. 'A giant man with muscles and a rounded belly with a bruise? Should be the same man who tried choking Aileen in that alley in Loch Fuar.'

Rory paused. 'Do we now ken who tried attacking ye?'

'We already knew. As I told Aileen, they had hound tattoos.' Callan explained.

Folding his hands, Rory dipped his chin. 'Ye sure?'

Callan stubbed a toe into the gravel. 'Aileen saw this giant man twice. First at Marley's neighbour's place and the other time when we went to Morticia Luna's lair. Aileen couldn't remember it then, but I'm sure it was the same man with Morticia Luna. He was the one threatening the neighbour, and he was the one who made sure those suitcases were in the boot and that everything was in place. His muscles and broad frame make him look like a giant. But he isn't much taller than I am.'

Rory huffed. 'Well then, it's clear enough what ye and Aileen must look into next. Speaking of her, where's yer partner? Ye two have been joined at the hips recently.'

Rory guffawed at Callan's angry glare. Nosy bosses!

However, Callan did wonder what his partner was up to…

CHINA CLATTERED AND TEASPOONS TINKLED WHEN knocked against the ceramic floral cups. There was a steady whisper of voices laughing, tattling and some even flirting. In the fragrant warmth of Barbara's Tea Room, exchanging secrets and rumours was always in vogue.

Aileen stepped into the room where old ladies' perfume mixed with the warm traditional cuppa. She glanced around at the cosy setting, much like she had when she'd just driven into Loch Fuar.

Despite the early morning hour, the tables were engaged by old ladies and young lads gossiping nineteen to a dozen.

Aileen's right cheek lifted, musing at the scandals these walls have heard. She took a seat in the corner where she'd have the view of the entire tea room.

'Aileen!' A throaty voice greeted.

She smiled at the woman who owned that voice. Barbara had her white-blond hair pinned neatly, her skirt was well-fitted and ironed. And her blouse swayed around her slim physique.

'How are ye, ma dearie?' She came to a stop at Aileen's table.

'I'm fine, just busy.' Aileen shrugged.

'Ah, I heard ye're helping our boy Callan in his investigation.' Barbara smiled.

It was obvious she knew all about the investigation. Barbara ran this place, the hub of gossip in Loch Fuar. And there was always plenty to go around.

Without asking for an invitation, she sat gracefully. 'How's it going?'

Still uneasy with the ways of the locals, Aileen licked her lips. 'Dachaigh's good and so am I. We shall open soon.'

She dismissed Aileen's comments with a wave. 'Dachaigh's always doing good. I'm asking about Callan and ye. That poor boy needs someone, ye know. He's too lonely.'

Aileen's cheeks warmed. Did everyone assume they were an item? That they had… 'Um, I'm sure he's quite capable of taking care of himself.'

'That's what they all think, but they aren't. It's good that ye're helping him out.' Barbara winked.

Desperately, Aileen steered the conversation away. 'Have you seen a woman, perhaps she came here last week?'

Barbara chuckled. 'We have a lot of customers.'

Aileen felt around in her satchel and produced the notebook. 'This woman?'

To her credit, Barbara didn't ask about the notebook. She peered at the photo, studying it closely.

Five minutes later, she folded her spectacles and pursed her lips. 'I'm sorry I haven't seen this woman before.'

Aileen's shoulders sagged. If Morticia Luna hadn't come here, where had she gone?

'Although.' Barbara lifted a finger and continued. 'I heard Ginny say something about a difficult customer last week. Let me think. It was around the time that girl was killed. She said how this strange woman had come into her shop. She'd seemed eager at first. She'd tried everything on, put none of the clothes back in place and at the end purchased nothing.'

'By Ginny, do you mean at the antique shop?' Aileen enquired.

Barbara shook her head, her long earrings clinking. 'No, no, Ginny has purchased the apparel store now, right next to the antique shop. And she's doing a good job of it, too!'

Aileen was lost in thought. 'I'm sorry, but I've got to go.' She shoved the notebook back into her satchel and hurried away.

A couple of minutes later, Aileen stood in "Ginny's Jeggings."

They didn't just stock leggings though, but also lovely skirts and dresses. Well, if Aileen ever fancied shopping, she could come here.

'Hello! How may I help you?' A cheerful voice asked from behind a shelf.

'I was looking for Ginny.' Aileen called out.

The woman stood and rounded the shelf.

She was slightly younger than Barbara, perhaps in her fifties. A pair of spectacles dangled around her neck. She wore an assortment of bangles, and her short black bob was the epitome of chic. And her smile lit up the room. 'You must be Aileen Mackinnon.'

Aileen bobbed her greeting. Everyone knew everyone in Loch Fuar, apparently. Aileen had never set foot in this shop before and couldn't have recognised Ginny if she ran into her elsewhere.

Choking the burbling uneasiness, Aileen pushed through with her investigation. 'I was just down at Barbara's and she said you could be of help.'

Ginny scrutinised the image, but it didn't take her long to recognise her. 'That's her alright. Made this place a mess and bought nothing. She spent half the time frowning at the other customers and staring at her hand. Oh, not her hand, that smartwatch on her wrist.' She huffed. 'The vixen tried everything on, even the shirts that couldn't possibly fit her! Slim as a willow but eyes sharp as a witch's.'

Aileen had to ask. 'You mean she had bi-coloured eyes?'

Ginny nodded solemnly. 'Had them hidden behind sunglasses first. But of course, she took them off at the antique store. She wouldn't have been able to see the items clearly otherwise! Loch Fuar attracts all sorts.'

Excitement bubbled in Aileen's gut. 'The antique store?'

'Oh yes,' Ginny scowled. 'Made a mess here and then waltzed in there. I have a connecting door in my office at the back. So, when I went through and greeted her in my antique store, she wasn't happy to see me.'

Aileen pulled out her yellow notepad, taking notes. 'And what did she do there?'

Ginny tapped a finger on her chin. 'Took off

her glasses and shot me a stink eye. And then she looked around at some antique jewellery that I'd just acquired at an auction. And she wanted to know about some coins and a few pricey antique vases that will be on auction soon. I don't have them here, of course, but there's talk in the auctioneer community about those pieces.'

Scribbling it all down, Aileen asked, 'What time did she come here?'

'Right about one in the afternoon, I'd reckon. Spent a good three hours here.' Ginny grimaced.

Nodding, Aileen asked. 'And did you see where she went next?'

Ginny bit her lip, thinking. 'Back towards the main square. I suppose she was making her way towards Isla's Bakery.'

Aileen grinned, she was finally making strides in the case. She had traced Morticia Luna's steps the day of the murder.

Waving Ginny goodbye, Aileen left her shop, promising to return soon.

It was just past noon now, but clouds had gathered in the sky. The potted plants at the roadside swayed in the light breeze. The tiny sandwich shop grilled warm sandwiches for lunch.

Lifting her head to the sky, she grinned.

Progress… That was all that counted. Now they could brainstorm and figure out the next step. And she knew it, *felt* it in her gut. They were really close to figuring out who murdered Marley and TJ.

Just then the door opposite to "Ginny's Jeggings" opened and a chime sounded.

'Ms Mackinnon! Ye are the spitting image of yer gran, did I tell ye before?' A croaky voice came through the door.

Frank Walker, a man who'd been one of her suspects from a previous case, stepped out. He greeted her with a nod and walked off. But it wasn't he who'd called her. It was his uncle.

The uncle, Sam Walker, was as old as her gran. He sat at his customary position behind the counter, his body so ancient it slouched with age.

Uneasy, Aileen smiled back at the man. She had had too many human interactions today. Her insides itched to run back into the safety of her inn. But he gestured for her to step in.

Not wanting to seem rude, Aileen entered. 'Hi. Um, what can I do for you?'

He stooped over the counter. 'Heard ye were solving another case. Someone killed that rude bampot, eh? Ye did the right thing by firing her.'

Aileen smiled. She wasn't sure what to say. Wasn't it ill to speak of the dead?

But Sam had other ideas. He beckoned her closer with two fingers. 'I dinna bite! Come here.' He lowered his voice. 'Thought ye might be interested in a bloke who's rented that flat above this office.'

What was he going on about? 'I'm sorry?' Aileen frowned.

He swatted a wrinkly hand. 'Oh lassie, this man isn't the right sort. Dangerous, more like. Look into him. He came dun here, the day after the murder. And he's been renting a room too, for the past week. But he'd gone off somewhere for a couple of days. Returned yesterday, he did.'

Aileen listed it down and assured Sam she'll have Callan check it out. There was no way to know who this man was. Sam didn't remember, all he knew was that this man wasn't "civilised" and smoked a lot.

Aileen thanked the old man and clicked the door shut behind her. The sky was overcast, the beautiful day they'd had disappearing under thick grey clouds.

Much to her agony, thick droplets of water landed on her beige coat. Families scattered, seeking shelter as the Heavens opened.

Aileen checked the time. It was one in the afternoon. She couldn't afford to wait for the rain to abate. In her slightly heeled boots, she wasn't sure she could run for it either. After all, Loch Fuar was an old town with uneven cobbled roads.

Standing here would do her no good, she had to get moving!

The droplets came harder, and the crowd dissipated. The pitter-patter thundered in her ears. And then she heard an angry roar. It grew louder by the second and soon a *crack* sounded.

Pain ripped through her as the entire world

tipped. Everything swirled until it flipped onto its head and went dark.

Callan paced in his tiny office. It hadn't always been tiny. He'd once had a bigger office and a bigger team too until it had become too much.

Outside, the pleasant day had turned into a moody one. It was pouring now, droplets pounding against the roof. Typical Scottish weather.

He stared at his murder board. Why had someone gone to such lengths to murder a woman who was essentially nobody? She had no relatives or friends except for a lad who'd helped her gather intel on people.

Morticia Luna… Hopefully, Aileen would have made some progress by now. Where was she?

He heard heavy footsteps and his boss emerged. 'Hey, so after ye left I went to the market. Ran into Sean buying some imported fruit for his wife. Says it's her new diet.' He shuddered.

Callan raised both eyebrows.

And Rory got to the topic at hand. 'Oh, sorry. I wanted to say, Sean told me the day he arrived at the lot the night of the murder. He noticed that red-haired man. Said he was doing something to our victim's car. Something in the boot. He thinks he lugged a suitcase from there into his own vehicle before driving away.'

'A suitcase?' Callan scrunched his eyebrow.

Rory hummed. 'Aye, the man was apparently struggling to get it out of the tiny car. Sean thought it must have been heavy, but he had no time to stop and help, he was late for his shift.'

'Why didn't he mention this before? He spoke to Aileen and me about this man at the pub last night.' Callan grumbled.

Rory tsked. 'He said he only remembered it after talking to ye last night.'

'Hold on.' Callan uncapped his marker and scrawled "suitcase" on the board. Where was it? 'Did he have anything else on him, this red-headed man?'

Pushing his hands in his pockets, Rory hung his head. 'Sean doesn't remember. He was late and in a hurry.'

Scrutinising the board, Callan confirmed. 'This is the same man, is he sure of that?'

Rory crossed his legs at the ankles. 'Aye, the red-haired one who followed Marley.'

Callan caressed his chin. 'Strange, it's all very strange.'

'Not that strange. I heard ye had a fancy time with Aileen last night. It'll do ye good, lad, spending time with that lass. She's a good one. Hasn't had her share of fun either.' Rory smirked.

Callan didn't want to think about Aileen Mackinnon and her citrus perfume in that way. Or the way she'd leant into him to listen to what Sean had to say.

That reminded him... 'Where's Aileen got to?' He muttered.

Rory uncurled his legs just as the front door slammed open.

'Callan! Callan!' A flustered Isla ran in. 'Why the hell don't you answer your damned phone? Aileen! It's Aileen, she's been hurt!'

What?

His limbs acted before his brain registered what had happened. Callan tugged on his jacket, ready to sprint out. His phone beeped as he was about to shove it in his pocket. He had five missed calls from Isla and one simple text from an unknown number.

I asked you to stay away. Sorry about your girlfriend :)

CHAPTER TWELVE

The car's tyres screeched as he brought it to an abrupt halt. Flinging the door open, he ran full throttle into the hospital with Isla and Rory trailing behind.

He barely registered the bewildered nurse behind the emergency counter gawking at him. Nor did he notice the ubiquitous antiseptic that every hospital reeked of.

The emergency area was relatively quiet apart from a few children sobbing in one corner, clutching their hands. It was perhaps a broken arm or leg.

'Aileen Mackinnon.' His breaths came in short puffs as he clenched and unclenched his fists.

Someone placed a hand on his shoulder whilst the nurse spoke with her colleague.

After what felt like an eternity, someone from the hospital staff approached them. 'Inspector.'

Callan gave the man his full attention. He was wearing a white lab coat, which Callan assumed meant he was a doctor. Callan hated the lot, dispassionate creatures who didn't give a damn if you died! He seethed.

'Are ye here regarding the accident?' The doctor's voice was monotonous.

Isla hugged herself. 'Yes.'

He nodded. 'If ye could please wait a minute. Ms Aileen Mackinnon's in surgery. She was bleeding when the ambulance arrived. Thus, we had to get her into surgery at once.'

Not wanting to rage at the apathetic robot, Callan slid into a chair and rubbed his face.

Aileen was injured. They'd hurt her. He'd failed to protect her.

A sharp pain zinged through his heart.

'Deep breaths, Callan.' Rory's voice was thick.

He pushed the hand away. 'I don't give a bloody damn about breathing!' He snapped. Something heavy clotted in his heart, making it difficult to breathe.

But he slowed his raging thoughts and took a few calming breaths. Then he raised fraught eyes to Isla's. Desperately he asked. 'What happened?'

Evidently distressed herself, she sat next to him. 'From what I heard, Aileen was walking back when it rained. A bike came from nowhere and hit her.

The person didn't stop and just continued to ride on.'

'A hit and run. Deliberately done.' Callan gritted his teeth.

What was it about this damned case? Why hurt Aileen?

His heart thundered, wishing to jump out of his throat. What if she was so badly hurt that she didn't make it?

Callan rubbed his face and buried it in his hands. He sat there, energy drained.

'She's a strong lass, Callan.' Rory sat in the opposite chair.

Bloody hell! If he's paid attention to the threat the killer had left them after killing TJ, Aileen wouldn't be here.

It was his fault.

Why couldn't she just stay away?

Damn that woman! A magnet for trouble she was.

Callan rubbed at his eyes. The sadness gave way to anger. Red hot boiling anger. He refused to sit on his arse and let the perpetrator get off scot-free.

Aye, he cared about Aileen. And he would not lose his girl. He couldn't. Wouldn't. 'I'm going to the station.'

Rory shot him a confused look.

'We need to find out who tried to hurt her. And we need to be quick about this before he disappears.' Callan growled.

Rory leant on his elbows. 'It could be some stupid lad who lost control of his bike in the rain.'

Callan shoved his phone towards Rory. The message he'd received flashed on the screen.

'Oh,' was all Rory said, his wrinkles more prominent than before.

Callan nodded. 'Just call me if there's any progress with Aileen. We should crack on.'

If something happened to Aileen, he'd make sure this man and the blasted lot of his suspects never lived to see the light of day again. He stalked outside, his face resembling thunder, heart pounding in his chest.

At a breakneck speed, he arrived at the station and in front of his murder board.

Aileen had been outside Barbara's Tea Room when she'd been hit. She was chasing after Morticia Luna, so what had Aileen found? Or was it just being at the wrong place at the wrong time? No, he couldn't believe that. That text proved someone had hurt her intentionally.

He glanced at the text and ground his teeth hard. 'Bampot!'

Shutting his eyes, he imagined the market place. Aileen had been walking back to the police station. She couldn't have been at Barbara's Tea Room if she was on her way back.

Beyond that spot was the barber's shop, Ginny's antiques and the post office… And aye, there was an apparel shop, Ginny's again.

Most women could spend hours in one store, but that woman wasn't Aileen, not when she was on an agenda.

She had been on Morticia Luna's trail.

The front door of the station creaked open and Robert Davis appeared at his door.

'Hey!' He frowned. 'Ye heard about Aileen, didn't ye?'

At Callan's stoic face, Robert got his answer. 'I took witness statements. It was a hit and run, but I think it was deliberate... And ye already ken that.'

'Did ye find out where Aileen had been before she was hit? Callan questioned.

Robert flipped through the pages of his notepad. 'Aye, a couple of witnesses said she'd just stepped out of the post office. Sam Walker confirmed it.'

'Post office?' Callan clenched his jaw. What the hell was she doing there?

'Aye, old Sam said he called her in and said something about a suspicious new tenant living on the flat above the post office.'

Robert pointed at Morticia Luna's photograph. 'Could've been her.'

Callan faced that woman again. Aileen must have got close, uncomfortably close, and Morticia Luna had decided to... Well, she'd warned both of them off.

But until Aileen regained consciousness, they wouldn't know what she knew.

He dialled Rory instead.

'Any updates?' Callan didn't waste time on pleasantries.

'She's still in surgery.' Rory sounded tired.

But there was no time to slack. If Aileen knew something, she was still in danger. 'Look, I need ye to keep an eye on who goes in Aileen's room and who comes out. I believe whoever tried to harm her might do it again.'

'I've already told the doctor who came to talk to us. Aileen's a witness and is under police protection.' Rory said flatly.

'Not just a witness, she kens something Morticia Luna wants kept hidden.' Callan hissed. It irked him that he didn't know what it was.

Callan directed Robert to get to the post office and search the flat above.

He considered making coffee, but for the first time didn't have the stomach to gulp down the sludge or anything else. Rubbing his pricking eyes, Callan sat and let his mind wander.

Marley Watson had arrived at Loch Fuar with another car in tow. It had been a man. She'd gone with him to a rundown cottage and celebrated something. Yes, that's what Sean had said. This red-haired man had followed her that morning. But Marley could've only died after four. Another man, presumably Morticia Luna's goon, had followed them. No one had seen these three people for the rest of the day.

Where had they disappeared off to? Had the goon killed Marley and threatened the red-haired man?

But Sean had said this man had taken a heavy suitcase from Marley's car. How did he ken she had carried a suitcase? Unless she was trying to run from her old life or had plans to go on holiday in the Highlands?

A holiday? That was unlikely, but running away from that dump she'd lived in? Plausible.

He thought about each of their suspects: Charlie, Freddie, Martin Luther Hussey and Morticia Luna. So far, they'd only looked at Morticia Luna and found a lot of evidence pointing to her.

But what about Charlie? He too could've been Marley's potential "target." But Aileen had had all of Marley's books with her in her satchel.

Damn Aileen. What was she thinking, walking back in the rain? Why hadn't she jumped away when she'd heard the bike charging towards her? Insufferable woman!

Oh, Aileen…

Callan stared at the ceiling. She would be back soon, with her fiery reprimands and questions. He knew it. She was indeed like Siobhan, not one to back down.

As for himself? He was out for blood now. He'd get that bastard.

Maybe he had to dig into their other suspects.

He needed those damn notebooks. Where was Aileen's bag?

He phoned Rory again.

'Robert logged it in as evidence, Callan. It was drenched and had blood splatters, he sent me pictures. But by the looks of it, it was light surely with just her wallet. No books. At least Robert didn't mention any, and that lad is meticulous.'

Shit!

Had this man stolen the notebooks? How had he known about them?

Slamming the phone on his desk, Callan glared.

When his phone rang again, he looked at it with hope, but it was Walsh.

'No way! Someone hit her?' The sod seemed genuinely concerned.

Callan told him about his idea that it might be one of Morticia Luna's goons.

Walsh listened patiently and then added, 'There's been no hard evidence suggesting she keeps such accomplices. But the thing is, she is into all sorts of criminal activities, but we can never pin her down. The authorities are desperate for evidence. She's escalated over the years. It started with tax evasion, and now they say she's sitting on an enormous pile and not paying authorities a dime. That money is channelled into her rings. But it's all whispers with no proof.'

That meant Morticia Luna was capable of all these things.

Walsh exclaimed. 'I almost forgot why I called. I suppose you are busy, but I got some data for you, you might want to check out.'

'Data?' Callan asked.

'Whenever you have the time, you'll need to come to Loch Heaven for it though. I had someone look into it and she's ready to hand it over to you.' Walsh explained.

Callan grunted and told him he'd be there after Aileen was home from the hospital.

As soon as he clicked the phone off, the door opened and in jogged Officer Robert Davis. He was panting. 'I checked the rental flat, but it's been wiped clean with bleach. And he's run off.'

'Damn it!' Callan slammed a hand on his desk, rattling it.

Now he knew this man was Morticia Luna's. He had to be.

After half an hour of raging and gnashing his teeth, Callan's phone rang. It was Rory. 'You best come to the hospital, lad.'

Weary, Callan walked into the abode of pungent antiseptic and bandages that gave him nightmares with Egyptian mummies.

Braving his demons, he walked towards Rory. Isla was still there and to his surprise ten other residents of Loch Fuar, including Barbara whose usual calm demeanour was displaced by sobs.

Rory had dark circles under his eyes. 'The

doctor just came by. He says she lost some blood. She rammed her head onto the footpath's edge.'

Callan swallowed. 'She's got a thick skull.'

For the first time since they'd got here, Rory smiled. 'She just might, because the doctor assured us the surgery went well. She's got a fractured hand and stitches on her forehead. Nothing major.'

'How long till she gains consciousness?' Callan asked.

'She is under anaesthesia. Twenty-four hours and she should feel better.'

A day… Oh, thank God!

Callan's gaze swept the waiting room that was unusually brimming with people. 'What are they all doing here?'

Isla came over and hugged him. 'Everyone's outraged that someone hurt one of our own in broad daylight, or in a downpour, but you get my point. First, it was murder, and now our Aileen. Between ourselves we got Lesley, the local artist, to sketch a portrait of this man.'

Callan raised an eyebrow. 'Wasn't the rider wearing a helmet?'

Isla gave a teary grin. 'Luckily for us, he wasn't. Either he was too sure of himself or didn't think anybody'd notice.' She raised her chin. 'We don't need surveillance in Loch Fuar, we've got eyes as sharp as any.'

And wagging tongues, luckily.

Still holding on to him, Isla said, 'The sketch'll

be ready any minute. We order you to find this man, Callan. Aileen is one of our own and we'd be crushed if, if...'

Tears overtook her, and she shuddered. Callan knew exactly how she felt. He felt it tenfold.

In a rare gesture, he hugged Isla back, and they both prayed for Aileen's good health.

HE'D TRIED GOING HOME TO GET SOME REST, BUT IT was a futile attempt. Heavy pouches hung under his eyes, and his hair stood in all directions as if he'd been electrocuted.

'Blast!'

He found himself in his office chair, massaging his right knee.

He'd wanted an intellectual exercise, hadn't he? A challenging case? He'd got it.

Be careful what you wish for, Cameron.

He needn't have worried about Aileen though. It was as if all of Loch Fuar had descended in that waiting room.

Callan chuckled. They needn't have asked Robert to stay back. Everyone in Loch Fuar was ready to keep watch, wanting to give the criminal a piece of their mind and also of their rolling pins and hammers.

Aileen was well protected.

Callan's gaze fell on the sketch the people of

Loch Fuar had drawn up. The artist had done a damn good job. Usually, too many cooks spoilt the soup but well, ah damn. It didn't sound right. It wasn't soup, was it? Aileen would ken.

He saw the muscled man, tattoos on his neck and a sinister determined face.

Recognition hit him. It had been the same who'd come here with Morticia Luna and the same person who'd assaulted Aileen at Loch Heaven.

Thinking quickly, he sent the picture to Walsh asking if he knew the man.

He didn't have to wait long. Walsh worked long hours as well. His respect for the detective increased tenfold. A man after his own heart.

The phone shrilled.

Walsh didn't waste time in greetings. 'That man's not a stranger at the station. He's got quite the sterling record. Several breaking & entering charges, vandalism and of course hit-and-runs.'

Callan asked. 'Manslaughter?'

Walsh was quick in responding. 'No, nothing like that or anything close to it.'

Callan spoke almost to himself. 'But he could've escalated.'

The line went quiet for a while before Walsh spoke, 'He's never been seen with Morticia Luna before. It doesn't surprise me it's him. Although she's never been associated with a man such as him. Her records are squeaky clean.'

Callan's blood boiled, and frustration seeped into his pores.

Walsh continued, 'and even if we can make a connection between him and Morticia Luna, we can't charge her guilty by association.'

Callan's lips pursed. He gritted out. 'No, we can't but I promise ye, I'll find a way. She doesn't hurt someone… Aileen, and get away with it.'

Snapping the phone down, Callan slammed a fist onto his desk.

'Bloody hell!'

What was happening to him? He didn't need Aileen to bloody breathe!

Callan took deep breaths. Damn it!

He had to be objective. This was just a stressful reaction.

A reaction that had him entering the damned hospital before dawn broke. He'd forsaken his morning run which left his muscles aching.

This "reaction" had him gingerly walking into Aileen's room. It had his heart doing somersaults at the sight of her—tubes attached to her slight frame. She was tiny, too thin in that bed. Her face was bruised and pale.

Swallowing, he took a seat and covered her unhurt hand. The other, he shuddered, was in a cast. The back of her hand had a sinister needle attached to it, supplying IV.

He sat there for a while, unsure, caressing her hand while his mind churned. Past events and facts, filing away and sorting in place by the beeps of the various monitors attached to Aileen's body.

Lost in thought that he was, he never realised her fingers twitched until… 'Ca-Callan?' Her voice was soft and groggy.

'Aileen!' He looked at her. 'Hold on, let me call the nurse.'

But the adamant woman that she was, she demanded water and then started. 'I-I found Morticia Luna's…'

'Not now. Ye've been hurt.' He told her sternly.

But did she ever listen? Aileen opened her mouth to speak when the nurse arrived.

After checking all the monitors beeping around Aileen, the nurse checked her vitals and left them alone.

'Just cannae stay away from trouble, can ye?' Callan pressed his hand on her uninjured one. 'How are ye feeling?'

Aileen licked her lips. 'I'll feel better when we catch whoever hit me and put Marley and TJ's killer behind bars!'

He narrowed his eyes. 'How come ye never heard the bike?'

Aileen mumbled, staring at her lap. 'I heard it, just never thought it would ram into me.'

Callan stood and walked to the one window her room had. It looked onto the small walking track in the hospital's backyard. 'Ye definitely ticked these people off.' He faced Aileen. 'We haven't told

Siobhan officially, but she called Rory. He's asked her not to worry.'

Aileen gawked. 'No! Don't tell my family! The last thing I need is them descending here.'

She sat straighter and winced. Her shoulder's slouched, pain clear on her face. 'Oh, that reminds me! Sam Walker at the post office said a man was living in the flat above. There's a chance…' She trailed off when she noticed Callan's clenched fists.

He shook his head. 'Robert checked the place out. The sod checked out the morning he hit ye. He's wiped the place clean. I think he was waiting for an opportunity to hurt ye. Hurt me and he faces more trouble, me being a police officer.' Callan walked to the bed. 'Ye need to get some rest.'

'No! We need to figure this out! I'm perfectly fine.' She winced.

Queen of impatience!

Determined, Aileen persisted, telling him what she'd found out. He took notes, grateful for her thorough analysis.

'I'll go to the station, put it on the board.' Callan said when she'd finished.

Now a little weary, Aileen bit her lips. She settled back without complaint. 'Could-could you get me my satchel?'

'About that…' Callan began.

But Aileen cut him off. 'You can't deny me some light reading. Maybe if I sit here quietly and read the notebooks, something might stand out that could help us! I won't be throwing myself in harm's way!'

'The goon who hit ye stole the notebooks.' He deadpanned.

Aileen's eyes represented saucers. When she wrung her hands, dejection on her face, he tried reassuring her. 'Hey, it's okay, we ken what we ken.'

'I'm sorry to mess this up and hamper the investigation.'

To his horror, tears leaked from her eyes. She hiccupped and knuckled her eyes like a little girl.

Damn pain medication!

Similar to a deer caught in headlights, Callan's mouth went dry. He sank into the chair, not knowing what to do. 'We'll find a way.' He spluttered.

Suddenly she stopped. 'Of course, there's a way, Callan!' Aileen yelled. 'I have backups. I scanned all the notebooks. I'm not dumb! It's just that the original copies would have served as evidence in court.'

Callan stood so abruptly that the chair screeched. 'Aileen! Ye genius woman!' He bent to her eye-level but immediately pulled back. 'Where did ye store them?'

Narrowing her eyes, she glared at him. 'In the cloud, duh. Get Isla to bring my laptop. I will read those notebooks whether you like it or not.'

Not being able to keep pace with her emotions, Callan simply nodded. 'But yer head-'

'Has never been better.' Aileen nodded. 'Get me the laptop.' She ordered.

Callan left the hospital feeling revved. Even a good night's sleep couldn't give him this much energy. He felt so much lighter to see Aileen being herself again.

But energised or not, he needed a nap before he could give his all to catch the sod who thought it was okay to run Aileen off the road.

Not on Callan's watch!

CHAPTER THIRTEEN

That afternoon, Callan sat in his office muttering expletives at Douglas's cat. He'd gone and prodded over Warren's vegetable garden again. Didn't that fluffy eejit understand boundaries?

Callan had been so excited that Aileen had copies of the notebooks that he hadn't got any sleep.

Slurping coffee, Callan eyed the murder board.

What did they know so far? Marley Watson had driven to Loch Fuar, and a car had followed hers. This hound-masked person had sported red-hair when he'd parked the car at the lot. Then there was another slick car which followed them. That one belonged to Morticia Luna. Her goon had accompanied her.

As far as he knew, Marley had plans to extract

money from Morticia Luna. But a simple handoff could take an hour or two at the maximum. What were they doing at the cottage for the entire day?

Callan caressed his prickly beard.

Taking a deep breath, he approached the board. Who was this red-haired man? Did Marley know him or was she running away from him?

Neither Sean nor Josh at the parking lot knew whether they had met up later.

And what had Morticia Luna been doing at Loch Fuar all day?

'Ye look like shit.' Rory stood in the doorway to his office in his uniformed plaid shirt and trousers. He'd got some shut-eye since he didn't sport heavy pouches under his eyes.

'Rory.' Callan greeted his boss.

His head ached from all the stress of the last couple of hours. If only they could figure out where the sod who'd hurt Aileen had gone off to, things would be much better!

'Go home and get some sleep. Isla's at the hospital. They're sending Aileen home.' Rory informed him.

Callan narrowed his eyes. 'Already?' Only twelve hours ago, Aileen had been unconscious.

Rory shrugged. 'Let's just say, Siobhan's granddaughter is just as stubborn and persuasive. She wants to go back home to a better, stronger Wi-Fi connection. She said it's something to do with the case.'

That made Callan groan. When would she understand the importance of patience? She needed rest, not work! He'd like to give her a piece of his mind. Since she wasn't here to do just that, Callan chuckled sarcastically. 'Next, she'll demand I move my office to Dachaigh so she can take part in this investigation.'

Rory laughed. 'Ah, ye read minds. That order, my lad, has already been placed. Ye've been asked to move yer board and yer arse, although I think she said "behind" to Dachaigh.'

'Hell I will!' Callan frowned, slamming his hands on the desk.

'It's not an official investigation, Callan, and Aileen's been hurt. Be there for her.' Rory advised.

When Callan scowled at his superior officer, Rory shook his head. 'Something ye should ken, Callan. Ye never say no to a woman. They have ways to get back at ye.' The older man shuddered. 'Once I told my wife I wouldn't mow the lawn that morning, that same night all the whisky from the house was gone!'

Callan made a face. Rory and his whisky. He'd never found Rory drunk, the man just loved the drink.

'Aileen has no control over me.' Callan announced.

'*Yet.*' Rory smirked, waving at Callan as he walked out the door.

Callan sat dumb folded.

Yet.

Bloody hell! He stood.

It was time to make his way to Dachaigh.

LATE IN THE AFTERNOON WHEN THE SUN WAS A little milder and the sky was clear blue, Callan left the police station. It had showered, leaving behind a damp road.

Birds chirped, hidden in the trees, and an elderly man lugged a trolley towards the grocery store.

A typical calm day in Loch Fuar.

Callan got into his car and adjusted the mirror. He was buying time.

Huffing, he cast one last look in the mirror and frowned. What was that?

A car was parked some ways from the police station. He hadn't seen it hereabouts. Callan shrugged. Could be a tourist's.

Purring his car to life, Callan pulled out on the street.

Fifteen minutes later, his car rumbled down the road to Dachaigh, murder board in tow.

Dachaigh stood as it had for the last six decades —a traditional Scottish inn with whitewashed walls and pastel blue window frames and door. Flowers bloomed around the house and on the window sills, pleasant as spring.

When he bumped down the road and parked in the small parking lot belonging to the inn, he heard a soft wail of a bird. He knew little about bird species, but it was a wail, nonetheless.

Groaning, he hefted the board out. His right knee hurt, but he bit the pain away.

That's what ye get for not going for that jog!

He bent over to lock his car when a glint caught his eye. It had come from the foliage that faced the inn.

Dachaigh stood on a wee mound, a good ten-minute drive from the rest of town. That meant the inn had no neighbours. So what was that?

Callan stuffed his board back in the car. He had to investigate.

Locking his car, just in case, he peered at the exact spot where he'd seen something shine. He shuffled his feet and bending low, assessed the trees.

Nothing.

Maybe he was seeing things thanks to his lack of sleep.

Callan rubbed his eyes and was about to turn back when something glinted in the trees again. He had seen it this time, as real as day.

Making sure his gun was in the holster, Callan crouched and tiptoed to the bonnet of his car. Hiding behind it, he tried to see through the trees. And rightly so, something glinted again.

It had to be the sun reflecting from a glass surface or even a mirror. It couldn't be a lost tourist, given that there was an inn right here to seek shelter in.

Besides, there was nothing in that foliage that a tourist would want to explore. That too at Dachaigh? There was Aileen. Callan didn't like coincidences.

Was someone keeping an eye on her?

Carefully, to make little noise, Callan ran towards the hedges to the side. If this person hadn't made him out yet, Callan still had the advantage to surprise this spy.

Pulling the gun out, Callan was still bent low as he approached the spot he'd seen the glint. Dry leaves crunched under his feet and twigs and leaves poked his black coat. He ignored it, grateful that the coat covered his injured arm.

Snap!

A larger twig cracked under his leg.

Bloody hell!

Something rustled in the trees. Knowing the perpetrator had made him, Callan ran through the foliage towards the sound.

More trees rustled until he saw it. The same car that had been parked near the police station. Now it sat on a narrow mud road behind the foliage. And this time it had a driver. This driver wore a hound mask.

Shit!

Callan lunged for the vehicle, but the driver had already started the car. It roared to life, shattering the silence and raced out, spewing damp mud on Callan.

'Heck!' Callan cocked his gun and fired, but he was too late. The eejit driver ploughed through the thinning hedge and raced down the tar road. The car hurtled out of view, towards the Highway.

Struggling with his damn phone, Callan put a call through to Robert. Yelling the car's license plate, he snapped at the officer. 'Follow the damn vehicle to wherever it goes! But if ye lose it, find the surveillance footage and try to put a BOLO on it!'

Still spitting expletives, Callan jogged back to the car when the door to Dachaigh opened. It was Isla. The Highland breeze playing with her wild red hair. 'Callan! We heard the gunshots. What is it? Are you hurt?' Her eyes were wide, panicked.

From inside the inn, he heard a baby crying. Callan tugged his hair. 'Sorry.'

Isla inspected the now serene Highlands behind him. But rightly so, she saw the trampled hedges.

'Come in!' She told Callan. 'Let me go settle Carly. The shots startled her awake. Are you sure you aren't hurt?'

He nodded. 'I'm fine. Aileen?'

Isla gestured for him to enter and jogged towards the crib. Shrill wails assaulted his ears but used to toddlers and their tantrums, Callan made his way towards Aileen, ignoring the cry.

Aileen sat on the sofa, surrounded by several

cushions, her left hand placed in a brace and a bandage around her head.

Well rested, her eyes twinkled when she saw him but scrunched up seeing the thunder on his face. 'What happened?'

Callan snarled at himself. 'I was followed and never even noticed!'

At Aileen's questioning look, Callan explained. 'The hound-mask wearing man. I saw the car parked near the police station, but the feartie has fixed another license plate to it. It never struck me as being the same car. There are plenty of compact vehicles with the same make and model. Bampot!' Callan ploughed a fist into his thigh. 'I was this close to getting the sod.'

Aileen shuffled her way towards Callan and patted his back. 'There's always a next time.' She winced.

Callan turned his attention to her. 'Are ye alright? Do ye need rest?'

Aileen nodded. 'I have something to-'

They were interrupted by the loud ringing of Callan's phone. It was Robert.

'What?' Callan sniped.

Robert's voice was hard. 'The sod got away. But there's a problem with that BOLO. That car isn't connected to an official case we are solving, is it?'

Heck! 'Just let it go. Instead, dig up data for that license plate as well as the license plate the driver previously used. Get me as much as ye can.'

Callan sat back, gritting his teeth.

Aileen pointed at the coffee table, brimming with hot chocolate, sandwiches and pastries. 'Eat. It'll make you feel better.'

Callan only scowled, but when his stomach growled, he picked a pastry and gobbled it. 'I'll get that murder board.'

When he returned with the board, Isla instructed him to place it away from toddler's eyes. He wasn't sure how much little humans understood about murder, but he didn't want to chance another loud protest.

He reached for a sandwich and chewed on it.

Aileen started almost immediately. 'I was thinking…'

Isla groaned. 'Aileen! Let the man eat! Here, sip your tea!'

Aileen punched a cushion and scowled. 'I don't want tea.'

Isla huffed and took a seat. 'These pain medicines make her slightly…' She pointed her forefinger to the side of her head and twirled it.

Mouth full, Callan sniggered playfully. 'What's there to go crazy? She's already *aff her heid*!'

'Hey!' Aileen pulled an indignant face at her two snickering friends. 'I'm smart.'

'Ye are, Ms Accountant. What were ye thinking?' Callan questioned.

Aileen sipped her tea. 'I was thinking about Marley Watson and that beam. Who fixed it? With the right tools, she could have done it herself. But why fix it?'

Callan told Aileen about the suitcase Sean had seen the red-haired man heft from her car. 'And I was just thinking: If this was some handoff for money, what took them the entire day to get it all sorted?'

Isla cleared her throat. 'Could Marley have plans to stay at the cottage overnight? I mean I know it was dilapidated, but what if she was camping out that night? That would explain why she fixed that beam. If it holds the roof in place, she could've wanted to stay in the cottage overnight. Didn't you say she was supposed to hand her car over the next day?'

He mulled over Isla's words. 'That's plausible. Now the question is: Was the red-haired man accompanying her or was he hunting her?'

A loud silence followed when all three sat thinking.

The sky had turned purple with a hint of pink, almost like candy floss.

Isla dusted her hands. 'I'm spending the night, but I've got to put Carly to bed. We've to keep a watch on Aileen, make sure she's in her senses and all.'

Callan chuckled. 'Sure.'

When Isla left, Aileen plucked a pastry and munched on it.

Walking up to the murder board, Callan faced

her. 'Charlie, Freddie, Morticia Luna, Martin Luther Hussey are our primary suspects. Why Charlie? Marley was spying on him.' Holding up two fingers, Callan said, 'Freddie because he was Marley's neighbour and had access to her flat. They might have had a spat about the money he was taking from Marley.'

Aileen interrupted. 'But he's a hermit and if they had a spat, it would have been in either of their flats and not at Loch Fuar. It's unlikely he's that red-haired man. Besides, if he's a science geek and likes testing potions, it's more likely he'll use poison or something more, I don't know, science-y to kill.'

Callan nodded. 'Makes sense. Besides, if someone tied that noose, they had to be tall and strong enough to hold Marley down. Freddie isn't a fit sort of person. He doesn't do much lifting apart from lifting a test tube. And then there's Morticia Luna. She was seen around town that day. Was she securing an alibi for herself for the murder? Or perhaps, this red-haired sod is her goon doing the dirty work for her. And this other man with Morticia Luna could've ensured that the deed was done.'

Aileen picked up. 'So then why did she dash across town to get to the parking lot and hurtle out of there? What sent her in a frenzy? Something unexpected, like murder?'

Shrugging, Callan pointed at the last suspect. 'Martin Luther Hussey. He was romantically and professionally linked with Marley. He's threatened us to stay away multiple times, and he's got a bucket-load of cash in the recent days. Is that Marley's money that, like her neighbour and TJ, he helped himself too, or is it one of his nefarious activities?'

He thought back to the last meeting with the man. He's sported an angry gash on his neck and had one hidden under his sleeve. A bruised lip. But it was the expensive perfume and the golden chain he's specifically told Callan about that intrigued him. Why point out that he'd purchased the chain with cash and not stolen it?

Was it just to get a police officer off his scent?

Aileen spoke softly, 'Besides, he's always camped outside Marley's house. Most likely he gets his cash from her apartment too.'

But there was something about that man. Just like there was something about Charlie. Unlike Martin Luther Hussey, Charlie had a motive. Perhaps Marley had been bleeding him dry for a while now and he'd snapped.

Callan thought out loud. 'Charlie. Didn't Roland say their "rat" told them stabbings in the area have increased? What if Charlie is a rat for the police? Being the pub-owner, he'd hear things. Definitely helpful for the police to monitor the area.'

'And a good reason why Roland wants to keep this case closed. He wants to keep his rat safe.' Aileen suggested.

As one, they spoke. 'Charlie. Let's look into him.'

Both grinned when Aileen huffed. 'I hoped we'd have some concrete physical description on that red-haired man. But all we know is his hair colour.'

'He wanted to be inconspicuous. Hence that strange hair colour. Most people would notice it instead of his features. Plus, he could have added features, ye ken, a pot-belly for example, or contact lenses, longer ears. There's plenty available, and he went shopping for a hound mask.' Callan observed.

Pulling out his notepad, Callan scribbled all that they had discussed. 'Walsh called. He has something for us but says he wants to hand it over in Loch Heaven instead of online. I told him I'll be there when ye get discharged from the hospital. So, I think I'll make my way there tomorrow.'

Aileen opened her mouth to argue when the windows lit up with car headlights. Isla pranced in, an overnight bag in tow.

'Isla, you don't have to stay. I'll take care of myself.' Aileen told her.

But Isla swatted her hand. 'Think of it as a girl's night.' She pointed to the murder board. 'Any progress?'

Callan, hands in his pockets, nodded. 'I'll be going to Loch Heaven again. Meet with Walsh and search for that blasted car that followed me.'

'Hey!' Aileen huffed. 'I'm coming too!'

'With a hand in a cast and a banged-up head?

If I wanted to cart something around, I'd rather wear a weighted vest.' Callan crossed his arms.

Aileen shouted. 'I'm not-'

'At least a weighted vest doesn't talk back!' He admonished.

Lifting her chin, Aileen said, 'I'm perfectly capable of taking care of myself.'

Callan refused. 'Not like this, ye aren't. Ye need to take rest, get healed.'

'I'm fine!' Aileen slammed her hands on the cushions.

He snapped. Didn't she care about her own life? 'Are ye an eejit? This woman would stop at nothing to keep you quiet! Ye are a sitting duck if ye come along with me.'

Aileen sat mum.

Callan winced. Perhaps he'd been too rude to her. But he shouldn't encourage this. She was in danger with a target on her back. 'I should get going.' He packed his murder board.

Wincing, Aileen stood and walked him to the door.

Callan warned. 'Don't start again, I said no.'

'Thank you.' She was barely audible over the sound of the crickets. Aileen held onto the cool metallic door handle with her good hand.

Callan shrugged. His hand landed on her shoulder. 'I'm asking ye to stay safe, that's all. Walsh told me in not so many words that Morticia Luna isn't someone ye mess with.'

Aileen played with the hem of her shirt. 'Callan if there's anything I can do with the finances or the tech stuff.'

Feeling a little guilty of cutting her off, Callan suggested. 'Maybe you can go through the notebooks? Perhaps there's something we've missed?'

She smiled thinly. 'I will.'

He squeezed her shoulder one last time. 'Take care.'

Raising her chin, she said. 'You take care of the oaf. We need him hereabouts.'

'What'd ye call me?' Callan cocked an eyebrow.

'Oaf!' She muttered.

As unexpected as the blue moon, he cracked up guffawing with belly hurting fits of laughter.

'God, Aileen! There's only one of ye.' He waved at her.

Aileen called after him. 'Bampot!'

The light breeze carried his continued laughter. 'Keep the same company and ye might expand yer vocabulary.'

He smiled all the way to his flat where he collapsed into a dreamless sleep.

CHAPTER FOURTEEN

Grinning, Aileen clicked the door shut only to find Isla pulling a cheeky expression.

'Match made in heaven….'

Aileen rolled her eyes, but it didn't deter Isla. 'Ever since you've come back from Loch Heaven, you've been different, the both of you.'

'Yeah, we saw a man die in front of us! Why is he so stubborn?' Aileen crossed her arms.

Isla sighed. 'He was really worried when you were in the hospital. We all were. And he's right. This man or woman is dangerous.'

Aileen leant against the door and her shoulders slumped. 'So why would Marley associate herself with such people?'

Isla frowned, thinking… 'Perks?'

'What kind of perks?' Aileen asked. She

couldn't think of any perks that could make her want to join forces with criminals.

Biting her lips, Isla guessed. 'Money? Accommodation?'

'Yes, money.' Aileen hummed. 'But what do you mean about accommodation?'

Isla shrugged. 'As rent payment. Morticia Luna was Marley's landlady, wasn't she?'

Aileen walked towards the sofa and sank into it. 'Yes, she was. And in that pocket-sized diary of hers, Marley doesn't mention any rent payments. So that is possible.'

Suddenly, she sat straighter. 'Callan's right. These people will stop at nothing. No wonder Marley had her finances written in code. She knew who those people are that she paid money to. But there should be a detailed account somewhere.'

Isla sank into a chair. 'I think you should catch some sleep.'

Aileen huffed. 'I'll have time for that later. Isla? What if Callan's wrong in going to Loch Fuar? What if he gets hurt?'

Being the good friend that she was, Isla came up to her and squeezed her shoulders. 'He's a detective, not some rookie who'd hurt himself. He's a smart man, give him credit for that.'

Aileen's voice was barely above a whisper as she recalled the stench, the metallic knife, TJ's glassy eyes and Marley's bare feet dangling in the bitter air. "I saw them, Isla. It was so easy to kill that lad.

One moment he was here and the next? He was as old as me!'

Isla helped Aileen stand. 'Off to bed now. Don't tax yourself.'

She let Isla guide her to the bed.

When an hour later, she just couldn't sleep, Aileen blinked.

This is what that person had wanted. To scare her off. Would she let them win?

Wincing, Aileen wiggled into a sitting position. No, she wasn't some scared little wimp. She was a smart woman and she would help Callan.

Aileen booted her laptop and cosied up in bed, tucking the blankets around her. She accessed the notebook on Charlie.

First, she went through his log, but it led her nowhere. She already knew his schedule. She then opened the other larger book Marley had maintained.

This one she'd gone through once. It had Charlie's health record, height, weight and an approximation of his income.

Then Marley had drawn a floor layout of Sláinte. Why a map? What did she want in Sláinte?

Aileen scrolled, bending over her laptop. The late-night reading made her injured head throb, but she persisted.

Apparently, there was a staircase from behind the bar that led to the floor above. This staircase was much sturdier than the rickety ladder that sat outside the back door.

Marley didn't have a floor map for the storehouse above, but she'd marked it with a red cross.

What did that mean? Aileen bit her lip.

Was Charlie hiding something there?

Aileen's question was answered almost immediately when she scrolled to the next page.

Using a faint pencil, Marley had scrawled in the margins "Convicts planted."

What did that mean? Was it something misleading or a slip-up? But Marley hadn't been wrong so far, her information about Morticia Luna's lair had panned out.

Then these convicts had to be something pertinent as well. They had to check it out, especially if this could help crack the case. Perhaps these convicts are what killed Marley.

And hadn't TJ died outside Sláinte as well? It gave Charlie a good vantage point and no one would question what he was doing lurking outside his own pub.

Aileen shut the lid of her laptop. Adventure awaited her.

BIRDSONG BROKE OUT IN THE QUIET HIGHLANDS. The town stirred as sunlight swept across the loch and its surrounding mountains.

A little stiff despite his morning run, Callan stopped at the police station to grab the papers he wanted.

He brewed himself a cup, filled in his leave application—which he was sure Rory would consent to—and bid a sleepy Robert goodbye.

It was best to get a head start and meet with Walsh.

Shouldering open the door, he strode towards his car and stopped.

'What are ye doing here?' He questioned the brunette.

'Packed and ready to leave!' Aileen smiled a little too sweetly.

Seeing red, he barked. 'Aileen! Where's Isla?'

'She gave up at about three am.'

Isla gave up? No wonder Aileen had taken after her gran.

He huffed. There was no point in telling this woman to stay put because she wouldn't listen and might even go off sleuthing on her own.

'I've got something for you.' Aileen smirked. 'A possible break in the case.'

Callan narrowed his eyes. 'Get in the car.'

After a lot of wriggling, Aileen managed to click the seat belt in place. Then she turned to him. 'I couldn't sleep last night thanks to those weird pain medicines and anaesthesia. So I scanned through those notebooks again and guess what I found in Charlie's?'

Giving her his full attention, he listened and took notes. 'So we need to see what these convicts are in the storeroom. And there's a staircase from inside Sláinte. Got it.'

Aileen laid her head on the backrest. 'But it's unlikely Charlie will just let you walk in.'

'We'll find a way to get in there.' Callan dismissed. 'Let's just hope this information is genuine and won't mislead us.'

Saying that, Callan started the car and cruised out, heading for Loch Heaven.

The road to Loch Heaven had become familiar now. Rolling hills and the fresh countryside made him imagine he was on holiday.

All the while, Aileen's gaze was riveted outside the window. Halfway there she dropped off into slumber before she awoke, blinked her eyes and then promptly nodded off again.

Why didn't she admit that she was tired? Stubborn woman that she was, but he was glad she'd come along. Two heads were better than one.

Taking the exit off the highway, Callan entered the town of Loch Heaven.

When they parked in the parking lot in the centre of town, Aileen raised an eyebrow. 'What's the plan now?'

Callan checked his watch. 'Sláinte first. It's early still, which means no one should be in.'

He went to the boot and took out a bag.

'What's this for?' Aileen studied the bag.

Callan beckoned to her. 'You'll see.'

Aileen didn't ask what it was again. She seemed lost in her thoughts. Taking his proffered arm, she let him guide her towards Sláinte. Neither of them was interested in their usual banter. Both focused on solving the case.

It was a wee hike, one that made the area seem more dilapidated than horrendous. Holding her closer, he surveyed the streets. Nothing had changed.

The locality was littered with the same kind of people, still exchanging the same kind of nefarious items. Only in the morning hours, most were still hidden underneath blankets. Those who were awake huddled in the darker corners where the sun never touched the earth.

Tilting his head to Aileen's, he whispered. 'Let's use the back door. Fewer people to see us get in that way.'

Aileen licked her lips; her shoulders had bunched up.

He patted her arm. 'It's broad daylight.'

The sun was high in the sky, its harsh rays scorching his exposed skin.

'Of course.' Aileen mumbled.

Eyes followed them, others loitered in the shadows of awnings. All structures either sported broken window panes or at least peeling paint.

Callan led them to the back alley where only a

few days ago TJ had breathed his last. Aileen's breath hitched, but she didn't stop.

The air was sultry. At the edge of his vision, bodily fluids ran into a drain.

The back entrance of Sláinte was littered with overflowing dustbins. Their bottle green colour faded into mucky black. Amidst the dirt was the ladder. If one could call it that. It was more like two rusted rods joined by smaller rusted rods. It led to the door of the storeroom. Thanks to Marley's books, they didn't need to use it.

The harsh sun didn't help with the odour of the garbage sprawled on the road.

Jogging towards the back door, Callan sought refuge in the darkness. Aileen stuck to his side, hidden from view.

Callan worked quickly with the lock-pick in his bag.

A soft hand landed on his shoulder. 'How much longer?'

Just then the door clicked open. It creaked loudly in the silence, but when he heard no sound from inside, Callan ventured in. He had to blink to adjust his eyes to the darkness.

The pub stank of malt and nicotine, but unlike last time, the floors were wiped clean. There were no glasses on the well-worn bar table. The wood though sported some cup stains.

The chairs were turned upside down on the tables, and the front door was bolted from the inside. Weren't they lucky Charlie used the back door?

They tiptoed over the stone floor and rounded the bar. On the other side, glass bottles with various amber liquids sat quietly in the dark.

A chink sounded, and a light beam struck the other wall. Aileen flicked her torch across the room. 'According to Marley's notes, the staircase is behind the bar.' She whispered.

Thus, they went to the end of the bar where a door with a peep-hole was. And there was no lock on it. It swung open without noise.

Callan held the door open for Aileen and they stepped through to a concrete flight of stairs. There was nothing there except for blank cemented walls on either side. The stairs led straight up. Aileen went first, flashing her torch.

Their footsteps echoed in the empty stairwell, making them sound like smacks on an anvil.

When Aileen emerged from the stairs and into the boarded-up room, her torch spotlighted a dirty green wall with peeling paint. 'It's just stacks and stacks of cheap booze.' She observed.

Callan fired his torch and surveyed the room.

Aileen had observed correctly. Cardboard boxes were stacked on top of each other, a couple of shiny cans glittered in the dark.

He strode over to an open box and muttered. 'Shit!' It was nothing but full of cheap cans and some dry snacks. Some snacks, Callan observed, had reached their expiry date. The miserly Charlie didn't believe in serving his customers fresh food apparently. Expired food was much cheaper.

What did he expect to find in a pub's storehouse apart from food and beverages anyway? Callan huffed.

'Do you think Marley made a mistake?' Aileen spoke in soft tones, echoing his thoughts.

He grunted, but it just didn't add up. 'Why would she have made a mistake? Especially being so thorough? All her other tips panned out.'

Knitting her brows, Aileen asked. 'What are we searching for exactly?'

That was a good question. Callan didn't know the answer to it, but he knew what they weren't looking for. 'Check for something that isn't alcohol or food sachets.' He suggested.

'I wouldn't-' Aileen began.

Just then Callan's ears perked up. 'Hush!'

He gestured to Aileen. They sank to the floor behind a couple of boxes, just as the door to the stairwell downstairs swung open. Footsteps thundered as they walked into the storeroom.

Aileen poked Callan in the ribs, mouthing, 'You are hurting me.'

He scrunched his face. 'Sorry'

A fat man emerged. It was Charlie. What was he doing here so early?

The answer came when DCI Kevin Roland followed closely behind.

Shit!

Roland had his hands in his pockets, and he lugged his weight as he walked. 'Sheesh man! Couldn't you find a better place than this stink hole?'

'Money, better money 'ere.' Charlie grunted.

Satisfied, Roland trotted over to one box and plucked out a can.

'Hey! Nay, withoot paying.' The pub-owner shouted.

Roland chuckled. 'As if I'm interested in this piss.' He dropped the can back inside carelessly. 'What did you find out about this man?'

Charlie snarled, 'One of yers, nosing abut.'

'I never sent anybody.' Roland countered.

Charlie wagged his hand. 'Course ye did, ya bampot.'

'Mind your language, man!' Roland reprimanded. 'I'll sort this out. Blasted Walsh! He's under bad influence letting that detective and his wench nose about.' He muttered the last part to himself.

But Charlie caught it and responded. 'I dinnae care abut yer Walsh. I dinnae want boabies nosing abut ma business. I dinnae get any customers.'

Roland waved a hand. 'It doesn't matter. Why would he be snooping hereabouts? What have you got here?'

Charlie pointed at the cardboard boxes Aileen and Callan were hiding behind. It took all of

Callan's willpower to sit there without charging at these men. 'Just beer and the occasional food.'

Glaring at the pub-owner, Roland snapped. 'Nothing else?'

Charlie shook his head. 'Course not! I've been clean fer a while now.'

Roland tilted his chin. 'Keep a watch! And I'll keep unwanted guests away. Bloody Loch Fuar detective!'

Abruptly, he turned towards the stairs and thundered away.

Cussing like a sailor, the tattooed Charlie followed on his heels. Their voices drifted from downstairs until the back door slammed shut.

But Charlie didn't leave. His pacing could be heard in the storehouse, as he kept hurtling expletives at Roland.

Shit, how could they get out now? Charlie was right there.

Aileen whispered. 'We'd have to use this door.' She pointed to the door on the other side that was attached to that flimsy ladder.

'Let's dig out these convicts first. There's something here. And let's hope Charlie leaves.' There had to be something in here. Marley had thought this out too well for her to go wrong.

They switched on their torches and began checking.

Callan massaged his right knee. It hurt again. Eejit knee.

He tiptoed towards a lone table in the far corner. A thick coat of dust lay over it, undisturbed. Another opened box of cans sat beside it. There was nothing on the table, except for a few scampering cockroaches.

Callan flashed his torch underneath the table, only to be met by spiders hanging on cobwebs and more cockroaches.

Aileen's light footsteps treaded to the box. 'There's nothing except al...'

He raised his eyebrows when she trailed off.

'Callan! Give me a hand, will you?' She was standing near one box, studying it.

Shuffling to her side, he handed her a pair of gloves. Despite the brace, she used her other hand too. Best they don't leave any prints behind.

Together, they pulled out the cans. Then he saw it, papers, stacks of them underneath the cans.

He removed them carefully, blowing away the dust which settled on them. He shone a light on the papers.

'Gotcha!' Callan exclaimed.

Her head near his upper arms, Aileen peered into the paper. 'Callan, they are Morticia Luna's tax records! And her ledgers, although they are photocopies. But they seem genuine records.'

Excitedly, she flicked through the papers, her sharp gaze flying over the numbers. 'Let's check the other boxes.'

Carefully, he placed the papers in an evidence

bag and moved on to help Aileen with another box. It was empty.

It took them almost an hour and a half to get through the opened boxes.

'I'm surprised Charlie didn't notice these boxes had been opened.' Aileen commented.

'He's a pea-brained eejit.' Callan muttered.

Callan's bag was almost full to bursting. 'Let's get back and study them.'

Since Aileen couldn't climb down that rickety ladder, Callan hoped Charlie had long gone. He tiptoed downstairs, bag slung over his shoulders, and peered out the peep-hole.

'Damn it. He's still here.' Callan whispered. He thought for a moment and then handed the bag over to Aileen. 'Take this. I'll go distract him.' Callan flashed his teeth. It would feel good to plough into the man. He longed for a good fight. 'And make a dash for it when-'

Aileen rolled her eyes. 'That's such a typical response. Think, Callan! If someone hears you and walks in to help Charlie, you are toast. Follow me.' She handed the bag back to him.

Crouching low, Aileen nudged the door open. Since it was well oiled, it made no sound.

Charlie was still busy raging at everything that was wrong with his life. But he was pacing just beside the bar on the customers' side.

Being petite, she only needed to open the door a couple of inches.

Suddenly Charlie halted. Aileen froze, stuck in between the door.

Frowning, he went back to his pacing. 'Bloody boabies dinna let the likes of us make money. Marley now? Eh? That eejit wench…' He rambled on to himself.

Carefully Aileen nudged ahead and made a dash for the counter. Hidden behind it, she gestured for Callan to follow.

Bending low, he too opened the door when his bag clanked against the door frame.

Bloody hell!

Charlie stopped pacing and swivelled around. Thinking fast, Callan shut the door and hunched behind it in the stairwell.

Aileen was all alone outside. *Shit!*

Footsteps led to the door, and it opened just a crack. Charlie peeped in.

Wearing black, Callan was almost camouflaged, but when Charlie turned around, Aileen would be in plain sight behind the counter.

Clenching his fist tight, Callan was ready to strike the man when a glass smashed against the other wall.

Charlie jerked away and ran into the pub.

Acting at once, Callan gently pushed against the door to see Charlie at the other end of the room. But there was no Aileen behind the counter.

Where did she go?

WHEN EYES DON'T LIE

AILEEN WAS BREATHING HARD. WHEN SHE'D SEEN Charlie walk towards that door, she knew he'd make Callan out.

Thinking quickly, she lifted a glass and hurled it against the front door. Before Charlie could turn around, she'd skirted the bar.

When the man reached the front door, Aileen looked around for another glass. She saw it dangling above the bar counter but hell, she was too short to reach it.

Her eyes turned towards the glass bottles.

Hands trembling, she plucked one from the stands. Charlie was still inspecting what the noise was. Muttering, he flicked on a switch and the entire room lit in dim light.

Aileen aimed the bottle at Charlie's back. She let it fly. It travelled through the air, but it wouldn't hit its target. However, the "pea-brain" that he was, Charlie moved right in the way of the missile.

The bottle hit him on his head. The massive mass of muscle and the bottle both crashed. But Aileen had no time to inspect the damage. She yelled at Callan. 'Come on!'

They were out the door and into the bright sunlight.

Blinking at the sudden change in the light, Aileen had to stop. Callan grabbed her hand and tugged.

Not giving a damn to her aching head or hand, they dashed out onto the stinky road and ran full throttle. Aileen's lungs burned, but she kept pace with Callan.

He'd slowed to match her shorter strides. Panting, they didn't stop until the footfall increased and the traffic on the road thickened. Only then did they come to a stop.

Aileen was red in the face. Callan hooted with laughter. 'Oh god! There's never a dull day with ye!'

Despite her pants, she joined him and they both lugged their way back to Callan's car. 'Let's find a hotel and get something to eat. All this exercise has made me hungry.'

This time they tried another hotel and haggled one room out of the irritated receptionist. All hotels were booked for the weekend, but Callan had "mistakenly" flashed his badge.

Anything for justice.

Once inside, Aileen inspected the small space. 'Are we paying for this? Or is this the closet?'

'Come on, we've got no time for your snips.'

They'd bought some packaged food for lunch. Munching, Aileen sat on the floor, the papers scattered around her.

Callan sat beside Aileen. The yellow notepad rested on the floor as she hunched over it. Her lips moved, tracing the words, and she made notes in the margins simultaneously.

Such a nerd! Typical Aileen. But her habits had

stood them in good stead. They wouldn't have got these papers otherwise.

'What have we got so far?' Callan asked. He was no good at all the jargon.

Aileen pointed to a couple of sheets. 'Marley found Morticia Luna's original files. Look here, these are tax records that Morticia Luna's filed. And here are the accounts she submitted with them. But here's another set of books, even though it's a photocopy these are the Houndress's actual books of accounts.'

Her eyes twinkled as she rambled on. 'And it's got all her real incomes and expenses. Look here, there's an income from the sale of old paintings. Stolen, illegal paintings! And, and there's income from money laundering too!' Excitedly she pointed at more incomes, the amount ten times what had been reported to the authorities.

Morticia Luna had income from various illegal projects and she also had international bank accounts where she'd hidden the money.

When Aileen was done, Callan tutted. 'That's Morticia Luna's entire life behind bars. Wow! It's definitely worth killing for.'

But Aileen wasn't done. She pointed to the expense side of the accounts. 'And there's payroll, Callan! And Marley's attached the list of all the names in the notes to these accounts! I can bet the goon who hit me is on there. And Callan, there are payments to various other projects, illegal ones. We hand this in, and we've got her cornered!'

Aileen pumped her fist in the air and then grimaced. 'I forgot about my arm.'

He had to chuckle at her. 'This is good.' He conceded. He didn't understand much of the accounting jargon, but he understood that this was hard evidence that pointed at Morticia Luna's nefarious activities.

Curious, Callan lifted a few sheets and leafed through them. 'Hey, there's a list of people on her payroll, isn't there? Let's go through it, search if there are any known names.'

They read the names together, arms brushing, heads pressed. They poured through the list.

It was a long one, and most of the names were foreign to them both. They turned the page and continued to read, the names blurring into one another until…

Callan's breath hitched, and his finger landed on the name. 'Is that?'

Aileen pursed her lips. 'DCI Kevin Roland.'

CHAPTER FIFTEEN

'I knew he was a Detective Creep Inspector.' Aileen muttered.

Callan gnashed his teeth. 'That bastard! Now we ken why he was so interested to keep the case closed.'

Stacking all the papers, Aileen placed them in the safe in the hotel's cupboard. Carefully, she followed the instructions and locked them. They would be safe here than in her satchel. Lesson learnt. She wouldn't carry pertinent evidence around.

She faced Callan again, her mind churning. 'Callan, what if this red-haired man is Roland? What if Morticia Luna made him do it? That's even more motive for him to keep this case closed.'

Callan walked to the window. 'Feartie! That's

entirely possible. But where does that bring us with Walsh?'

Aileen didn't know. But all that Walsh had done was help them thus far. He'd saved their lives and helped Callan when he'd asked for information.

'Why don't we meet him, try to discern what his intentions are?' She suggested.

But right then, Callan's phone beeped. It was Robert.

Aileen could hear Callan's side of the conversation. All he did was grunt. In less than two minutes, Callan hung up.

'The second license plate this driver used was stolen. It belongs to a car an old woman gave to the mechanic for repairs. The license plate was reported missing on Sunday, the day after Marley's murder.'

She noted the details down. 'Being extra cautious again.'

He hummed his agreement. 'And the first license plate belongs to "Houndress & Co." and the car's registered to a parking lot. The vendor says it was a second-hand sale. All made in cash.'

'Robert's done a lot of work.' Aileen appreciated the young officer.

Callan scowled. 'He'd got twelve hours to do so. But this parking lot, it's within five-minute walking distance.'

So as the sun burned their skins, Aileen and Callan hiked to the parking lot grateful for the GPS.

Aileen led the way because Callan didn't know how to navigate using GPS. He'd insulted the technology until, exasperated, Aileen had plucked the phone out of his hands.

The few shops and restaurants they passed were crowded with people, all enjoying the bright sunlight.

Ice cream vans had long queues and the parking lot was packed to maximum capacity.

Precisely ten minutes since they'd left, they met the manager, a Mr Will Jones.

The man had dark hair with a few white strands sewn like a silver thread. He smiled widely at Callan, perhaps the first person in Loch Heaven to smile at them with genuine glee. 'What can I do for you?'

Callan asked him about the car that the masked driver had twice driven into Loch Fuar.

Mr Jones consulted their digital log but shook his head. 'I can't find such a car in our system. It's never been here.'

Then Callan asked if he'd ever seen a red-haired man loitering about. But Mr Jones hadn't.

Finally, just when they thought they'd be leaving the lot empty-handed, a lass walked in. She wore a dark blue coat with the name of the car company "Rent Your Ride." Unsure, she smiled at them. 'I heard ye asking about this red-haired man. This might interest ye.'

She gestured for them to follow. She led them

outside the parking lot and round the bend into a quieter alley. It seemed like a car dump because lots of broken engines and tyres were scattered everywhere, some even buried under a creeper.

Ducking under a tree branch, the lass pointed to something behind a tree. There it sat, the white compact car with its original number plate. But there was no driver inside.

She pointed at a stone fence that hid the car from view. 'That's the fence where the lot ends. I was here one morning, painting the parking lines when I noticed the car. It stood out because even though it's old, it isn't rusted. Most people leave their rusted cars here, dump them. But this one wasn't that bad. Still has some miles in her.'

She paused, eyeing Aileen and Callan. 'I saw that badge hidden under yer coat. I ken ye're from the police. My grandpa, mum and bro all serve. So, I don't lie to the police. The other day, when I was done painting the lines, I heard the car's engine, but it wasn't one of the cars in the lot. It was getting dark, and I saw the headlights. It was from this car. I saw a man, at least I thought he was one, wearing a Hound's mask. He drove the car away.'

Aileen and Callan thanked the girl. She might have given them another big clue.

Callan approached the car and asked Aileen to stay put. He surveyed it and made sure it was safe.

Here in the secluded lane, they had only the

wind, sun and leaves for company. Callan gestured Aileen to the driver's side.

After emptying the papers they'd found at Sláinte in the safe, Callan had brought the bag along with him again.

This time he pulled out a long metallic ruler.

Aileen eyed it. 'What are you doing? Measuring the car?'

He grinned at her and pointed to the car's door. The white car was old-fashioned. It had a keyhole and would require a simple key to unlock it. And Callan could see a strand of red hair peeking out from under the seat.

'Haven't ye ever broken into cars before?' He jested.

Aileen huffed. 'I don't go about breaking the law.'

Callan chuckled. 'Watch and learn.'

Using the long ruler, he inserted it into the tiny space between the window and the car's metallic body. The ruler slid in right about the area where the keyhole was on the door.

Wriggling the ruler, Callan felt for something and with one easy push, the car's door unlocked. 'Voilà!'

Aileen gaped at him. 'How? Goodness, Callan, you are a police detective.'

'Don't forget I was a lad before that.' Happy with himself, he pulled on a pair of gloves and opened the car door.

Callan flashed his torch around the car. The driver hadn't bothered to decorate it, and the seats were hard and worn. The plastic on the steering wheel and the dashboard had gone sticky with age.

An empty packet of chips and a pack of six emptied Irn-Bru cans strewed the bench.

Aileen, wearing her gloves, opened the other door and looked about. 'Callan!' She exclaimed, holding up a wig with red-hair.

She bent lower still and brought out a mask that was shaped like a hound. She inspected the thing. 'It's supposed to be worn over the head like a glove. It's got openings where the eyes, ears, mouth and nose should be. Genius.'

He opened the glove box. It carried an olive-green pouch. He pulled out the binoculars inside. Ah, this is what had reflected the sun that day outside Dachaigh.

'Hand me the evidence bags.' Callan instructed Aileen.

They packaged it all: the red wig, the hound mask, a pair of binoculars, even an empty packet of chips and the pack of six emptied Irn-Bru cans.

Callan zipped them into the evidence bags and tucked them into his bag.

Aileen reached across and pulled open the lever for the boot. She rounded the car and opened the boot. 'Callan!' She called him.

In the small storage compartment sat a suitcase

and beside it worn boots sticky with mud. The suitcase was heavy but locked.

'That's Marley's suitcase and boots.' Aileen whispered.

They looked at each other. 'This is the car of Marley's murderer, isn't it?' Aileen questioned.

'Aye.'

One last time, they searched the car again, but there was nothing else to find.

If this case was official, a simple DNA sample would've led them to their killer. But since it wasn't, Callan faced Aileen. 'It's time we speak with Walsh.'

WALSH WAS ALREADY WAITING FOR THEM AT THE cafe. This time it was crowded with youngsters and families. Aileen's stomach rumbled at the cheesy grilled sandwiches most of the customers were eating.

The detective stood out in the crowd. He wasn't just older, but he'd kept his trench coat and hat on.

Aileen slid into the seat opposite. Callan sat beside her, thighs pressed against hers.

'Who are you hiding from?' Aileen asked Walsh.

Walsh squinted down his nose at her. He leant across the table. 'This is no joking matter. We're in deep muck and you better watch your six. How are you feeling?' He asked Aileen.

Aileen huffed. 'I'm perfectly fine.'

Callan hunched his elbows on the table. 'What do ye mean? Who's after ye?'

The detective hung his head. 'I got a call from Roland. He wants me to keep the investigation closed. I don't know where he figured out that I was helping you.' The man sighed. 'But I want to help you out especially since Roland's trying his best to stop you from re-opening the case. Besides, the last couple of days have been shit.'

Callan cocked an eyebrow. 'Why? What's gone wrong?'

Walsh spread his hands. 'Roland's got friends in high places and I won't have him throwing dirt at my career, but I can't sit back and let him snub justice either.'

Aileen watched the exchange between the two men. Callan stared at Walsh for a while before nodding in understanding. 'I see.'

She hissed, exasperated. 'What do you see? If Roland threatened you, you can complain to another superior officer or Roland's superior.'

Walsh glowered, his face contorted in a withering frown under that large hat. 'Theory's easy but reality is dangerous.'

'Are you giving up? Besides, don't you think Roland has something to do with this? He doesn't want us investigating this for sure.' Aileen pressed.

Callan nudged her, hoping she'd keep her mouth shut. Callan didn't want to tell Walsh about Roland yet. He said, reiterating what he'd said after their visit with Roland, 'Statistics, that's all Marley and TJ are to him.'

Aileen slammed her hands on the table, speaking between clenched teeth, 'I can't believe this. You took an oath to protect people but-'

Callan tugged her sleeve. 'Oh, shut it.' He focused his attention on Walsh. 'Why have the past couple of days been shit?'

Walsh rubbed his forehead, which gleamed a rich cocoa under the bright natural light. 'There have been burglaries around here. Four jewellery stores in two nights and a handful of artefacts from an antique store. And it's all worth a bomb. They started the day after Marley's death. That's why I had to rush back here. We needed more officers on the team. Our local museum was broken into as well, although nothing was taken. They were supposed to have an auction there next week. They've hired more security for the event now and installed more security cams.'

Callan sat back. 'Burglaries hereabouts, ye say?' A memory flickered to life. Hadn't they seen Morticia Luna's men carry heavy suitcases the other night? 'How heavy can all these items be together?'

Walsh frowned at Callan, confused. 'Weigh? Judging by the items stolen, pretty heavy I should think, especially those antique vases and brass statues.'

Aileen leant in. 'Any that are particularly noteworthy?'

'I don't know much about those, but the museum directors say there was a lot of talk in the auctioneer circles about a set of porcelain vases that will be coming up for auction soon.' Walsh flicked a hand. 'Let's get to the matter at hand. If Roland doesn't want you investigating this, then you can use a better techie. And I can't be seen with you.'

He pivoted as a young teenager prodded in. The girl had cropped electric-purple hair, a pale face with slumped shoulders and vivid blue eyes behind large round spectacles. Silently, she slid in beside Walsh.

'This is Purple. She's a hacker.'

Purple dipped her chin in acknowledgement and slammed a drive onto the table between them. A laptop followed.

Her cream-white fingers flew over the keyboard and her eyes followed the screen. She plugged the drive in and turned the laptop to face them.

Callan muttered a few expletives and reached for the device. Before his hand could touch the screen, Purple swatted it away.

'Dude, no touching.' Her voice was high pitched and her gaze steady with confidence. He harrumphed.

'What are you showing us?' Aileen asked.

Walsh gestured, drawing their attention to him. 'I asked her to go to Vicky's and check out the computer TJ worked on. She's got some intel for us.'

Purple pushed her specs up her nose. 'TJ

searched a lot of shit, but he's got a file on that gal, Marley Watson. He's also got info on a bloke called Charlie, and, if you ask me, Charlie's a big softie. He gorges on ice cream sodas in case you wanted to know and is a lightweight.'

Purple tsked. 'But you want to know about this Marley Watson person. I hacked into TJ's email and he'd emailed her a few times. In the last email he asked for his money and where she'd gone and all that.'

Aileen leant in. 'Had he been to her flat?'

Purple shrugged nonchalantly, 'didn't say but because I got your gal's email, I hacked into that. Now that's an interesting woman you've got, takes after my elder sis, blackmailing and such.'

Gosh, where had Walsh found this girl? Callan liked her. She was certainly smart and good at her work.

Purple clicked a few keys. 'The Marley Watson person had a lot of emails, guess she was old-fashioned that way. And there's a log, a cash ledger of sorts that she'd emailed to herself. I guess you'd be interested in that sort of thing.'

Purple slapped a small bundle of papers on the table.

Aileen reached for them, leafing through. 'I knew it! I knew she'd have a detailed copy. Thanks for this.'

Purple squirmed in her seat. 'Don't get ahead of yourself, lady. There's more.'

Aileen raised surprised eyebrows. 'How much did you manage to dig in a day?'

'Five hours. I'm good that way.' The girl raised her chin. 'I got access into her emails, but her phone would've been a better option. This old man doesn't have it.' She jabbed a thumb at Walsh.

Walsh scowled. 'I'm not old! The phone's logged in as evidence. I cannot get it out without raising suspicion.'

Purple dropped her shoulders. 'Doesn't matter, I dug into the junk. She used email for everything.'

Walsh grinned at Aileen and Callan. 'Amazing, isn't she?'

Instead of grinning with pride, Purple rolled her eyes. 'I need to leave. Enough small talk.'

Callan smirked and muttered. 'Ah, I admire this woman.'

Purple didn't pay him any heed. Instead, she said. 'Marley had a calendar entry the day she hanged herself, just one. The rest of the calendar is empty. It said—in her words, not mine—she was about to be "a very rich bitch".'

Walsh frowned, 'No other hint of blackmail?'

Purple simply snapped another drive on the table. 'That's all the time I've got. The drive's got all the info. You can keep it.'

Without a goodbye, she slid out of her chair and walked away.

'An oddball but effective.' Walsh sat back

without explaining where he'd got acquainted with the girl.

Aileen produced her laptop and popped the drive in. Just then, Walsh's wife placed their steaming beverages and quietly excused herself, not before giving Walsh a sly smile.

Aileen slurped her mint tea. 'Purple's collected a lot of information-emails, financial records, and a list of TJ's clients…'

She pulled up Marley's emails and passed the laptop to Callan before lifting the printed booklet containing Marley's financial records.

Callan skimmed through the plethora of emails and turned to Aileen. 'What've ye got?'

Flipping through the pages, Aileen was busy studying the numbers.

She said, 'From what I can gauge from this cash ledger, Marley's just recorded who's paid her, not why. Her expenses are minimal: The regular pizza payments are so cheap that I wonder where the pizza place gets the money to purchase the flour from.'

Going through a few more pages, Aileen observed. 'There are no other regular payments, no payments to the grocery store nor any entertainment expense, but yes, she's paid rent to Morticia Luna every month. But for a single woman of Marley's age, these expenses are very unusual.'

On the other side of the table, Walsh was going through the other data.

'She's got a ton of emails.' Walsh observed.

Callan grunted but jerked a thumb at Aileen. 'What else do the finances say?'

Aileen peered over the papers, reciting her observations. 'Marley pays a portion of the money she receives to Martin Luther Hussey. But it isn't twenty percent like Hussey told us, it's approximately ten percent. These payments are like clockwork, every time she receives the money, she pays around ten percent to him.'

Walsh intertwined his fingers on the table. 'She could've been lying to Hussey and paying him less than she promised. Motive for murder.'

Callan made a note of this. 'Is there any other name of the list that matches with our list?'

Aileen shrugged. 'Charlie's but she's paid him for drinks she purchased when she was at Sláinte. What do the emails say?'

Callan landed her laptop back to her. 'Check for yourself.' He nodded at Walsh. 'Thanks for this.'

'As I said, I want to see justice. Now, if that's all, I've got to get back to those darned burglaries.' Walsh pushed away from the table.

'About that,' Callan raised a finger. 'It's linked to Morticia Luna.'

Walsh crossed his arms. 'How do you-'

Callan shared a look with Aileen. She nodded. Aye, it was safe to share information with this man. If he wanted to snub them, he wouldn't have risked his job this way. 'Sit down.' Callan told Walsh.

'Haven't got the time.' Walsh huffed and sat. 'Fire away.'

The crowd in the cafe had dwindled. Only a few groups remained, most of them huddled together.

Reaching into his bag, Callan pulled out the papers they'd found at Sláinte. 'We've found evidence that'll put Morticia Luna in prison.'

A server came and refilled their coffee cups.

Meticulously Aileen and Callan went through the papers with Walsh, and he listened with a patient ear.

'Ah hell.' Walsh had set his hat on the table a long time ago, his coffee gone cold. He ran a hand through his hair and sighed. 'You know this makes it all *really* difficult.'

Callan tucked his chin and nodded sympathetically.

Walsh continued. 'He's my boss and we have no proof on his underworld activities apart from this sheet. But I don't think he's above this. And with this data,' his eyes twinkled as he flipped through the papers. 'The tax authorities are about to have a field day, especially with Morticia Luna. We might even have a nice long celebration at the office.'

Callan raised a finger. 'Do not let Roland get away and grill Morticia Luna about the murders. She was there the day of the murder. We have several witnesses who placed her around Loch Fuar. We want to know if her goon killed Marley.' He also told him about what they'd seen at Morticia Luna's lair with the gentleman.

When Callan was done, Walsh patted the heap. 'Thanks for this. I'll get on with it then.'

He waved at them and took off.

Aileen went back to work over the emails.

Callan's calloused finger tapped the paper. 'These payments to Hussey. How does she make them?'

Aileen pursed her lips. 'Cash. It's got to be, judging by all the cash we found in her safe.'

'Bloody hell!' Callan crossed his arms. 'And the sod told us he'd never seen her in months. Of course they met to hand over the cash.'

'Why would he lie about seeing her?' Scowling at the screen, Aileen navigated to the emails.

'He's got something to hide. For example, he might be stealing more from her from the ATM that's her neighbour.'

Callan peeped into Aileen's laptop. She was reading the emails Purple had marked "MLH." All of them contained nothing more than six sentences. No greetings, no attachments. 'Strange.' He observed.

'What?' Aileen blinked. She pointed to something at the screen and explained. Marley's sent emails to an ID called MLH. It has no name, but a strange set of numbers used as suffixes. It's all very unusual and secretive.'

Callan read through each of the emails on screen.

Wire the money. A day late and I'll hit send.

Want to experience life in prison? Where's my money?

All the emails were threats to share data. With the police? Callan wasn't sure. None of the emails mentioned the sum of money Marley wanted MLH to wire.

They were all blackmails too.

'They are all succinct, taunting as well.' Aileen observed.

In another email Marley had simply written, *I'm not scared of your hounds.*

Aileen drummed her fingers on her thighs. 'Has to be Morticia Luna.'

Callan draped a hand over the seat, pointing at another email.

Heard your hounds sniffing, quit it. You know the account details, wire the money. All I have to do is send your files.

The last email ended with, *See ya soon at our place, Mars*

That email had been sent a day before her murder.

Callan scratched his chin. 'How much did she ask from Morticia Luna? It has to be a large amount if she was about to be "a very rich bitch".'

Aileen rubbed her forehead. 'It could've been. And the cottage was the drop off point. So where is the cash?'

Callan stared out front. 'Aye, where is it? Unless she didn't hand the money and killed Marley off. Morticia Luna could've paid the blackmail money but what's there to say Marley won't send this data to whoever she'd threatened to send it to in the first place.'

Aileen realised what he was saying, 'So killing her off means she won't speak, ever.' She shivered.

A waiter placed a plate of muffins on the table. 'Mrs Walsh would like feedback on these. She's trying out a new recipe.'

The muffins were fluffy with sprinkles and chocolate icing.

Callan grinned. 'Thank ye.' He dug into one, moaning. 'Wow, this is good!'

Aileen rolled her eyes. 'We're solving a case, remember?'

He nodded, wiping the icing stuck to his lips. 'It's hazelnut chocolate. Sorry, can't resist.'

Chuckling at him, Aileen tried a bite. 'Yes, it is delicious!'

Done, Callan tapped a finger on the table 'Morticia Luna's never been associated with goons. Thus, if she were to murder Marley, why do it herself when she's got people to do it for her. And if she had plans to do the deed, why would she go about showing her face around town? For one that "Houndress and Co." thing is a red flag.'

Aileen sighed and sat back. 'You mean that Morticia Luna could have gone to Loch Fuar, but we aren't really sure whether she actually killed Marley.'

'Something like that. I think we need to head back to the hotel room and go through our notes, brainstorm. We might even find the answer.'

CHAPTER SIXTEEN

Aileen sat on the chair and sighed. Her head was pounding, but her gut told her she was close. They had all that they needed to crack this thing wide open.

Callan plopped into the other chair and pulled out his notepad. 'What do we ken?'

Sipping a glass of water, Aileen stared at the floor. 'Marley Watson came to Loch Fuar on Saturday morning with a suitcase. Another car with the red-haired man followed her. She parked the car at the parking lot and had arrangements to turn it in the following day, since it was a rental. Marley didn't take her suitcase along but had equipment with her to fix the beam.'

Callan gestured for her to halt. 'At this point we have Morticia Luna and her goon pull into the lot.

She left for the town and her goon took the hounds with him. And let's assume he had the money too.'

Aileen nodded. 'Then in the evening someone murdered Marley. At around five, Morticia Luna made a dash for the parking lot. She got in and raced away with the same man along with her hounds.'

Callan took over. 'But her goons attacked us, and we found her at Freddie's a couple of days later. And we have mounting evidence about her rings, thanks to Marley. TJ was killed at the same time he said something about Hounds. And someone hurt ye when ye asked around for Morticia Luna.'

Flipping the pages of her yellow notepad, Aileen read through the notes.

She stood, pacing as she thought. 'Morticia Luna is also connected to DCI Kevin Roland. He has the power to solve this crime and hence the power to commit it. But would he risk an illustrious career? Even if that illustrious career was a hoax?'

'Unlikely, but he might have been confident that no one would find out.' Callan answered.

Tugging at her ears, Aileen continued to pace. The carpeted floor muffled her footsteps. She'd sprayed some of her refreshing lemongrass air freshener that never failed to calm her nerves.

Suddenly, she paused. 'Why don't we eliminate each suspect? Morticia Luna's on there. So, what about the others?'

Callan went to the window and stared out. It was a pleasant afternoon, and the tourists milled about, enjoying the day with not a care in the world. 'Freddie is the least likely of the lot.' Callan announced.

Aileen seconded that opinion. 'Marley was an ATM for him. Kill her and his cash inflow stops. Unless this is a crime of passion where he killed her in rage. But then why would they be at Loch Fuar and not in that building?'

She ticked Freddie off her list and moved to the next. 'Martin Luther Hussey.' She announced.

Callan turned to her. 'He's got the bruises and the money. Alibi? Dinnae ken. Add in the motive of receiving only half the money Marley had promised.'

Aileen circled his name. 'He stays on our list. Then let's move on to Charlie. I can't see any other motive rather than blackmail.'

Pushing his hands in his pockets, Callan walked to her and peered at the notepad. 'What if Marley had planned for two drop-offs that day? Charlie in the morning and Morticia Luna in the evening?'

'Two of her targets paying her on the same day? It would make her very rich, as she'd wanted to be that day. That's entirely possible. Instead, one of her targets did her in.'

Aileen made a note of this theory.

When her arm cramped, she placed the notebook on the coffee table. 'We are left with Kevin

Roland, Martin Luther Hussey, Charlie, and Morticia Luna's goon.'

Callan plopped onto the other chair and shut his eyes. 'Put yerself in Marley's shoes.'

Aileen shut her eyes, too, and did as he told her.

Was Marley scared that day or excited?

Scared. Aileen's mind said. *Why?* Marley wasn't an independent woman.

How did Aileen know that? *Thanks to those social media posts about women being dependents.*

But Marley had been celebrating. She hadn't been scared. Aileen spoke aloud. 'Marley wasn't scared that day, she was celebrating. Because she got the money from Charlie? But what did she blackmail him with?'

Aileen reached for her laptop and scanned those notebooks again. Then she pulled up the emails. 'Marley's made a copy of the information she had on Charlie. But there is nothing here that is incriminating and that the police don't know. And she hasn't sent any emails to Charlie.'

Callan sighed. 'No, she hasn't. I got an email from that colleague whom I had asked to search *ilovemurder*. It's a dormant account now. A dead end.'

'What's Charlie's connection to those eyes? Is he smart enough to find our emails and threaten us?' Aileen questioned.

'Course not. That was all Morticia Luna. So, if

Marley hasn't emailed Charlie, she has to have asked him in person,' Callan said.

They each fell silent. Until they both shook their head. 'But what did she blackmail him with?' Aileen asked.

'Nothing.' Callan stood. 'Because Charlie was never at the cottage.'

Aileen stood as well. 'No, it was someone else.'

Callan took a step closer to Aileen. 'Someone Marley *trusted*.'

Aileen too took a step towards Callan. 'Someone who wanted more money than Marley was willing to give.'

He nodded and bent to look Aileen in the eye. They were almost nose to nose. 'Aye, Marley was celebrating with her business partner that day.'

Now beaming, they said in unison, 'Martin Luther Hussey.'

Aileen grabbed Callan's arms, forgetting all about the pain. 'He is the one who took the money, the cash that Morticia Luna paid Marley. He was the one loitering outside Sláinte and Marley's house. And he was the one who asked us to stay away.'

Callan agreed. 'He spent cash, as he pointed out to me, on that gold chain and the perfume. And he reeked of cigarettes, just like the person who killed TJ did. Hussey didn't want us to figure out about those papers at Sláinte because then Morticia Luna would point the finger at him. Her goon witnessed the murder, that's what made her run for it and hightail out of Loch Fuar.'

Aileen took a deep breath. 'Now all we need is evidence.'

They sat silently thinking about how they could extract evidence. The red wig and the hound mask were burning a hole in Callan's bag, but damn it, he couldn't wait for a DNA report.

For once in his life, Callan planned. He turned to Aileen, who snoozed on the chair, the yellow notepad still perched on her thigh.

The woman was tired but didn't say so. Callan nudged her awake. If everything went to plan, he'd get Martin Luther Hussey behind bars.

His phone rang, and startled Aileen awake. 'What?' She mumbled, confused.

Whipping it out of his pocket, Callan greeted. 'Hello?'

There was a pause before Walsh spoke. 'Cameron. We got Morticia Luna in for questioning. It looks bad for her. I'm sure her lawyer will try to get her out of it, but we've got solid evidence now and a warrant's coming through for her place. I'm sure we'll find originals there. But she won't confess to killing Marley or TJ. She says it was the boyfriend.'

Callan sat back. 'We ken it's him. I was wondering if ye could get him in.'

Walsh sighed. 'Too late, he's AWOL. My officers can't track him down.'

'How is that possible?' Callan barked.

'We found his house empty. He had plans to take off for a while now, at least that's what we think.' Walsh explained.

'I've got a plan, but I need yer help.' Callan ventured.

It didn't take long for Walsh to respond. 'What do you need?'

'First, we need to type a letter to the killer.' Callan began.

WHILE WALSH UTILISED THE TIME TO ASSEMBLE A team and work on getting Morticia Luna arrested, Callan wrote the letter.

Aileen, they'd mutually agreed, was far too polite to word it in such a manner as to cause offence. Callan, on the other hand, had no qualms about hurting someone.

Posing as another thug, they'd written to their potential killer, saying they knew who'd killed Marley and propositioning to keep quiet in exchange for cash. They'd meet the killer under a famous bridge in Loch Heaven, which would be just dingy and dark enough.

Walsh called in the late afternoon, saying all the plans were in place. 'Roland's not happy about this. He's denying ever meeting Morticia Luna. But most of our team's at her house and the lair now. I just got a call, Morticia Luna Ltd is coming down, thanks to you.'

Callan waved him off. 'It's our duty as officers of the law, Walsh.'

'Not everyone's.' He said and went back to clean the mess Roland had created. They'd deal with him by the book.

Aileen and Callan too prepared for their stake-out. It was Aileen's first, and she only hoped the blasted pain medicines didn't tire her out.

Callan chuckled. 'I doubt ye'll sleep for a week.' He was dressed in his all black and could easily pass off as a rough goon himself.

He hadn't worn his badge prominently to stay incognito.

When Walsh pulled up outside the hotel to pick Aileen, she squeezed Callan's arm. 'Be careful.'

He waved her off. Callan wasn't worried, he was invigorated. It had been a while since he'd staged such an operation.

Rubbing his hands together in anticipation, Callan followed Walsh's car till he reached a fork in the road. Instead of driving uphill, he drove towards the secluded underpass.

It was barely half-past eleven, and he was to

meet Hussey at one in the night. He had plenty of time.

This area was just like the one surrounding Marley's flat. Most squatters huddled out of the cold, warmer under the bridge.

A street light hummed like a bee and flickered.

He parked the car and sank into the shadows. To someone passing by, the car was parked here. The dark interiors and his black clothes made him invisible.

Satisfied with the position he'd parked the car in, Callan cut the engine. He could see all the vehicles that entered or exited the underpass from here. And he also had the opportunity to sneak on someone while staying in the shadows. It was a good vantage point.

He kicked back and mused to himself.

Walsh had succeeded in getting Morticia Luna behind bars. His team had found a lot of incriminating evidence against her at that fortress she called home.

It was because of that operation that Walsh couldn't spare more men or the equipment. Callan was connected via the radio to Walsh, but he hadn't worn a vest. It was dangerous, but more wasted time would allow Hussey to get away. And they couldn't let that happen.

Now all that remained were Roland and Martin Luther Hussey.

WHEN EYES DON'T LIE

And he could not wait to see them both behind bars.

CHAPTER SEVENTEEN

Aileen pursed her lips and looked around her. 'Well, this is fun.'

It was half-past eleven, and they were ready. A few of Walsh's officer pals had agreed to help, ready to face Roland's wrath if it came to that. They all wanted justice, and they were riding high on Morticia Luna's capture.

Aileen couldn't sit with Callan, as he was to meet with the killer. She would be with Walsh.

The Loch Heaven detective had already stationed some of his men incognito around their meeting spot. Their murderer wouldn't know what hit him.

Walsh stationed his black car over a mound overlooking the bridge. He had a pair of binoculars with him.

The detective cackled with laughter at her sarcastic tone. He was so loud, Aileen shuddered. 'There's no need to whisper. I hope you have patience because this will take a while. Our killer has an hour and a half to show up.'

As Callan had pointed out many times before, Aileen never had enough patience. She wasn't just cut out for it. The suspense was killing her. She wanted to witness the showdown.

Half an hour in, a yawn escaped. She bit her lips, no she couldn't sleep.

Walsh, at home with this stakeout deal, sat munching potato crisps. Aileen didn't bother to point out the crumbs he'd littered over his seat.

Instead, she gazed at the starry sky. It was magnificent, as if a little girl had sprinkled glitter on black paper.

The moonless night caused Aileen's nerves to jitter thinking of Callan down there, all alone in that dingy area. Albeit, he had police officers guarding his back, but they weren't *his* people. Despite the common uniform, he didn't know them.

As if you could guard him any better.

Aileen loosened her tensed muscles. Callan had been acting strange lately. He had complimented her and hadn't picked as many fights. She enjoyed their verbal sparring, but this softer side of his made her heart flutter.

Warmth flooded her cheeks as she thought of their wrestling match at the cottage in Loch Fuar. It had been foolhardy, but the compliments Callan had paid her a couple of days before still reverberated in her mind.

He thought she was as playful and strong as the ninety-year-old Siobhan? Aileen would be glad if she was even a wee bit like her gran.

But what he'd said had been true.

Aileen had caught some eminent people embezzling cash and cheating their customers, and she had caught a murderer. She internally scoffed. Here she was on a stakeout, the former "risk-less" accountant, awaiting a criminal.

The radio crackled, and Callan's drawl came through. 'We've fifteen minutes till the moment of truth, don't doze off.'

Walsh chuckled. 'Wide awake, Cameron. We're ready for a ball.'

The radio was a respite for Aileen. At least Callan could communicate with them through it.

There hadn't been time to call a tech team to give them eyes and ears into Callan's car. And arranging a team meant a lot of paperwork. Instead, they'd just grabbed basic gear.

Time ticked by rather slowly.

Aileen took to twiddling her thumbs and fidgeting. She didn't know how to start a conversation with DI Declan Walsh. And the detective sat mum, lost in his own thoughts, devouring that same bag of crisps.

At least he ate in a civilised manner. Aileen cracked a small smile. Callan, God, that man ate as if he were a starved ape. But what did one expect from oafs?

An oaf who'd work his guts off to give someone justice. Even put his life on the line for a stranger.

The clock struck one, and Aileen's heart began its nervous dance.

She intertwined her fingers tightly and bunched her shoulders. Her throat was dry, and she was desperate for a glass of water.

The darkness under the bridge was silent, and yet Callan sat in his car patiently. Their "meeting spot" was lit by the mere golden hue of a street lamp.

Aileen could almost taste the horridness of human fluids.

The clock struck five minutes past one, and there was still no movement.

Involuntarily, she drummed a rhythm onto her trouser clad thighs. Her heart frantic, she wished Callan would speak through the radio, check in and assure them he was doing okay.

Why was he so silent, sitting alone in that dark place?

Her hands were clammy. They were cold against the warmth of her thigh.

Another ten minutes passed. The silence stretching into an abyss of nothingness.

Just as a huge yawn threatened to escape, a bike pulled up in front of Callan's car.

Aileen straightened, peering through the darkness at the scene unfolding below her. Her heart went wild, beating more than she could take. Fear rose, gripped her throat as a man clambered off the bike.

Leaning on the dashboard, she observed with unblinking eyes.

The man stood to his full height, shaking a long curly mane. He wasn't any of their suspects. Worry built inside her.

Walsh had binoculars trained on the scene.

Even though she couldn't make out the details, Aileen saw the man twirl before peering at Callan's car.

Aileen wanted to do something, anything. But Callan was too far away. How could he be so patient?

The bike-man shook his head, his hair bouncing, and strode away into the dark.

What in the-

Beside her, Walsh laughed. 'The sod's peeing! Good God.' He rubbed the tears from his eyes.

He thought this was a joke? That man could be a murderer for all Aileen cared, and Callan was a sitting duck.

Outraged she was about to rebuke when the man staggered into the dim light, fixing his trousers. He mounted his bike, its purr alive in the silent night. And without a backward glance, drove the way he'd come.

Aileen blinked just as the radio came alive again.

'False call, I say we wait fifteen more minutes.'

Walsh responded in an affirmative.

The time on Aileen's watch told her it was a quarter to two.

Her heart beat quieted as the night waned on. Fifteen minutes could've been three hours. With Aileen barely breathing, anticipation was tangible in the air.

Where was their killer?

At precisely two am, Callan's car purred to life, and he pulled out of the waiting area. Walsh loitered as Callan circled the small mound and came to a halt beside them.

Aileen pushed the door open and scrambled out. Her throat was parched as if she'd been in the desert, and her limbs ached.

Cold air slapped her face. The summer air was light, a small breeze playing with the grass under her feet.

Callan climbed out of his rugged vehicle. He had refused to "dress for the showdown." They'd agreed that he'd better suit the situation in black. The scowl he wore on his face was his own patent—apart from that annoying smirk—but it gave him an air of being nasty.

Aileen wanted to fling her arms around him and assure herself he was okay. Instead, she shuffled her feet. She was being unnatural, this entire situation had her in a mess.

Walsh rounded the car and came to a halt in front of Callan. 'What do you think?'

'He either saw through us or he's a coward. Or he's dead.'

Walsh scrunched his face, 'Don't think so. This person's a sucker for money and wants to keep himself isolated. But I don't think Hussey's got the brains to figure our plot out. Unless... Unless someone tipped them off.'

WALSH DROVE OFF, BUMMED THEIR PLAN HAD LED TO nothing. But he had bigger fish to fry. He'd probably be up all-night.

As his car disappeared down the road, Callan kicked a stone in front of him. 'Bloody hell! I make one plan and it fails!'

She clenched her fist. 'I know we spent the entire day planning it-'

Callan cut her off as he raged. 'An entire day we could've caught the killer. And now? He's slipped away. An entire day. He sat laughing at us when we've been running around like headless chickens. Where does that lead us? We've no leads and no way to ken where our killer is.'

'Hussey isn't that brilliant, but we are, especially

together. I'm sure we'll figure something out.' She reassured him.

Callan kicked his car's wheel and slammed his hands on the hood. 'Let's get back. Eejit!' With one last kick, he slid into the driver's seat. 'Walsh should wait for those DNA results and then they can search for the eejit. He'll be long gone then, mark my words!'

Aileen'd never seen him rage this way. She rounded the car and took her seat. 'Deep breaths, Callan.'

He started the car's engine. 'Shit!' He swore one last time and took three deep breaths.

They started for their hotel in silence.

Callan's gaze was riveted on the road, but Aileen smiled to herself. He wasn't gripping the steering wheel as if his life depended on it.

A few minutes in, Callan sniffed the air.

Aileen raised an eyebrow.

'Ye stink.' Came the bland response. So much for the compliments he'd given her the other day. At least he was back to jesting.

Aileen appraised herself. She stank. The weird chemical mixture of adrenaline and fear had made her sweat profusely. Adding to that, her head throbbed, and her bandaged arm itched. For that, all he had to say was she stank.

'Crude oaf!' She muttered instead and made Callan laugh.

He surprised her by playing along. 'I really like that name. What should we call ye?'

Callan was on a roll. 'Stinky—Ouch! That hurt.' He guffawed with laughter at her scowl. She'd only lightly punched him in the arm.

'I'm not stinky.' She reprimanded him.

'Aye, ye aren't. Ye are a petite warrior. Though I need a better name than that.' Callan shrugged.

Aileen smiled. 'You'll get there.'

Callan licked his lips, thinking. 'How about Clever Clogs? Or Accountant Logs?' He chuckled to himself.

God, this… This… Infuriating man!

Aileen raised her chin defiantly. 'How about Ms Holmes?'

Callan opened his mouth to answer when a distinct click sounded from the back seat. It was a distinguished snick of a gun.

CHAPTER EIGHTEEN

An involuntary tremor snapped across Callan's back when the cold barrel touched the base of his neck. A hand encircled Aileen's throat and squeezed.

'Drive as I tell ye or yer sassy little wench is dead.'

It was Hussey.

The barrel left Callan's neck and touched Aileen's head instead. She whimpered.

Callan grasped the steering wheel tighter. His first goal was to keep Aileen safe.

'Move down the Highway.' Hussey ordered.

Quenching the unusual heaviness in his heart, Callan did as he was told. Hussey wouldn't keep them alive any longer than it would take to dispose of them. Doing something stupid now would endanger the few civilian cars on the road.

Callan drove awhile, Hussey still breathing down his neck. Aileen sat petrified by his side.

Light painted the inky sky. It was almost dawn, but would they live to experience this new day?

Callan cast a sidelong glance at Aileen. He hoped she didn't do something stupid.

'Take the trail here.' Hussey instructed.

They swayed as the car took the unkempt mud road.

Hopefully Hussey had a good grip over the gun's trigger. Even if he cursed Aileen's mind more often than not, Callan wanted her brain intact.

Aileen's voice was a murmur. 'Why are you doing this?'

Hussey pressed the gun tighter into the base of her skull.

A water body glittered in the early light. It was dark grey under the nascent morning sun; the rays shining on the oscillating water.

'Out!' Hussey spat.

Callan obeyed, his eyes spying around them.

Dense foliage still thick with spring leaves made the entire scene darker than the dawn lightening the sky. They seemed to be in a forest of sorts with not a soul to hear their pleas.

If he could get the sod away from Aileen, he'd be able to turn the tables, hopefully.

Aileen trembled as she got off the car, keeping a straight face. She was indeed a strong woman. And he needed her to keep her cool at this moment.

Callan sneered. 'Come on, Hussey, bullying a woman to get me to do yer bidding? Tell us what ye did.'

Hussey growled. 'You think yer smart, eh? Sending me that email as if I'd walk right in yer trap. I'm telling ye no nothing. I'm going to kill ye.'

But Callan didn't back down. 'Who's yer spy?'

Hussey snarled. 'I don't need one, bastard.'

'Let the woman go and let's fight like real men: hand to hand.' Callan baited.

Hussey pressed the barrel tighter to Aileen's head. Her face was stoic, albeit a whimper slipped through. Aileen's body was rigid, and her hands clenched so tight, her knuckles had gone white.

'I told ye, I'm no fool. Enough of this chatter.' Hussey gestured to Callan's police issue. 'Drop yer gun.'

Callan complied and carefully placed the gun on the ground.

Hussey held Aileen in front of his chest at such an angle, he couldn't dare take a shot that might hit her.

Somewhere a bird greeted "good morning," waking its friends. So far, this dawn had been anything but good.

'Lay on yer stomach.' Hussey commanded. Damned if Callan listened to that. This eejit would shoot him through the chest.

Instead, he raised his chin. 'Ye might kill us, but Walsh knows it's ye.'

Hussey grinned as he towered over Aileen. 'Who said I'd be here waiting for him? Get down on yer stomach!'

When Hussey tightened his grip on her, Aileen struggled. 'Shut up, ye wench!'

Seeing Hussey distracted, Callan took his chance. He had a precious few seconds. Lunging forward, he gripped his gun and shot.

It was a wide shot, but it startled Hussey.

Aileen—thank God for her presence of mind—slipped out of his grasp. She collapsed into the foliage and rolled away.

Callan pounced. Paying no heed to his aching knee, he kicked the gun out of Hussey's hand.

Both men landed on dried leaves and fallen tree branches, grunting their protests.

Hussey barely had time to deflect Callan's blow to his ribs. Instead of fighting, the man scrambled trying to free himself from Callan's muscled weight.

In a vain attempt, Hussey punched Callan in the side. More kicks, punches, and groans sounded in the secluded forest, at contrast to the beautiful birdsong.

Callan hoped Aileen had the street smarts to get away to safety. She was the last thing he needed to worry about.

Hussey tried to push Callan away, but he merely wrestled the man onto his back. Now if only he could pivot this poor excuse of a man onto his stomach.

Just when Callan thought he'd got a good grip over Hussey, the feartie slammed a stone on his head.

Blinding pain disoriented him, enough to lose his grasp on Hussey. Instead of finishing the deed, the ruffian scurried away.

Callan touched the side of his head gingerly, before steadying himself as best he could. It wasn't a deep wound, but his vision was slightly hazy. Blinking, he righted his blurring vision.

The forest now gradually came alive under the dim morning light. The songs of the birds could be heard and the sound of a gun clicking.

Pushing against the dry leaves, Callan managed to stand in a warrior stance. Pain zinged through his entire body. The cuts he'd got from falling on the tree branches stung tremendously.

Hussey aimed his gun at Callan, ready to fire.

Callan tried mocking him. 'Scared to fight like a man, eh, Hussey?'

'Shut up, shut up ye! Get down.' Hussey hissed.

Callan spread his hands wide. 'Come on, ye ken ye'd enjoy a bit of a tussle. It'll make ye feel good.'

Hussey fired, aiming straight for his chest, but Callan anticipated his move—the result of his years of training and experience—and dived to the side.

The leaves rustled beneath him. The bullet missed his chest but scraped his already injured arm.

Callan stifled a groan of pain.

That eejit!

He leaped, eyes darting for his own issue, but it was nowhere to be seen in that dry foliage littering the ground. It was still too inky to see clearly.

Hussey fired another shot. The man was a lunatic. Gunpowder littered the air. But he hadn't aimed it well. The shot slammed somewhere above Callan's crown.

If Hussey was expecting Callan to flinch, he'd be sorely disappointed.

Callan cursed his damned arm and prepared to combat the sod.

But Hussey cackled with laughter and wagged his gun. 'Drop on yer knees and prepare to listen to this story.'

'Telling me how ye killed Marley, eh?'

The sod smirked. 'Ye wanted to ken, didn't ye? I'll indulge yer dying wish.'

'Marley Watson was a greedy wench. She wanted to milk Morticia Luna for her cash. And she'd planned it out well for someone as stupid as she was. Got that rat, TJ, to do her stuff for her. She had it all, showed me too, all those records that could put Morticia Luna behind bars. What an opportunity! But she couldn't do it alone now, could she? We were business partners. Marley had it in her mind that we were something more. Eejit.' He spat on the ground.

Callan didn't dare move. He wanted Hussey to

confess. He'd tackle that man into submission anyway he could. 'How did ye do the deed?'

Hussey snarled, showing his teeth. 'Marley fixed the cottage for us to spend the night. She wanted to camp out there. Then she had TJ email Morticia Luna asking for cash.'

'So Morticia Luna could drop off the money?'

'Aye. And I'd get my share. I cracked open a bottle of champagne to celebrate. We were going to be rich! But guess what?' He snarled. 'That wench says she'd only give me ten percent. Ten percent! Says I didn't do much to help. Then she tells me she'd always been paying me ten percent from all that blackmail money she got regularly from her cows. We'd agreed I'd get twenty!'

Hussey's roar reverberated through the forest, startling a few birds.

'Lost it then, I did.' He brandished his teeth. 'No woman one ups me! Especially not a rag like her. I taught her a lesson. She was no match to me, trying to stop me from choking her. I tied a loop around her neck. And wow, she died right there, hanging.'

Callan gritted his teeth. 'What did ye do after ye killed her?'

Hussey smirked. 'Put that light on. Marley was afraid of the dark.' He chuckled. 'She'd not be afraid anymore. She was the dark now. I left her hanging there, took all the cash, all mine! It'll help me get away now. They'll never find me.'

He pointed the gun right at Callan's chest, but something stopped him from shooting.

Aileen's sharp voice broke through the birdsong. 'Drop your weapon or I'll fire.'

So much for her street smartness…

Callan's arm stung now, so did his head, but he'd be damned if he'd let pain win this round. Callan was a trained detective for God's sakes, and he'd taken an oath to keep civilians safe, civilians like Aileen.

Now all he could do was observe as Hussey contemplated taking the shot.

Aileen was barely visible from behind the thug, but a gun was powerful, even in the hands of the tiniest of tigers.

Her voice was steely. 'Come on, Hussey, you know you've been caught. Surrender.'

Hussey's outstretched hand shook, sweat beaded his forehead.

Aileen nudged him. 'The police know what you've done. Everyone knows. I've recorded that entire confession. There's no point in running away. Surrender.'

She faked that confidence because her voice held a slight tremble, but Hussey, in his quaking terror, could never call her bluff.

Instead, he dropped his hand.

As Callan stepped forward to arrest him, Hussey raised it again.

But Aileen was quicker. She slammed her foot

into his knee.

He staggered and collapsed on the ground.

Shouting a war cry, Aileen kicked his ribs. Hard. *Banlaoch*...

But Callan was too sleepy to witness the show. His limbs grew tired and the need to sleep overpowered him. There, in that dry foliage, he sat on the ground. Perhaps he should nap for a while...

TREMBLES OF FEAR RACED THROUGH AILEEN'S BODY, but they didn't hold a candle to the adrenaline pumping through her veins. Her rage roared. She wouldn't let this sorry excuse for a man injure Callan. Not when he'd saved her life!

Not sure of what her online classes had taught her, she did the only kick she'd ever been successful at. She kicked Hussey below the belt.

He howled and writhed in the mud.

Aileen picked up his fallen gun. On shaky legs, she stepped back one leg after the other when she heard another thud.

Good God! Callan was sprawled on the ground. He appeared to have taken a bath in his own blood! His forehead sparkled red and his black shirt was drenched in sweat and more blood. His arm, just where it had been sliced, had split open again and was bleeding too profusely for her liking.

She rushed to his side. Where was Walsh? She'd

called him before running back to grab Callan's gun.

Seeing Hussey point a gun at her oaf, something had snapped inside her. Before she'd known what she was doing, Aileen had threatened the man.

Pride bubbled in her heart. She'd succeeded in tackling a criminal and had saved her man! Seeing a gun trained on him had almost shattered her heart to pieces. Yes, Callan meant something to her.

This was not the time to analyse her emotions though. Aileen snapped out of it. Callan needed her.

She approached him just when he muttered something unintelligible and twitched his shoulders.

Using his injured arm, Callan slapped his leg only to grimace and let out a string of expletives. 'Damned leg!'

'Are you out of your mind? Stop, stop!' Aileen held his injured arm in her grasp. Her head hurt, and her left arm was of no use.

When he continued to lean on his arse and swear, she rebuked him with a stern voice. 'That's only making it bleed more! I'm no good at first aid. Hold on, Walsh's on his way.'

'Hold on? This... This freaking prick of a leg! I'm a police officer-'

'Who saved my life-'

Aileen couldn't believe this, he'd been so calm,

so collected. His one wrong move and she'd be dead before she knew it. And here he was, cussing himself.

But Callan's tirade didn't stop. He yelled at her. 'What were ye thinking coming back here? Are ye okay? Why didn't ye run away? Damn, I have to snap the handcuffs on him!'

She rubbed his back. 'Callan, you need to calm down. Give me the handcuffs.'

She plucked the handcuffs from where they'd fallen on the ground and jogged over to Hussey who was still on the ground, crying.

For her safety, she kicked him in his ribs again before snapping on the handcuffs.

Behind her, Callan groaned. He was still agitated but his eyes had drooped. And he was losing a lot of blood.

Aileen searched her trousers and produced a neatly pressed white handkerchief. Carefully, she wrapped it around Callan's wound. Grimacing when he whimpered.

Callan tugged his arm lightly but was too oblivious to protest. From what little she knew, it was best he didn't lose consciousness.

'Callan! Callan! Stay still, stay awake.' She demanded of that infuriating oaf.

As if he'd taken a vow to never listen to her, his eyes almost entirely closed.

In a desperate attempt, Aileen did what she'd

wanted to do from the first time she'd encountered him—she slapped him hard.

Callan groaned, his eyes fluttering. His weak hand tried pushing her away.

When his head lolled back, slipping, she back handed his other cheek.

She must have hit him hard enough for his cheek to turn red. But she was at the brim of slipping over into hysteria. Somewhere, the sensible portion of her brain told her she was harming him and that patting his face was a better idea.

To Hell with that sensible part.

In Callan's own words, she wouldn't let this eejit sleep.

With more force, she slapped him again.

Callan raised a trembling hand as sirens drowned the forest in shades of red and blue.

'You are *not* sleeping! You work your arse off and now sleep? Lazy!' Another slap.

At once several uniformed men and women rushed towards them.

Someone plucked Aileen off the ground and led her away. People dressed in green uniforms hunched over Callan.

A blanket was draped over her trembling shoulders, but her throat was parched, and her palms stung.

The paramedics loaded Callan into the ambulance, but he was still incoherent. Refusing to be left behind, Aileen boosted herself beside Callan.

She breathed—through the hysteria, her pain and her spiralling thoughts.

Eventually, she glanced at her bright red hands, wincing when they smarted. Her cast hung loosely, her injured arm ached.

The paramedic said something, but Aileen couldn't pay him any heed. She regarded the unconscious Callan, an oxygen mask attached to his face.

Where was his scowl? His smirk or his cussing?

Aileen closed her eyes when tears threatened to escape.

Alone in that ambulance, she silently wept.

THE REST OF THE JOURNEY TO THE HOSPITAL SPED by until they rushed Callan into surgery.

Aileen paced in a waiting room of sorts. When another paramedic tried assisting her, she pushed him away but allowed him to wrap another blanket around her.

Callan hadn't been coherent when they'd taken him inside, and no matter how much she tried swearing at him, he wouldn't wake.

A sombre Walsh plodded in. 'Got Hussey in custody. That kick did a number on him. He's still sobbing.'

But Aileen wasn't in a mood to listen.

Walsh thrust his hands into his pockets. 'I'll need statements but um, those can wait.'

They'd better wait. A sudden rage overtook the fear. Everything better wait till Callan got better. And when he did? She'd have a word with that oaf. Putting his life on the line for her and then lying on the ground bleeding? That was... That was the scariest thing she'd ever witnessed.

Callan would be fine, he had to be. That... That... *Her* oaf!

Who'd asked him to leap into harm's way? Good God, what if he hadn't stayed calm? They'd all be lying dead in a ditch.

Walsh stepped into her field of vision. 'Do you need someone to inspect that arm?'

Aileen shook her head, her heart swelling with fear for Callan.

Walsh shuffled his feet, clearly uncomfortable.

They lapsed into silence.

Callan, Aileen's entire being screamed, prayed that he was okay. Between prayers, Aileen sent an uncharacteristic profanity Callan's way.

After what seemed like hours, a white-jacketed doctor strode in with a clipboard.

'We stitched the wound. Mr Cameron needs rest, but he'll be fine.'

Aileen let out a relieved groan and crumbled into a chair. Shutting her eyes, she drifted away into oblivion.

A few hours later, Walsh flashed his badge and

asked to meet with Callan. They let him in, and Aileen strode along.

The nurse tried to object but one glare shut him up. Beside her, Walsh chuckled but didn't say a word.

Someone pulled a pastel blue curtain aside to reveal a very sleepy-eyed Callan.

Despite his disposition, he picked on Aileen. 'Ah, the angered demon from Hell has arrived.'

Walsh assessed her appearance. 'You've got blood and dirt all over you.'

Aileen lifted her chin. She'd saved Callan's arse, hadn't she? She had finally made the right decision in tagging along and pointing the gun at Hussey. A heavy ball of fear had settled in her gut, but she'd done it. She'd taken the right decision and got justice for Marley and TJ. Her mission was complete.

Aileen swallowed. 'Nice outfit.'

Callan was covered in a thin blue blanket and wore a polka dotted hospital gown.

His voice was gruff, but he managed a smirk. 'Ye wore something like this not so long ago.'

Aileen made a mental note of teaching that crude oaf some manners and the magic of gratitude.

Walsh pointed at Callan's face. 'Nice tattoo.'

For the first time, she really gazed at him and gasped aloud.

Callan's cheeks had an imprint of her hand from when she'd slapped him!

His blue orbs flashed, narrowing on her. 'They showed it to me.' He grimaced. 'Someone definitely took all their rage out on a poor disabled man, especially when he could not fight back.'

Aileen bit her lip. Her relief at seeing him alive broke through her haughty persona. That oaf was as fit as a fiddle, healthy enough to taunt her. If he was expecting a rise from her, he'd be sorely disappointed.

She was knackered and the machines beeping around Callan, mixed with the sterilised stench of hospital, doused her anger. She trudged towards him, glaring at the lopsided grin on Callan's face.

He'd scared her even more than Hussey's stupid gun. If she'd let him fall unconscious back in the forest, he wouldn't be taunting her now. Perhaps he wouldn't even be breathing.

Aileen cleared her mind of those obnoxious thoughts. She slid onto the stool that stood by his bedside. The curtain shuffled next to her as the nurse and Walsh left them alone.

She chanced another glance at Callan's bruised face and wagged a finger at him. 'You deserve it, you know.'

Callan's lips lifted in a small smile, but it ended in a grimace. He was covered in aches and bruises caused by rolling around on tree branches.

Aileen gulped. 'You could've died! You... Thank you for saving my arse.'

With a rough voice barely more than a whisper, he said, 'I've taken an oath to protect.'

'Yes, but there are a few who go above and beyond. And you go above and beyond, every time.'

The shock of the last few days caught up with Aileen; the terror at being accosted in an alley, choked, held at gunpoint, being run off the road and seeing the dead bodies. And to tie it up, Callan almost lost consciousness.

Aileen grabbed onto his calloused hand, just staring at it, glad to take in his warmth and share hers with him. She pressed his hand to her forehead, desperately trying to keep the tears from escaping.

'You slap really well.' He joked, still weak.

Taking a moment to thank anyone who was listening for keeping Callan safe, she sat up.

Swallowing the lump of fear that had taken a permanent residency for the last few hours, Aileen whispered. 'If you were hurt, who'd I argue with?'

Callan snorted and coughed. 'Hurt? You mean died?'

Aileen gripped the mattress. She refused to even say that dreaded word. 'Loch Fuar needs you to protect its people.'

A grim smile came over Callan's face. 'Hardly, I'm not special.'

She narrowed her eyes. 'Yes, you are. What would Douglas's cat do without you? You are a part of Loch Fuar, Callan. And you are well appreciated for what you do for the people. Why, Isla just sent me a bunch of messages from everyone you could think of, old Sam included. They are all worried for you.'

He fell silent, but emotion misted his eyes. Ultimately, he asked. 'And ye?'

Aileen shuffled closer. 'I need you to keep Dachaigh safe. I can take care of myself.'

Playfully, he sniggered. 'As if-'

Aileen raised her chin. 'Just so you know, I saved your arse again.'

'Arse, Ms Mackinnon?'

She smirked at him. Raising her voice an octave, she said, 'Aye, yer arse. Remember that next time ye taunt me, Detective Cameron.'

'Ha! Never.'

Aileen gave him her best glare before leaning over and pressing her lips to his cheek. Trying to hold in a giggle, she said, 'I'll just have to slap you again then. It was quite fun, you know.'

Callan's eyes were a stormy shade when he responded. 'I'm arresting ye for assaulting a police officer.'

'It should be noted: I did that to keep his hide warm and alive.'

Callan laughed a deep bellied laugh, despite the pain that contorted his face. 'God, Aileen! Ye're something else.'

'Yes I am, Callan. That's why you need me.'

He grinned, the pain vanishing from his face,

making him appear younger and carefree. He squeezed their joined hands. 'Aye… Partner.'

Partners they are but could they be something more?
Turn the page to read the next novel in Aileen and Callan's world

THE NEXT BOOK IN THIS SERIES

A cold case threatens to shatter Callan's career

Blaine Macgregor vanished on a summer's night fifteen years ago. Now Detective Inspector Callan

THE NEXT BOOK IN THIS SERIES

Cameron is investigating his case one last time. But for Callan it means unearthing a bygone summer he'd rather forget.

Amateur sleuth Aileen Mackinnon overhears a guest's puzzling conversation and can't stop asking questions. Is she being duped again? With Callan refusing to open up about his case, Aileen needs a distraction. What better than a case of her own?

As Aileen and Callan balance on a thin rope of betrayal and trust, one question haunts them: Is Blaine still alive?

Turn the page to read more...

CHAPTER ONE

'Oh God!' Her body braced and muscles shuddered. Dripping with sweat, Aileen blinked at the man looming over her.

Detective Inspector Callan Cameron's electric blues, with their special hint of grey, assessed her with an intensity enough to burn through paper. They clearly didn't like what they saw. 'Fifty times in as many minutes, Mackinnon! What's wrong with ye?'

What's wrong? Her stomach growled, ready to eat itself. Her clothes stuck to her like a second skin, making her body itch, and her breath raced faster than the speed of light. That's what was wrong!

Aileen tried to turn onto her side. The mat underneath should've been comfortable, but after this torture, it was akin to a hard stone grinding into her aching arse.

CHAPTER ONE

Another moan slipped through her clenched lips. Her dark brown locks, now appearing pitch black thanks to all the sweat, had broken out of their militant ponytail.

Bloody detective! Now she had to deal with this haystack for the rest of their—

'Up!' The word lasered through her constant pants.

Aileen muttered a few curses between shallow gasps.

They didn't sound as muted as she'd thought.

'If ye'd channel some of yer frustration here, ye wouldn't be on yer arse all the time.'

She continued to huff, a steam engine with no signs of stopping. Aileen's legs quaked, so she pushed against the mat with shivering arms and landed on her rump. She'd be able to use her legs sometime tomorrow, she hoped. 'Can we call it a day?'

Callan folded his arms, muscles bulging like taut balloons. Had they grown overnight? Unlikely.

There wasn't a hint of perspiration on his scowling face. A soot-black mop and scruff jaw with the barest of prickly beards gave him an edgier, dangerous look – never mind those defined bones. 'Ye can't ask yer enemy for a timeout. For all ye ken, they'd finish ye off in two minutes, given yer less than average stamina.'

Aileen gritted her teeth. 'I'm not going off to war. Help me!'

CHAPTER ONE

Still, the infernal man didn't move. His sharp eyes scanned the barn, which was fitted with fitness tools, searching for more torture equipment.

She wouldn't give him the chance. If she wanted to get back to Dachaigh using her own legs, she had to end this.

Aileen crouched on all fours and gripped Callan's forearm, then used the last millilitre of fuel left to heft herself up.

The ground quaked, those torture-buffers – aka blue mats – providing some cushion for her legs. White light blinded her, beating onto her damp back. Was it suddenly hot in here?

Aileen's throat pleaded mercy. A woman lost in the desert was better hydrated.

This had been a bad idea.

Callan had taken it upon himself to teach Aileen self-defence. For the four sessions they'd practised together, Aileen had found herself on her arse more than her feet.

The detective never promised to be a gentle person; he represented his features: all muscle and not an ounce of fat to spare. Add this to Coach Callan and diamonds could be more yielding – he showed as much mercy as Henry VIII to an adulterous Anne Boleyn.

She didn't want to listen to his instructions. Her pumping blood and ceaseless pants obstructed her hearing, Aileen only hoped to get out of there in one piece.

CHAPTER ONE

Callan muttered a jab. 'If ye don't do as I tell ye, this is useless!'

Aileen peeked up at him, her petite height nowhere near his six feet plus. Damn him! Her tiny frame meant he often picked her up and dropped her on the mats, as if she were a twig. It frustrated her, to say the least. How do you hurt a boulder?

He cares enough to want to protect you.

'I don't have the time to follow your ridiculous exercise regime.' She spewed a few more curses. His fitness mindset hadn't rubbed off on her, although his affinity to curse had.

It caused him to scowl harder. 'I ken what ye're trying to do. Ye can't distract me. Move! Fifty push-ups followed by fifty squats.'

'I'd be dead on the floor!'

His lips twitched as he waved her off. 'Get moving!'

Was he trying to hold a smirk? She could manage some kickboxing, especially with him as her target.

Crossing her arms across her chest, she pursed her lips. 'Not doing it.'

Callan tipped his chin, as if contemplating her argument. 'I won't let ye solve cases with me if ye don't.'

Hell, he drove a hard bargain. No more sleuthing?

'Five squats and two push-ups.'

CHAPTER ONE

'Twenty and ten. I'll let ye have an extra piece of the chocolate-hazelnut tart.'

A fool would refuse it. She might learn to walk without her legs. Or a generous serving of chocolate with hazelnut might resurrect her.

An agonising eternity later, Aileen slipped on her normal shoes. They trained twice every week at a barn belonging to Old Brun, someone from Callan's past. She hadn't met the man, nor did she know anything about him.

She stared at her blotchy face in the mirror. She'd been able to calm her racing heart after a freezing bath. Callan said it would soothe her sore muscles; Aileen wondered if they'd divorce her for all the torture she'd put them through.

Most people had a palpitating heart and red face from *other* activities on a date.

Was this supposed to be a date? Or had he brought her here to appease her gran?

Siobhan had negotiated with Callan months ago: answers in exchange for a date with her grandwean.

Aileen shook her head. This was Callan's idea of taking her on a date – he'd said so. It suited him. They weren't much for sitting around discussing movies or the weather. They hashed out murder investigations. Neither of them pretended to be normal.

It still plagued her, what a man like him saw in

CHAPTER ONE

her. His loyalty and respect for his badge would make any sane female swoon. Then came the icing on the cake: muscles paired with a grumpy, chiselled face crafted to perfection, and topped with military-cut black hair. The epitome of swoon-worthy.

And her? A recovering overworked accountant who, at twenty-eight, wanted adventure to spice up her life. She'd achieved her goal after coming to Loch Fuar a few months ago. Despite being more adventurous than when she'd arrived, Aileen couldn't fathom how Callan thought she resembled her grandmother: witty and mischievous.

Siobhan was famous in Loch Fuar for her boisterous yet loving nature. Callan sure adored her, despite the constant banter between the two of them. And Aileen suspected she terrified Callan a wee bit.

Aileen's stomach growled as she stepped out of the locker room.

A hungry, wannabe adventurous woman…

She turned to where Callan leaned against the wall, massaging his right knee.

Licking her lips, she dared. If they were dating, he'd tell her about *it*, wouldn't he? 'Is your knee hurting again?'

Callan jumped like someone had caught him nicking a cookie. He cleared his throat. 'Hungry? I'm starving.'

The hope in her chest deflated. Callan didn't trust her enough to share his ghosts. But then she hadn't told him everything either, had she?

CHAPTER ONE

Read More

READ AN EXCLUSIVE NOVELLA

When a storm cuts off the tiny town of Loch Fuar from the rest of the world, a murderer strikes. And it's someone among them.

Download your free copy:
Shanafrost.com/exclusivenovella

AUTHOR'S NOTE

Dear Reader Friend,

Thank you for taking the time to join Aileen and Callan on another adventure. If you want to discuss this story or just want to chat, you can write to me at author@shanafrost.com.

I would be very grateful if you could also leave a review for this book. Your review helps an independent author like me reach new readers. If you've never written a review before, you don't need to write a long literary essay, just a sentence or two on your preferred retailer store is perfect. And if you have the time, please also leave a review on Goodreads and/or Bookbub as well. Thank you.

Writing this story was an epic saga in itself. I learnt so much, from the craft to the power of perseverance. I shudder to think about the words that I've trashed and re-written, but in the end, all's well that ends well.

'When Eyes Don't Lie' was a hard case to crack, not just for Aileen and Callan, but for me as a writer. It took a lot of writing and re-writing to get this story to where it is now, and I'm proud of it.

The harder the story got, the more excited I was to solve this mystery. And it took a couple of people to make it as suspenseful and page-turning as it is now.

Thank you to my incredible Beta Readers: Jean Soderquist, Leonise van Reenen, Ingrid Vitalis and Laura Edwards. Your suggestions and comments helped me make this story so much better. Sometimes you need someone to point out the incorrect part of the puzzle to realise what's missing. Thank you for having the patience to help me sort out the story.

My deepest gratitude to my editor Charlotte Kane for her patience with the manuscript and my many questions.

A special thanks to my alpha readers: Sushma and Sharika Dhakappa.

If you enjoyed reading this mystery as much as I loved writing it, please leave a review on the platform you've purchased your copy from. It helps me reach more readers, and you get to tell the world how much you loved this story as well.

As you read this, I'm at my keyboard submerged in another whodunnit at Loch Fuar. Aileen is truly a magnet for trouble, I tell ye.

See ye soon,
Shana.

ABOUT THE AUTHOR

Shana Frost writes romantic mysteries as dramatic as the Scottish Highlands that inspire her. In every book, Shana shares the values she truly believes in: hope, justice, and love. Throughout her novels, you'll encounter a variety of characters—be their gender, ethnicity, disabilities, beliefs—all sharing their unique stories.

Always infused with a wee dram of the Scottish landscape and culture, Shana's stories take readers from Glasgow's gritty streets to the enigmatic Highlands. She promises that when reading her stories, you'll be at the edge of your seat, falling deeper in love with the characters.

To be enveloped in the world of Scottish romantic mysteries, visit Shana's home on the web at
Shanafrost.com

THANK YOU!

Thanks for reading thus far. I've got a surprise for you!

Partners they are, but what if they can be something more?

Join Aileen and Callan on their highly-anticipated first date ever. **Read this free short story** or type this URL in your browser **Shanafrost.com/wedl**

www.ingramcontent.com/pod-product-compliance
Lightning Source LLC
LaVergne TN
LVHW030312070526
838199LV00068B/6452